the

other

world

CALLISTA O'BRIEN

the
other
world

CALLISTA O'BRIEN

 Lucky Bat Books

A Lucky Bat Book

The Other World

Cover Design:
Nuno Moreira
http://www.nmdesign.org

Published by Lucky Bat Books
LuckyBatBooks.com

10 9 8 7 6 5 4 3 2 1

ISBN: 978-1-943588-23-7

This book also available in digital formats.

You can read more about this author at:
CallistaObrienAuthor.com

To MY FAMILY AND TO all the people who believe
that a book is never *just* a book.

CHAPTER 1

SITTING IN MY SOPHOMORE CHEMISTRY class, I silently curse *High School Musical*. It has completely ruined my high-school experience by making my standards unreasonably high. There is no singing (except in choir class), there are no dance routines in the middle of the hallways, and, despite popular belief, we are not all in this together. So you know what? Screw you, *High School Musical*.

My teacher drones on and on about atoms, which is another stupid thing about high school. The majority of us will never have to know that the nucleus of an atom is positively charged. I am not a chemist; I will never be a chemist and, therefore, I do not care.

I see the blonde hair of my best friend Cassie, who is sitting across class, and yearn to sit next to her. Being able to talk to her would make this class more bearable. But the cruel world (and my cruel teacher) has seated my friend on the other side of the room. Not to mention that my other friend, Matt, doesn't even have this class, since he has to be a genius and take advanced chemistry.

This is how it goes every day. I wake up at an ungodly hour, I walk to school with Matt, I haul myself through all of my classes like a zombie, and then I go home. This is followed by the short reprieve of the weekend, only to give way to yet another Monday, starting the whole banal routine again. Not to mention that every adult talks about high school as if it were the best time of their lives, which means that it only gets worse from here.

I know that I have a good life, so I shouldn't be complaining. I love my family more than a self-respecting teenager should, and I have great friends, but none of them are the problem. The problem is that nothing ever changes. I have gone to school with the same class since kindergarten.

I have lived in the same house my whole life. My parents expect me to go to college here, like the rest of my cousins, and then live here. Forever.

I wish that my life could actually be exciting—that there was still land to discover so that I could set out and find it. What I really need is just to graduate already, so I can travel the world. I have decided that adventure is not going to find me, so I have to go find it.

When the bell rings, finally releasing me to lunch, I leap out of my chair and through the hall as if the Olympic gun has just gone off. I make it out the doorway just in time to see Matt as he leaves his classroom. The boy is practically impossible to miss in the brightly colored Hawaiian shirts and khaki pants that he insists on wearing. I really don't know what goes through his head in the morning, but he just wouldn't be Matt if he didn't dress like that.

I follow his curly-haired head, bobbing in and out of my view as he navigates the crowded hall, and I'm about to call out to him when two juniors ram their shoulders into his, forcing him to fall to the ground. Oh God, why does something like this have to happen every day? I swear, that boy is bully bait.

The boys laugh and start walking off when my anger gets the best of me. I rush up to the both of them and grab the top straps of their backpacks. With one good yank, both boys fall back onto the ground in an explosion of curses.

"Touch him again, and I'll mess you up," I snap at them as they lie flat on the ground with me standing over them. The boys share an alarmed look before scrambling off the floor. I sigh, staring after them, before walking back to Matt and helping him off the ground.

"You're going to get yourself suspended again, Haylyn," Matt warns after thanking me for helping him up.

"What did she do this time?" Cassie asks with a grin as she joins us in the hall, just now making it through the mass exodus from class.

"Pulled two juniors to the ground and threatened them," Matt says, smiling even though he is feigning disappointment with me.

"Haylyn! This is why you don't have a boyfriend!" Cassie cries as the three of us make our way down the hall, surrounded by hordes of other students all shoving and pushing.

"Okay, he failed to mention that they pushed him to the ground first. I didn't do it for kicks. And don't even get me started with the boyfriend comment," I say. Cassie is always pushing me to date, but having a half-hearted, clingy, two-month relationship while everyone secretly hopes you break up isn't really my thing.

"Haylyn is a strong, independent woman who doesn't need no man," Matt says in his best stereotypically sassy, black woman voice. Cassie and I both crack up because there is just something hilarious about a scrawny white kid trying to wiggle his head and hips simultaneously in an attempt to appear sassy. Still laughing, we fight our way through the clumps of students and sit down at our regular spot in front of some lockers. Once I'm done wresting my lunch from the bottom of my backpack, I lean against Matt, feeling completely at ease in the familiarity of it all.

Sitting propped up between Matt and the lockers, I decide that we must look like quite the collage of personalities, sitting here together. We have Matt in his forever-a-Hawaiian tourist look, paired with a mop of reddish-brown curls. Then there's Cassie, who perfectly represents the stereotype of a white girl in her UGG boots, jeans, adorable sweater, and perfectly flat-ironed, shoulder-length blonde hair. Not to mention her Starbucks addiction. Then there's me in my sneakers, skinny jeans, and long-sleeved t-shirt with the Queen logo on it.

"Hopefully, I'll get a car tomorrow, so we don't have to keep eating here like freshmen, and we can eat in my car," Cassie says as we all start opening our lunch bags and eating. Tomorrow is Cassie's sixteenth birthday, and tonight is her party. She is the first in our little group to turn sixteen, so we are all dependent on whether or not she gets a car.

"I still don't see why I can't go to the party," Matt exclaims with a pout. Cassie and I exchange looks. Matt always brings this up.

"Because it's a sleepover, Matt, and Cassie's mom would never go for a guy sleeping in the same room as girls," I inform him as I impatiently push my long brown hair behind my ears. I don't really know why Cassie's mom is so afraid of Matt sleeping in the same room as us. Neither of us even considers Matt to be a threat to our virtue. Or any threat at all.

"Yeah, Matt, you know how my mom is," Cassie adds as she ruffles Matt's auburn curls before going back to ripping the crust off her

3

sandwich. Cassie can't stand crust, but doesn't have the heart to tell her mom this, so every day she rips apart the lovely ham and cheese sandwich that her mother made. Matt still looks upset, but stays quiet as he realizes this battle has been lost.

"Have you seen Heather's outfit today?" Cassie comments, changing the subject to our number-one mean girl. Every school's got one, and ours just happens to be Heather—a typical, popular name for a typical, popular girl. "Shouldn't a skirt be longer than your underwear? Somebody's thirsty."

I laugh, nearly making myself choke on my PB & J. "Dehydrated is more like it," I scoff, finishing off my sandwich and moving on to my granola bar.

"You guys are terrible," Matt says while smiling his signature goofy grin. "Do either of you have any food? I'm starving today—don't know why."

Cassie and I exchange another round of looks at each other and then laugh. This happens pretty much every day. Matt's mom is a nurse who, more often than not, has to work the night shift, meaning that she can't make Matt's lunch in the morning. This shouldn't be a problem; Matt is a smart, perfectly capable high-school sophomore. Except that he is hopeless in the kitchen. I used to think that anyone could slap some peanut butter and jelly on some bread … until I met Matt.

His mom used to try giving him lunch money, but he would have none of that. Instead, Matt always claims he's not hungry, which is such a lie—he's a teenage boy—and then asks us for food. Sometime last year, both Cassie and I started packing extra things in our lunch. I make the sandwich and Cassie brings the snack. I like doing it, though; it makes me feel so motherly when I make his lunch. I guess after all these years of friendship, I have become sort of protective of Matt.

"Yeah," I reply, tossing him the other PB & J that I've had ready for him all along.

"You know I do," Cassie adds, throwing a bag of chips at him.

"Thanks, you guys are the best!" he declares, tearing into his food.

"We know," Cassie answers, and then lunch continues on as normal, which means that we all share stories about our day and our worries about our next classes. I zone out during Cassie's rundown of last night's episode of *Pretty Little Liars*. Then suddenly a shadow slides into the corner of my eye. My skin raises into goosebumps, and I feel a chill run over me. I whip around, glaring at the lockers to my left, but see nothing. The bite of granola bar sticks to my mouth as it goes dry.

I choke down the bite and get up to go investigate, ignoring the calls of Cassie and Matt. I turn around the corner of the lockers but again see nothing. It feels as if something was here, though, with the stench of decaying roses left in the air. *Something* was watching me.

I jump when a hand falls onto my shoulder. I spin around and see Cassie giving me wide eyes. "What's the matter with you?"

I take a minute to collect myself. Geez, I just freaked out over what was probably nothing, and now I look like I'm crazy. "Nothing. I just thought I saw some freshman spying on us, so I decided to tell him to get lost, but he must have already left," I reply with a laugh.

Cassie eyes me suspiciously before shrugging and dragging me back to our lunch spot to continue her dramatic retelling of last night's episode. As I listen to Matt and Cassie argue over who "A" is *this* time, I eventually calm down and fall back into the boring swing of things that is my life.

I finish off my lunch and join in their conversation, the incident from before completely forgotten, when the dreaded bell ending our lunch blares to life.

"No," I groan as Cassie starts to haul me up off the ground. "I'm not ready!" I cry, being dramatic.

"Come on, Lynnie, there is only one more class, and then you are free," Matt says encouragingly, using my nickname.

"Ugg," I groan, using Cassie's hand to pull myself to my feet. I brush off my jeans before turning to face Cassie. "I'll be at your house around five," I say to her.

She throws her arms around me. "I can't wait! Thanks for helping me set up. Remember to bring your sleeping bag," she squeals in my ear.

"I won't! And I've got the Silly String all ready for our ambush!" I tell her.

Cassie holds out her fist to me in fist-bump style. "Potato," she says smiling.

I touch my fist to hers before we both pull back, opening our hands. "Fries!" we both say as our hands open. We laugh as Matt just shakes his head, smiling; this has been our thing for around two years now.

"See ya!" I call as she strides down the hallway. I turn to Matt. "Meet you outside of school?"

"Of course! Have fun in English," he replies.

"Always!" I respond sarcastically with a smile, yanking one of his curls before walking away.

I mosey my way through the sluggish crowds of procrastinating teenagers before making it to my classroom and sitting down at my desk. The bell rings, starting a long and grammar-filled hell, and I try to not fall asleep as we correct vocabulary. I constantly watch the clock, and when the final bell rings, I throw my bag over my shoulder and fight my way out the door.

I wait for Matt outside of school. The ice-filled air slaps against my cheeks, turning them pink. I dig out my beanie and pull it onto my head before pushing my hands deeper into the pockets of my puffy jacket, seeking warmth but finding none. It's as if all the warmth has left my body. I usually am fine with the cold. I have lived in it my whole life and have learned to ignore it, but right now it's impossible to ignore as every cell in my body seems to drop below freezing.

As the hairs on the back on my neck stand on end, I know that the reason I'm cold has nothing to do with the weather, but rather to do with the feeling that someone is watching me. I spin around and see a shadow ducking behind a tree. I squint my eyes, my wool hat falling into them, and try to search for any more movement.

I lift my foot to take a step after the shadow when Matt's voice startles me out of investigation.

"Is there any particular reason you are staring at that tree like it has the answers for next week's math test?" he inquires.

"Do you see anything by that tree?"

Matt leans forward, examining it. "Nope, other than the fact that the answer to number five is A."

I laugh and feel my tense muscles begin to relax. Of course, there is nothing. "Always the smart ass," I remark as we start to walk out of the parking lot.

The rest of the walk continues without incident; I calm down and listen to Matt as tells me about his adventures in band class. Apparently, some kid got hit with a tuba, but seeing Matt acting it out has me in fits of laughter. Together we walk through the harsh December air of Denver, Colorado, to my little brother's middle school. Avery runs up to us with his dark hair a hot mess atop his head; it's the same dark brown with undertones of red as mine. Avery babbles on about his day as we continue walking and somehow manages to get Matt to agree to play basketball with him this Sunday.

"Going to watch our game, Haylyn?" Matt asks as we say our goodbyes in his driveway, with Avery waiting impatiently on the sidewalk.

"Wouldn't miss it for the world," I tell him with a grin, hugging him goodbye before rejoining Avery at the sidewalk for our daily race.

"Ready?" Avery asks, getting into position.

"Go!" I cry as we both launch forward, running down the street. My long hair flows behind me like a flag as the cold air stings the bottoms of my ears, where my hat doesn't cover them. We turn onto our driveway, and I push my legs to move faster. I launch myself up the stairs to my porch and throw my hand against the door. "I won!" I heave as Avery gets there a second later, looking just as out of breath as I am.

"Only by a second! Monday, you're going down," he says with as much determination as a twelve-year-old boy can muster.

"Keep telling yourself that," I say as I dig my key out from my bag and unlock the front door. As soon as I push it open, our mixed-breed dog is charging out at us, nearly knocking us to the ground. "Hi, Foxy!" I coo as I run my hands through the features she was named for—an auburn coat and a tail that looks dipped in white, just like a fox's. She has been my protector and most loyal companion since we adopted her from the humane society when I was eight.

"I'll be in my room!" Avery calls from the kitchen, grabbing food before sneaking off to play as many video games as he can before Mom and Dad get home.

"Okay! I'm going to take Foxy for a walk, be back soon!" I call back. My mom said that I have to take her on a walk before I can go to the party, so I set my bag on the ground, grab the leash, and head back into the cold with Foxy in the lead.

I vaguely worry about the shadow that I have now seen twice today, before feeling reassured by the presence of my dog. Foxy walks about three feet in front of me, vigilantly sniffing the air for any hint of something suspicious. She would die before letting anything happen to me, and while I would do the same thing for her, she is a lot scarier in action than I am.

Vicious guard dog that she is, Foxy is still very well-behaved, so I stroll leisurely along the sidewalk, watching as we pass row after row of perfect white-picket-fenced houses. I know almost every person who lives in each house. The blue one across from my house belongs to Ms. Evalia, who has beautiful gardens in the summer, which I usually help her with. Matt lives in the tan one at the end, and every other house just adds to the picture-perfect look of my uneventful life.

I walk with Foxy to the towering trees at the back end of our neighborhood. Taking a deep breath, I let the familiar tang of pine fill my nose. I unhook Foxy from her leash, as I normally do once we are away from the street. Walking at a languid pace, I listen to my feet crunching on the snow until I get a prickling sensation all down my arms, as if the spines of a cactus are embracing them. Something is watching me. I look around, and out of the corner of my eye I see a shadow move. It is the same shadow from earlier today, but now I am in a forest with no people around. Guard dog or not, I have to get out of here.

Feeling completely freaked out, I turn to grab Foxy and run, but she isn't by my side. I look around, but she isn't anywhere in sight! She has never run off before. What do I do? The unnerving shadow now completely forgotten, I run through the trees, farther than I've ever gone. I am about to have a complete meltdown when suddenly my phone starts vibrating at my hip.

I look at the contact. Why is Avery calling? "Hello?"

"Haylyn? Where are you? I thought you were taking Foxy for a walk, but Foxy's right here," he says. I breathe out a sigh of relief. She is safe at home.

"Yeah, I was, but she went missing. I guess she decided to walk home," I say incredulously. "I'll be back there in a few," I add, walking around absently-mindedly.

"Okay, see you soon!" Avery calls before hanging up.

I sigh and slide my phone into my pocket. I am about to turn around when suddenly I hear a distinct cracking sound under my feet. Ice. I look down and see that while I have been distracted by my phone, I have wandered onto a frozen pond. Splintering cracks are already starting to form at my feet, meaning that this ice isn't very thick.

I try to take a careful step backward, only to scream as I am plunged into the water. Suddenly, everything is overtaken by the cold. It is so cold that it hurts. Every inch of my skin is burning. I try to swim back up to the hole where I fell through, but there seems to be some kind of thick current under the water, and I am being pulled down even farther.

I frantically struggle, but it is no use. My lungs feel like they are going to explode, and my vision is being blotted out with black dots. I am going to die. I desperately don't want to, but as the currents pull me down even more and I lose all movement of my limbs, it appears inevitable.

I think of my parents. I'm sorry that I can't save myself for their sake. The last thought I have before the darkness claims me is this: I don't want to die.

CHAPTER 2

DARKNESS SURROUNDS ME. AM I dead? Is this what death feels like? My chest aches and my wet hair is like ice against my scalp. Aren't you supposed to not feel any pain in death? What a rip-off. I have a distant memory of arms wrapped around my waist, but what I can't seem to remember is whether they were pulling me up to safety or pulling me down to make sure that I was really dead. I suppose it was the former one because, after several seconds, agitated voices start filling my ears.

"You almost killed her! Had I not jumped in…" a male voice that sounds like a perfectly tuned cello rants before he is cut off.

"It was merely a test to see how long she could withstand a lack of oxygen. Besides, she wasn't your responsibility at the time, Sam," growls a raspy voice that sounds as if it comes from someone who smokes a solid ten packs a day. "I find it curious that you seem to have forgotten that little piece of information in favor of rescuing her."

"And I find it curious that you would go to such lengths to get her, only to try and kill her once she was in your reach," the smooth, baritone cello voice replies sharply.

"Even now you continue to defend her," snaps Cigarettes.

"I'm not defending her. I'm just trying to figure you monsters out, like you do me," Cello voice drawls. "I saved her because, unlike you, I don't take pleasure in the deaths of others. However, next time, I'm just going to let her die if you're going to make such a big deal over it. It doesn't matter to me if she lives."

Well, that's reassuring.

"Very interesting," the smoker voice mutters, mainly to itself.

After the two voices remain silent for a few minutes, I decide to try and open my eyes and find out who these two people are and why they are acting like my death has the overall importance of a hangnail. My eyes slowly flutter open and drift over a small, plain room, like a guest room crossed with an infirmary. I lie in a bed with my damp clothes pressing down on me; waning light is filtering in from the curtained window. The smell of fabric starch and rubbing alcohol fills my nose, making it burn.

My eyes continue around the room until they stop on the horrible thing lurking in the corner. It has to be the living definition of hell spawn. The creature has a silhouette like a human's, but that's where the similarities stop. Rotting brown skin is paired with a long, curving beak resembling the mask of a plague doctor, but actually attached to its face. The eyes are squishy black orbs, and the hands are gnarled and boney, with the skin pulled as tightly as that of a person dying of starvation.

I scream and close my eyes tight. Thoughts race through my head. What is that? Where am I? The demon, shrew-like being clicks in annoyance as I begin to lash out. I flail around until strong hands clasp my wrists and push them to my sides. I continue to struggle against my restraints when that deep voice from before slowly fills my ears.

"Calm down," the voice urges in a whisper. I feel warm breath against my ear and smell the spicy scent of cinnamon. "You have to calm down. Just open your eyes, and then I can tell you what is going on."

I consider what the voice is telling me and decide to listen to it. I hesitantly pry open my clenched eyes and see that I am being caged by an attractive guy who looks to be about my age and human, with clothes just as wet as mine from his apparent swim to save me. He's not the fake kind of attractive that you see in the Abercrombie and Fitch advertisements, but the kind you see going by on a skateboard, with perfect bone structure and a mouth that instantly says, "I'm up to no good."

His lips curve into a small smirk, and his damp, golden-brown hair falls down to his eyebrows and curls out a little past his ears. Deep green eyes shine like sun-coated pine trees, and I have the urge to lean in closer to him, until I see the look in those eyes. He wears an expression much too serious for a boy his age, too distant and cold. Suddenly, that pull I felt for him a moment ago is being replaced by an icy wall.

"Will you not hit anyone now?" the boy asks. What did the smoker voice call him earlier? Sam?

"I won't make any promises," I reply, clutching the rough sheets of the bed. I will do whatever it takes to get out of here, and if escaping requires force, so be it.

Sam chuckles at my answer and releases my hands anyway. Then he sits back on the edge of the bed that I am lying in.

"Fair enough," Sam mutters, letting the air fall back into an eerie silence as my eyes drift over to the demon shrew standing in the corner. The thing glares into my soul, so I glare back, which, to my satisfaction, seems to ruffle a few of its feathers.

"So I opened my eyes. When do I get my answers?" I snap, trying to keep a level voice, my eyes never leaving the thing in the corner.

"Well, what are your questions?" Sam asks, the creepy human thing remaining silent.

"Well, first off, what is that?" I exclaim, pointing wildly at the shrew thing.

"That is a Lave," Sam responds flatly.

"And what the hell is a Lave?" I ask, exasperated.

"They are very similar to people, except they have bird influences. They are both smarter and stronger than humans," Sam explains in an informative tone.

"Uh-huh," I say doubtfully. "Well, at least that explains the beak," I add sarcastically, hoping he will tell me what is really going on.

"Yes," Sam replies hesitantly. I look over to him, trying to see the wavering in his eyes as he lies to me, because he has to be lying to me, but I see nothing. Either he is a really good actor, or he actually believes what he is saying. Why are the cute ones always crazy?

"Okay, so, then where on earth am I?" I demand, my voice growing louder as I start to get irritated.

"Nowhere," he answers.

"What?"

"Well, the thing is, you're not on earth."

I glare at Sam, and he holds my gaze back. A minute passes with us just staring at one another, and then I fully decide that I am done playing stupid brain games with these insane-asylum escapees.

"Well, I'm not sure what I just walked into, but I think you guys should lay off the drugs for a while. So, if you'll excuse me, I will just leave you to this cult meeting, or video game re-enactment, or whatever this and be on my way." I force my way up and swat away Sam's hands as he tries to restrain me. Considering that my hair is still wet, I can't have been taken too far away from that pond, so I can probably just walk home from here.

"Haylyn!" Sam calls. I turn around reluctantly, wondering how he knows my name. "You can't leave," he says.

"Watch me," I reply, making a run for the door. I hear Sam jump up, and after a few seconds he is bear-hugging me from behind. I respond by heel-kicking him in the shin and throwing my head back into his nose. Sam grunts and lets me go, and I sprint out the door.

I have barely made it a few feet outside when my chest starts to burn and my vision becomes speckled with black dots.

I collapse to the ground, only vaguely seeing feet storming over to me.

Escape attempt one: fail.

CHAPTER 3

MY EYES FLUTTER OPEN, AND I pray that everything I remember is just some crazy dream. My eyes open further, and I feel sick to my stomach when I realize that I am not in my bedroom. I almost feel disconnected from my body, like all this is happening to another person. I try to close my eyes and reopen them again, but the scenery around me doesn't change. I even try pinching myself, like they say to do in all of those cheesy movies, hoping that this is all just a dream, but I already know that it isn't.

The room looks similar to a hotel room. I lie on a bed positioned against a wall in the middle of the room, next to a small bedside table. Across from me on the opposite wall is a window draped with beige curtains; a plain upholstered chair sits in the corner. On my left are a pair of sliding doors that open to a small, empty closet. On my right, the wall has two doors: One leads to a bathroom, and the other seems to be the door that leads outside. The whole look is tied together with plain white walls. If this is a hotel room, it is the most boring one I have ever seen.

I slowly crawl out of bed and pad my way to the closed curtains. Sliding them open, I flinch as a spread of white light enters my room. Outside, I see other little cabin-type structures that appear to be about the same size as the room I am in. I can't see much beyond that, except for what might be a cluster of trees in the distance … maybe even a lake?

Slowly, as I start to process a bit more, I pat my pockets for my phone and pry it out of my jeans. I clap with glee when it turns on, even after my little unexpected swim. My face falls when I see that there is no service.

Well, isn't that just the cherry on top of the my-life-has-turned-into-shit ice cream? I try calling home, just in case, but I don't even get a ring.

My lungs rattle, and my eyes threaten to overflow with tears. The urge to drop to the ground in a ball and start hysterically crying and screaming is almost overpowering. The only thing that stops me from doing so is the fact that I have no idea what is going on or where on earth I am. I sniffle loudly and decide that if I want to get home, I have to talk to somebody here.

I look down and see that I am still in the same clothes I put on yesterday, before I almost drowned. They are stiff from water and crumpled from sleeping, and the jeans are still slightly damp. But at least they are from home.

I wander into the small bathroom and look at myself in the mirror. My long, dark-brown hair falls down my shoulders, ending at the small of my back. My cheeks look a little paler than usual, but otherwise, with my round, root-beer brown eyes and small frame, I look the same as I did the day before when I woke up in my own room back at home.

I comb my hair with my fingers and splash some cold water on my face, all in an attempt to calm myself down. I can't lose my head here. Isn't that what they say saves people in situations like this? Keeping calm and focused? I sure hope so because that is the only plan I have. Well, that and going bat-shit crazy until they decide I'm too much to handle and take me back home … I'll think of that as plan B.

I reach for the metal door handle, worried that what I will discover will be worse than anything my imagination could conjure up. I suppose that I could always turn around and hide in my closet or something else pathetic, but I can't give up before I even know what's going on. Gathering my courage, I swing open the door. The first thing that greets me is the wall to another cabin about seven feet in front of me. I look down and see that there is a small concrete path with empty flower beds that curls out from between the two cabins and stops at a street made of gravel.

I take a hesitant step out and immediately start to panic. The dry air is so thin it is nearly impossible to breathe. It feels like I'm at the top of Mt. Everest. The closest I have ever gotten to feeling like this is when I was eight and my dad took me to the top of one of the Rockies' highest points. This air seems even thinner.

Once I get over the initial shock, I force myself to calm down. Slowly, my breath grows deeper and less ragged, and after a second I get used to the lack of oxygen coming to my brain. At least I know we're high up.

I walk down the path to start searching for other people when a smooth, familiar voice slides out and stops me.

"Going somewhere?"

I turn around and see Sam leaning against the wall of my cabin, as if it is the most casual thing ever. I take a minute to study him, now that I am not so distracted. I see piercing green eyes surrounded by thick lashes that fan out like feathers and mussed-up brown hair. He wears a gray button-up shirt with dark jeans and Converse sneakers. All together with his lean, muscled body and cheekbones that any girl would kill to have, I have to admit that he's hot. Not that it makes any difference; he is probably in cahoots with the Laves anyway.

"Yeah, home," I reply once I finally get over the initial shock of him being here. Sam slowly peels himself off the wall and strides over to me.

He leans in close until I can smell the scent of cinnamon hovering around him and feel the heat of his lips above my ear. I think he does this just to fluster me. "You can't," he says in a low voice. I shove him away hard and he looks at me in surprise, his green eyes open wide.

"Bullshit. Take me home now!" I sputter, becoming more and more upset by the second.

"Like I just said, you can't. There is no escaping from here," Sam says slowly, as if letting me process.

"And where exactly is here? Mt. Evans?" I question sarcastically, naming the closest "fourteener" to Denver. Everyone is obsessed with climbing the 14,000-foot or higher mountains of the Rockies, so I am quite familiar with the name of the closest one. I know it's impossible for us to actually be on Mt. Evans, considering all of the buildings, but we have to be somewhere high up for the air to feel like this, and it seems that it's only been a day or a little more since I last passed out.

"Farther away than that," Sam mutters.

"Then where the hell are we? I'm sick of your dodgy answers! Just *tell* me!" I demand exasperatedly.

"You are in Die Andere Welt," Sam sighs, running his hand through his hair.

"And where's that, Switzerland?" I ask. The name sounds European.

"It's the closest dimension to earth's dimension," Sam finally admits. "Welcome to the other world."

I stare at Sam as his eyes remain on mine before he looks back to the ground and shoves his hands in his pockets. He doesn't look particularly crazy, but he has to be. Then again, I'm not an expert on crazy people. Don't they say sociopaths are usually charming and good looking? Well, lucky me, I've found one.

"Okay," I say, starting to back away. "Are you on drugs? Or should you be?"

At this, Sam's head perks up. "Why, do you want some?" he inquires with a smirk tugging at his lips.

My mouth opens in disbelief. I shake my head. Clearly, I am not getting anywhere with him. I start to turn and walk away when Sam lets out a groan and strides over, catching my arm in a loose grip.

"Get this through your thick head. I'm not crazy, or on drugs, or lying to you. This is really happening. You have been taken by the Laves to be studied, and you can never go home again. The sooner you can accept that, the sooner you can adjust to being here, and then we'll all get on with our lives." He says all this in an irritated tone, as if telling me that I've been kidnapped is wasting precious minutes of his time.

I stare at his hand casually looped around my arm and his easy posture. He has to be lying. But what if he isn't? Will I really never be able to see my family again? And what does he mean, "studied"?

All his words continue to tumble through my mind when I finally produce a logical answer. *Of course!*

"I'm being pranked," I state. Sam looks up at me and releases my arm. I look around, waiting for my friends or a camera crew to jump out at any moment.

"You're not being pranked," Sam replies.

"But…" I look around, straining to see anything that could give it away, but nothing comes. No laughing friends, no TV crews, and no smirking little brother. My mind struggles to produce anything else that will make more sense, but it is a feeble attempt. Nothing else comes to mind, and this place sure doesn't look like anything I've ever seen on earth. "So, you're not lying?" I try hesitantly, feeling insane for even considering what he is saying as a possibility.

"Would have been a lot faster if you had come to that conclusion in the first place," Sam responds in a superior tone. I glare, a special hate brewing up inside just for him.

"So, I'm in Die Andere Welt, another world. Where creatures called the Laves are going to study me. Study me for what?" I question, shoving aside my anger for the moment so I can get some answers.

"Laves are superior to humans and are the only creatures that have the knowledge and ability to travel through dimensions. They remained relatively uninterested with us up until World War I, when we unknow-ingly started developing weapons that could kill Laves just as easily as they killed humans.

"Laves then started studying humans to better understand us and, hopefully, to end our fighting and any chance that we could hurt them or each other. So the Laves created a little human colony, where at any given time about one thousand humans of various ages live. We can't ever go back because then we would talk about the Laves, and their whole plan for peace would be ruined," Sam explains lazily, as if he isn't really thinking about what he saying and these words are merely a rehearsed monologue.

I narrow my eyes as Sam continues to look distant. This doesn't add up. Yesterday, he mocked that Lave thing for taking pleasure in killing people; that doesn't sound very peaceful to me. Unless all of the voices were just a dream that I conjured up. But they couldn't have been, could they?

"Okay, so they rip innocent humans away from their families and study them like lab rats, all for the sake of peace?" I ask dubiously, taking out all of the sugar coating.

"Essentially, but the Laves are not the bad guys here," he replies in that same rehearsed voice, his eyes looking far into the distance, like he isn't even paying attention to this conversation anymore.

"And you're not going to do anything about it? You're just going to stay here like a caged animal?"

"Yes," he replies. Now I am starting to get angry.

"Whatever," I say angrily. "You may be okay with being here, but I'm not! I have family and friends to get back to. I need to get home! I—"

Suddenly, Sam's eyes are flashing with anger and he is rushing over to me, getting into my face and grabbing my arms.

"I've been here a lot longer than you, so don't act like you're the only one who will never see your family again! You can't escape—it's suicide. Over a thousand people have had to say goodbye to their past lives. You're not the only one. This isn't the Haylyn show. Get over yourself and move on!" Sam snarls. I look up at him in shock. The smooth, easy guy from just moments ago has suddenly disappeared.

Sam glares at me, his anger already simmering down again. My eyes start to sting, and I shrug off his hands before turning and walking purposefully down the pebbled street. I don't need this.

I walk onto the road of small black pebbles and hear them crunching under my shoes. I will not accept the fact that I will never see my family again, and I can't believe that a thousand people would accept that fact either. There has to be more to the story, and I am getting nowhere with Mr. Mood Swing.

I think about everyone back home. I wonder if they have reported me missing to the police yet. I nearly stop breathing as I am overcome with sadness with a sudden realization: I have missed Cassie's party. My best friend will only turn sixteen once, and I have missed it. Not to mention that Matt and Avery's basketball game has probably already happened, or has been canceled because of my disappearance. I said I wouldn't miss it for the world, and now mine's been turned upside down.

After a few minutes, I hear a fast crunching approaching me, and know that it is Sam running to catch up with me. I force myself to wipe any sadness from my face; I don't need to give him another reason to ridicule me.

"Save it," I tell him when he reaches my side. "I don't like dealing with you, and you don't like dealing with me, so spare the drama and let me find someone else to answer my questions."

"Trust me, if that was an option, I would have thought of it long before you ever woke up. Unfortunately for both of us, I have been assigned to be your mentor, which means I'm stuck with you," Sam simpers.

"Oh, goody, this day just keeps getting better and better," I mutter.

"Doesn't it, though?" Sam replies with a smirk.

"So when will I be able to get rid of you?" I don't know how much more of him I can take. With everything else that's happening, dealing with an annoying boy just isn't going to work.

Sam pauses, working his mouth. For a second, a real emotion actually passes through his eyes before it is replaced by his typical cockiness. "Hmm. I've never had this happen before. Usually the girls want me around; now one wants to get rid of me. Are you, by any chance, a lesbian?" Sam asks haughtily.

"No. Self-righteous jerks just happen not to be my type," I reply smoothly, making his eyebrows momentarily fly up. I grin. *That's right, pretty boy, not every girl is in love with you.*

Sam clears his throat as he tries to regain his usual confidence. "Well, uh, you get rid of me when the Laves decide that you no longer need my mentorship."

"Okay, so mentor me. Let's get this over with," I answer decisively. Somehow bickering with him is helping me keep all of my other emotions at bay. Sam now officially looks flustered. I have no doubt that no girl has ever treated him like this before.

"Okay, well … over there is the town, a few shops run by some of the older folk here who are mostly done being studied by the Laves now," he stammers. I look over to where he is pointing and see a few buildings that don't look quite as cookie-cutter as all the rows of cabins do.

"What is the currency here?" I ask, surprised that my mind is being so practical at a time like this. However, I do not expect this to last long. Soon enough, I will be running around in a full-on panic with lots of tears and screaming involved.

"Most things are free, and if they aren't, the Laves have money that they give you a certain amount of every month. It all depends on how many people you have with you, just like your cabin. You, being alone, get a cabin and money for one. But if a whole family is taken, then the

Laves would accommodate the extra people. However, if you've been here a certain amount of time and save up your money, then you can buy an upgraded cabin that's bigger and nicer."

I nod, my anger slowly fading as he now becomes strictly business-like. I remain silent for a few minutes, trying to soak everything up. Looking around, I feel exposed from the lack of mountains and hills. Growing up next to the Rockies, I always felt protected by their looming forms; now I feel bare. I squint my eyes and notice some tall, menacing trees in the far distance. I typically love the forest, but for some reason all I feel when I look at them is a sense of dread. That and the air, which is filled with the scent of dead roses, give me the impression that all beautiful things wither and die here. It is the same scent I got a whiff of that day in school. The connection makes my skin crawl.

Eventually, my calves start to burn from walking on the shifting rocks. The cabins we pass have a few personal touches, like flowers in the flowerbeds next to the walkways that look like they are struggling to live, or curtains drawn open. We pass a few people on the way, but we keep to ourselves. Everything feels so foreign.

After a few minutes, I finally get the sense to look up at the sky and figure out why I am squinting. I grow unnerved at what I see. The sky is solid white—a giant cotton sheet blaring light down on us. This can't be good for my skin. How is that even possible?

Why did this have to happen to me?

"Sam," I say, breaking the silence as my last thought starts to bother me. "Why me? Why did the Laves pick me out of everyone else in the world? Do I just have really bad luck?"

"All I know is that the Laves said they wanted someone with a temper, a strong will. Then, a few days later, I was being called to mentor someone, and you were there," he answers casually.

"What? I don't even have that bad of a temper!" I exclaim. Sam raises a perfect eyebrow at me. "Okay, so I get mad sometimes," I concede. "But I don't think that it's bad enough for me to get personally singled out, just for anger."

Sam shrugs. "Well, I don't really care to look into it, so it looks like that's the only answer you're getting."

I scrunch my face—some help he is. I have to have the worst luck in the world. I try to focus on my predicament from the outside, like it is all happening to another person, not me. I don't think that it has really set in yet. For now, it's easier than trying to wrap my mind around how terrifying this really is. Besides, part of me still isn't sure if I believe Sam.

We continue to walk, and it has now become obvious that Sam in leading me somewhere. "Where…" I start.

"Silence is a virtue, you know," Sam interrupts. I glare at him, but he continues to look ahead without a care in the world, his confidence completely returned by now and settling back in quite nicely. "It will be easier for the both of us if you could learn to just shut up."

"A virtue that I neither have, nor care to develop," I retort. "Now, answer my question before this has to get harder for the both of us." Sam lets out a huff in surrender. "Now, where are you leading me?"

"I'm taking you to the food court so that stomach of yours will stop performing the mating call of the male gorilla."

I am taken off guard by this. It's true that I am very hungry, but I haven't even noticed my stomach growling. And if I haven't, it's even more surprising that he has.

We finish the rest of the walk in silence, something I'm sure Sam is pleased about. My eyes are too busy taking everything in to be concerned with talking. I try to look for any distinguishing factors in the architecture that might give me a hint as to where we are, but everything is very bland, all clean lines and minimal colors.

After analyzing the architecture, I move on to the people. Occasionally, they talk to each other, bringing to my attention the mix of accents. The clash of cultures makes me think that this place should be bright and bubbly, filled with music and art. Instead, everything seems muted. My gaze follows every person we pass as I try to figure out each one's story, or whether they will tell me what is really going on. But no one pays us any attention. Most people just look at the ground and walk hurriedly. None of them reassure me that everything Sam has said is a lie.

It takes us several minutes before we walk up to a large, two-story building in the shape of an octagon whose roof reaches its highest point in the middle, with eight sloping slides falling down from there. It is by far the biggest building I have seen here yet. Over the double doors in the front of the building is a bright blue sign that reads "Food."

"Well, if that doesn't notify you that there's grub inside, I don't know what will," I remark, placing my hands on my hips as I study the building.

"They have to make it simple so even people like you will understand it," Sam responds.

I give him a look of death and decide that I don't care whether or not he's my mentor; I will get on without him. I stalk off and swing open the door to the food court, running right into someone on her way out. The girl has dirty blonde hair, blue eyes, and small teeth. A toxic cloud of sugary perfume excretes from her skin like a poisonous toad's. She is around five feet eight inches, judging from my own five-foot-four frame, so our collision means she's probably done more damage to me than I have to her. I also feel compelled to point out that she is wearing an outfit that a stripper would adore.

"I'm so sorry!" I sputter, but the girl isn't even looking at me; her gaze is glued to Sam as she twirls her hair with a thin finger and smiles like an idiot. The best part is that Sam obviously does not have the same feelings for her as she does for him.

"Hi, Sam," the girl says, batting her eyelashes, and I notice her voice has tiny traces of a Southern accent.

"Hey, Natalie," Sam replies, looking bored.

"How are you today?" she purrs.

"Fine," he answers airily, his eyes flicking over to me before he continues. "Hey, Natalie, will you do me a favor?" Here he sprouts a dazzling smile that makes two deeply set dimples appear on both sides of his grin. Natalie's eyes widen with such extreme excitement that I have to cover my mouth to keep from laughing out loud.

"Will you show Haylyn how to get food and all that? She just got here yesterday." He gestures to me, making my wide smile disappear in a second. I place my hands on my hips and get ready to sass him into his next life.

"You can't just—" I start before Natalie cuts me off with her annoyingly perky voice.

"Of course, Sam," she answers, smiling and looping her arm through mine, jerking me to her side without even looking at me, enveloping me in her bubble of perfume. I shoot Sam a fiery glare and grow even angrier when I see that his face is filled with amusement.

"Thanks, Natalie. 'Bye, Haylyn!" he calls, giving me a little wave. I frown deeply, and with that Sam turns around casually and starts to walk away. I hear him laugh to himself as Natalie pulls at my arm to face me.

I am so getting Sam back.

CHAPTER 4

"Hey, Haylyn, I'm Natalie! Welcome to Die Andere Welt!" she practically cheers in my ear. I raise my eyebrow. Is she for real?

"Hi," I mutter, not even sure how to handle this new, exploding mess of pep that is even worse than all of the girls at my school.

"I see you've met Sam," she says, staring, mesmerized, at his shrinking silhouette in the distance. "Isn't he dreamy?"

"A real charmer," I growl.

Natalie shakes her head and looks sad to turn away from Sam. She takes a moment to wallow in her emotions and then smiles at me. "So, what do you wanna do?"

I sigh. Some girls never change. I would think that being kidnapped and thrown into another world, away from their families, might help chip away that façade a little. Clearly, I thought wrong.

"Well, I was on my way to get some food. Could we do that?" I ask in defeat, even though Sam has already told her what she is supposed to show me.

"Of course we can! I do believe my friends are still eating. I just finished, but we can join them!"

Yay, more brats to deal with, I think. "Sounds great, thanks!" is what I say out loud, though.

I open the door, and a burst of warm air blows out at me. Natalie links her overly tanned arm with mine and hauls me inside. She obviously doesn't understand the meaning of personal space.

Once we are inside, I let myself look around. The building is huge, reminding me of the cafeterias they have at summer camps. A few wooden pillars stand out here and there, supporting the massive, slanted ceiling.

The floor is made out of a light-colored wood, and a few lame pictures of grass and rocks decorate the walls.

Moving all about the room are about two hundred people of all different ages. I let out a sigh of relief once I see that there are no Laves here. Natalie calls out to two other girls, and they begin to walk over to us. One has smooth, olive-colored skin with black hair and a calm expression; her left arm is in a sling, but everything else is perfectly done up. The other girl has short, blonde hair tied messily up in a ponytail, a style that reminds me of Cassie's. All of them look to be around my age, but I have seen clowns with more natural looks than the three of them are sporting.

"Tana, Emily, this is Haylyn. She's new," Natalie announces.

"Hi, Haylyn," says Tana in an accent that I can't quite place, while brushing back her black hair with her good hand.

"Hey," I reply, always the great first-impression maker.

"So, are you excited?"Tana asks, her accent now making it clear that she must be from the East Coast.

"Excited?" I question.

"Yeah! Excited to be here?" she continues. I eye her, wondering what makeup product that she must have accidentally inhaled while piling it on has made her so loopy.

"Excitement is not exactly the word I would use to describe how I feel about being here," I reply. Terrified? Of course. Confused? Definitely. Annoyed? Sure, I mean, I'm dealing with *these* people. But excited? Absolutely not.

"Why not? It's great here. Watching does sort of suck, and so does the food, but it makes dieting a breeze!" Natalie says with delight. My eyebrows scrunch together; they are worried about dieting? I don't even bother asking what the hell "Watching" is.

"You just need to adjust," pipes up the blonde girl, who must be Emily. Her words have no twang or apparent accent, which sounds more like what I am used to on the West Coast.

"Yeah, after the first week, you'll love it!" Tana agrees, breezing over her r's, in a Northeastern accent of some sort. "I've been here for about a year, and now I'm completely used to everything."

"I've been here six months, but it already feels like home," Emily adds, her blue eyes flashing remorse so quickly that I wonder if I'm imagining it.

"And I've been here longer than both of them," Natalie gloats, as though she prides herself on this fact.

"So that's it?" I ask. "You just accept that you can never go back? Don't you want to do everything you can to escape?"

"Why would we?" Tana asks in disbelief.

"You just need some time to adjust," Emily repeats, sticking to her same argument.

I stare at them. They can't really believe in all this, but all of them just continue to look at me with wide, honest eyes. "Why don't you show me how to get food now?" I ask Natalie, in an effort to break the awkward silence that has sprung up.

Natalie nods enthusiastically, smiling. "Yeah! Tana, Emily, go save us a table," she commands to her two followers. "You must be hungry," she says as she starts to lead me to where the food must be.

"Yeah, starving. I can't wait to get a hamburger in my stomach!" I exclaim. Natalie gives me a weird look, and I suddenly feel like there is something that I'm not getting. Natalie looks lost for a second and then smiles again, as if there has been some sort of mental lag.

"Oh, we don't have any of those. Sorry, it took me a second, I just haven't heard that word in so long. There actually isn't any meat at all."

No meat? I'm supposed to go vegetarian? Oh. Hell. No. I am not a tofu kind of girl. I demand to have my bacon! I start to panic again before forcing myself to calm down. I will get out of here, and when I do, I will eat all the hamburgers I want. Until then, I have to play nice and pretend to love whatever crap they try to force down my throat.

"Oh, okay, then I will just see what they have on the menu," I eventually manage to spit out.

Natalie turns on her heel at my word and starts to weave her way in and out of the throng of people. At first I worry that she has no idea where she is going, but then I realize that she is leading me to a counter that looks like any other counter at a café, with a small line of people.

"This is so weird," I declare under my breath. We wait in an awkward silence while I shift my weight from foot to foot. Normally, while waiting in line, I would be perusing the menu, but there isn't anything close to a menu anywhere. Eventually, I give up looking for one, and slowly the line moves forward until Natalie and I are at the counter.

The man behind the counter looks to be around sixty years old and has kind eyes surrounded by wrinkles and a bushy, gray mustache. I let out a sigh and ask for some peanut butter toast. It's delicious, and it doesn't contain any meat.

"I'm sorry, but the meal of the day is mash," he says with sorrow in his voice, like he knows that I'm new and hates to be the one to break this news to me. "That is the only thing that we will be serving today."

"Like mashed potatoes?" I ask.

"Um, no. Just mash," the man replies, sounding as if he comes from the Midwest. All of these different accents are starting to make it harder to come up with a logical reason for why we are all here, instead of the crazy reason Sam gave me.

"And what the heck is that supposed to be?" I demand, starting to get annoyed with everything about this stupid world.

"Just bring her a bowl, she'll know what it is when it arrives," Natalie announces from behind me.

The man shuffles away before I can argue further, and before I can wheel my anger over to Natalie, he is back with a paper bowl full of some suspicious substance. I take it in my hand and see something that looks like oatmeal, but with cold water. I absently thank the man for his service, even though I don't feel very thankful, and awkwardly stand there, not knowing whether this stuff is free or not.

"You don't have to pay, silly," Natalie speaks up from behind me. "All the food is free."

"Oh, okay. Sorry," I say. I guess it's good that I don't have to pay, considering I have no money from the Laves yet, but based on this meal's appearance, I don't know if I would pay even if I had to. Natalie gives me an encouraging look before skipping off to the table where Tana and Emily sit.

Since I don't know what else to do, I follow Natalie absentmindedly to a small table, where two of its four chairs are filled with Tana and Emily. Natalie doesn't hesitate at all before sitting down and joining them, but

I stand at the head of the table, clutching my bowl. I feel weird about joining their friend group, especially when I don't particularly like any of them and I can't imagine any of them particularly liking me.

All three girls lift their overly shadowed eyes to my looming figure, and I let out a small smile and sit down. "So what happened to your arm?" I ask Tana, trying to make everything less awkward.

"Oh, it's broken," Tana answers, her accent heavily lacing her words. Maybe she is from Boston?

"How'd you break it?" I inquire, remembering the time that I fell off the swing set in elementary school and broke my arm.

"I answered two questions wrong on the same day," she says, looking sheepish.

"What?"

"The Laves did it to me, for answering two questions wrong. I was being stupid."

"That's terrible! How could they do that?" I exclaim, causing all three girls to give me weird looks. How can all of them look so calm about this news, like I'm the crazy one?

"It's protocol. The Laves are no-nonsense," Tana adds with a shrug that makes her wince.

"No-nonsense? I think they're a little worse than no-nonsense," I comment.

"Don't worry, you'll get used to the Laves' rules eventually," Natalie soothes.

That's what I worry about—myself becoming just like these three girls. I worry that, after months of being stuck here, eventually I will become numb to punishments like this. This can't really be happening. They couldn't all really have been stuck here for that long, and I won't be either.

All three girls continue to watch me, so I quickly take a bite of my food, as if to prove that I am fine. Once the spoon touches my mouth, I instantly find myself regretting that decision. Forget what I said about pretending to like whatever crap they try to feed me because I can't do it. This stuff is nasty! Dry oatmeal with cold water—yeah, worst thing ever.

I shove my bowl away from me and try to pay attention to the Barbies' conversation, which includes numerous high-pitched giggles and an overload of very expressive hand gestures. One of them is waving her hand around so violently that I fear she will hit one of the others in the face. After a while, the call of hunger is too much, and I make myself take a few bites of the mash.

As I eat, my eyes study them. What I find most peculiar is that every single one of them has bitten-down nails. I can't picture any of these perfectly fake girls having a habit that would ruin her nails like this, but all three of them do it. The bad habit is usually brought on by anxiety, which makes me wonder what they are so anxious about. A sense of dread fills me as I imagine all the things they must be nervous about, if what everyone keeps telling me is true about this place.

I force myself to brush aside my fear and keep eating. I need to keep up my strength. I have completely zoned out of their conversation, but my ears perk up when I hear a name I am particularly curious about: Sam.

"Oh my God, you should have seen him today! He looked so fine!" Natalie exclaims, giggling. Tana and Emily swoon at her luck to have been able to talk to him. "I mean, he was practically all over me," Natalie continues.

I just roll my eyes; even I, whose love life is nonexistent, can tell that her love for him is unrequited. "I mean, don't you think he's hot, Haylyn?" Natalie inquires, suddenly making every pair of eyes flick over to me. I put down my spoon awkwardly and swallow another lump of disgustingness.

"Uh…" I don't know how to answer. I mean, well, yes, his looks are undeniable, but thinking about boys while I am stuck in this horrible world is just too absurd. Especially boys who are unfeeling jerks. So I go with the safest answer. "Yeah, I do, but he would look better with you, Natalie," Tana and Emily scowl at this, but Natalie is beaming. The other two may not like me now, but I have just earned some serious points in Natalie's book.

"You really think so?" she cries.

"Yeah, definitely," I reply, wishing desperately that I could just say no and ruin this annoying, overly cheerful charade. The three other girls continue their fanatic discussion of Sam, and after a few more bites, I give up on the mash and start to work on getting an annoying hangnail off.

I vaguely listen, since their discussion still involves Sam. Apparently, he has the top grades in class and is extremely toned. What I want to know is why he is extremely annoying. Unfortunately, why he has an attitude problem doesn't come up in their discussions.

"And tomorrow I can take Haylyn out shopping! Won't that be fun?" Natalie exclaims, turning all their attention back to me. I let out an embarrassed laugh at being caught not paying attention again. How exactly has their conversation gone from Sam's cuteness to shopping with me?

"Yeah, sure," I reply. "Hey, is it okay if I just head back to my cabin for tonight? I'm feeling pretty tired."

"Okay, see ya!" Natalie says, waving her hand and not turning to look at me when I stand up from the table. I can't help but feel slightly deflated at her lack of attention.

I lift my chin up and put on a brave face as I throw away my bowl and head outside. I shudder as the cold air nips at my cheeks. The whiteness is leaving the sky at a rapid rate, bringing in its place utter blackness. It is turning so dark that I can barely see more than a few yards ahead of me. The only light comes from a couple feet away, where a few street lights line the rows of cabins. I look to the sky to search for moonlight and see nothing but an inky canvas. There is no moon, no stars. My heart longs for the glittering sky dwellers, but I make myself look at the ground again. I begin to walk forward in what I believe to be the direction from which I came when Sam walked me to the food court earlier.

As I walk, an eerie feeling starts to chase me. I hunch my shoulders, trying to protect myself from the invisible threat, but it doesn't make the bad feeling stop lingering. The gravel crunching under my feet is the only noise in the still night. I can't shake the feeling that I need to hurry up and get back to my cabin before something bad happens.

After an immeasurable amount of time, it is official that I am lost. The light has long since left the sky, and I am left wandering alone in the dark. My ears long to hear something besides the constant grinding of gravel under my shoes. *Crunch. Crunch. Crunch.* I stop moving to take a quick breather, and to stop hearing the sound of gravel. I take a shaky breath in and let it back out when *crunch, crunch, crunch…* Footsteps pound into the gravel at a rapid rate from somewhere off to the side.

With fear striking into my core, I huddle against the closest cabin and peer back into an alleyway between two rows of cabins. I hug the side of the building, as though it can protect me while I search for whatever is running. I am about to give up looking when a figure runs out into the alleyway right in front of me.

I gasp. The closest street lamp is only a few feet away from the figure, making it easy to tell that it is definitely human.

Whoever this person is, he or she doesn't seem to see me in my hiding spot. As I watch, I wonder what this person is up to, running with a dark hood pulled up to obscure the face it covers. It certainly doesn't look like your typical evening jog. The figure sprints as though its life depends on it. And who knows, it could.

The person continues to run straight until black figures come out of nowhere and tackle it to the ground. I clasp my hand to my mouth to keep from screaming. The person lets out a screech, and the black shadows stand up again and grab the person's arms, holding them still. I focus in on the fast-moving shadows and feel an icy fear grip me. They are Laves.

Two Laves hold the person down, and a third walks out from the shadows to face it. I see several more against the walls of cabins, keeping guard or ready to jump in case that's needed. I know that I should get out of here, but the second I take a step away, the crunching of the gravel will alert every one of those Laves to my presence.

The Lave facing the person pulls off the hood, releasing long, bright-red hair. The figure is a woman. She gasps in pain as the two Laves holding her jerk her arms to force her to look up at the third Lave standing before her.

"What's going on?" the woman pleads. I want to run out and help her, but I can't even seem to breathe.

"Don't act stupid, Kat. We know that you are up to something," the third Lave hisses. I shrink back at the noise, but the woman shows no fear.

"Do you, now? And what exactly is it that you think I'm up to?" she drawls, switching from her innocent act to a more predatory one.

The Lave narrows its charcoal eyes and hisses in annoyance.

"Ha, you know nothing. If only suspicions were as easy as admissions; I'm not telling you anything," she snaps, provoking the lead Lave to wrap his gnarled hands around her throat.

"I can think of a few things that might loosen your tongue," he growls.

The woman's eyes remain hard. "I'm sure you can. But seeing as I'm a human, I know that you can't kill me. I need to be alive in order to tell you what I'm up to, so do your worst," she sputters through the death grip on her throat.

The Lave snarls. "Take her away," he commands to the other two Laves. They begin to drag her down the street, and the rest come out from the shadows to follow them ... all except one.

I stand there horrified as the woman is dragged away. I feel relief that they are gone until the noises come—loud thuds followed by piercing screams echoing from several cabins down. I feel sick to my stomach and tears sting my eyes. The screams continue for several minutes before finally stopping, and I can't help but think that it is not because they have decided that she's had enough.

I wipe tears from my cheeks and remain still, for one lone Lave is still across the street. It waits several minutes after the screams stop before taking one last look around and slinking into the shadows.

I heave in ragged breaths before standing up again. I wander around aimlessly, feeling incapable of emotion because I am too consumed by fear. I think I will be here all night, until I finally recognize one of the streets from earlier and find my way back to my cabin from there.

I approach my cabin, open its thick wooden door, and step in. As soon as I close the door behind me and confirm to myself that it's the same one where I woke up in this morning, I let out a long, terrified scream.

I claw at my hair until I finally manage to calm back down again. Who was that woman? What information could she possibly have that the Laves would want so badly? What happened to her?

It also strikes me how no one has come to check on me, even after my bloody-murder scream. Because no one in this world cares about me. I feel the loneliness start to eat at me, closing its hands around my throat, and know that if I stay here long enough, it won't matter how many deep breaths I take ... it will suffocate me.

I dig my phone out from where I hid it under my dresser earlier. I wait patiently as it turns on and feel sadness as I see that, yet again, there is no service. I didn't really expect it to change, though; I only turned it on so I could scroll through all of my old pictures. I need my friends' and family's strength now more than ever.

I crawl into the bed with my shoes and all my clothes on and scroll through all of my pictures and conversations with my friends. *How did all of this happen?* I ask myself, disbelieving that I could be stuck in this unfamiliar world. *I don't deserve this!* I feel my mind filling with an unsettling woe as I look down at all the smiling faces of the people I love dearly—people that I may never see again.

The thought sends me into a wave of depression. I wonder what all of them are doing tonight. What did they do when I didn't come back from my walk? Police and volunteers are probably searching for me. I want to scream at them, tell them that they aren't going to find me! My parents are probably in hysterical tears, and I can't do anything to help them.

I will never get to hug my mom again. There will be no more goodnight kisses from my dad on the very top of my head. I will never again get to ruffle Avery's hair and laugh when he protests. I will never get to tell them goodbye, or that I love them. Silent tears crawl down my face as I think of my family and of that poor woman I saw in the street. I turn off my phone to save its battery and fall asleep cradling it.

CHAPTER 5

I WAKE UP TO A loud pounding on my door and check the clock. It has only been an hour since I fell asleep. I rub my eyes as I start to stand up and head for the door, as though I can rub away the sadness.

I was dreaming of my childhood before the pounding woke me up. It was a memory from when I was ten years old, and dinner was minutes away from being ready. My parents had the Jack Johnson song "Do you remember" playing loudly throughout the house. My dad scooped me up from my room and carried me all around the house. I snuggled into his shoulder as he sang the lyrics to me: "Over ten years have gone by, but you're still mine." Even at the time this made me cry, though I tried hard not to show it, because I could feel how much he loved me. If I thought dealing with it then was hard, now it becomes unbearable.

I wipe my eyes as unwanted tears begin to fall. I want to crawl into a corner and start rocking myself in the fetal position while sobbing, but I can't surrender to it. I have to keep going. I will get home, and when I do, I don't want to have to spend all of my time in therapy.

I take a deep breath, regaining my composure before opening the door and getting a shock to the senses. Right there in front of me is Sam. My breath catches with a mixture of excitement and anger. His head is turned, his hair a dark chocolate in the black night. When he turns around, I know he must see my tear-streaked face, despite my efforts to wipe them away, because for a second he actually looks remorseful.

"Well, are you going to invite me in, or am I going to have to keep standing here all night long?" he asks smoothly.

"Depends," I say hotly, not in the mood for pity and not in the mood for him.

"And what would that depend on?" he inquires with a note of teasing.

"The reason that you're here. For instance, if you're here to apologize, then be my guest. Otherwise, I was trying to sleep, so get lost."

"I have nothing to apologize for," he states, shoving his way past me into my cabin. I let out a loud huff and slam the door.

"So leaving me in a strange world with some stripper wannabe and then making me find my own way back to my cabin in the dark doesn't deserve an apology in your book? Not to mention how incredibly rude you were!" I announce in a rush. For some reason, I don't feel comfortable bringing up the woman I saw getting attacked, so I don't mention it.

"Damn, what's your problem? Is it that time of the month?" Sam asks with a smirk.

Unbelievable! I take the closest thing next to me, which just happens to be my left shoe, and throw it at him as hard as I can. Unfortunately, Sam whips his hand out and catches it before it can hit his face. His eyebrows rise in amusement.

"Well, well. Here is that temper that the Laves were talking about," he says, the smirk on his face growing deeper as he swings my shoe around.

"I don't have a temper!" I exclaim. "I'm mad, and reasonably so, considering I'm being provoked by the biggest douche in the world!"

Sam looks around with fake interest. "Really? He's here? I'd have thought that you two would hit it off," he says sweetly, tossing my shoe to the corner.

"Well, considering that he's more annoying than Dora when she can't find the bridge that's directly behind her, you can imagine why I have problems dealing with him," I parry, both of us knowing that I'm talking about Sam.

"Hey, don't yell at me! It's not my fault you can't make friends. It all goes back to that temper of yours; you should really invest in some anger-management classes." He is smiling as if he's just given me great advice. My hands tighten and my nails are starting to bite into my palms. This boy gets to me like no one else can.

"Why do you have to be such an ass all the time? Do you really hate me that much? Or are you just naturally a jerk?" I question, finally having enough of this snappy banter.

He gives me a look, and I watch as he prowls around my room. I stand still, resisting the urge to turn around when he disappears behind me. I refuse to let him know how much he affects me. There is a moment of silence before I feel the warmth of Sam's chest pressing into my back.

"I don't *hate* you," he whispers into my hair, his voice stretching the word hate. I shiver at his breath and step forward to escape his proximity.

"And what is that supposed to mean?" I inquire. Sam steps around me so I am facing him again and gives me a wink, remaining elusive. I shake my head and suddenly just feel tired—tired of this place, of its stupid people and complicated head games.

"What are you here for, Sam?" I demand sullenly.

"Can't a guy just want to say hello?" he jokes.

"Not really."

"Well, if you must know, I'm here to tell you that you'll start Watching tomorrow," he says.

"And Watching is…?" I question, remembering Natalie saying how it sucked.

"Watching is basically the school of this world. It's where the Laves separate us based on age and teach us our basic core classes and study us."

"More school, because I was so great at that in the other world," I mumble, feeling angst.

"Exactly!" Sam beams, ignoring my sarcasm. "I will be here tomorrow at eight to pick you up; dress to impress!" He glances down at my jeans and Queen t-shirt. "That's not impressive."

I swing my hand, aiming for Sam's jaw, but he is already gone, slipping through my door without further comment. I let out a frustrated huff and fall back onto my bed. I begrudgingly set my alarm for the morning, so that I will have time to get ready. It doesn't seem like I have much choice in this.

I think about what Watching must be like and feel my intestines tying themselves into knots. I know that Laves will be there. How am supposed to walk right into their trap after everything I've seen them do? They broke Tana's arm, terrified three narcissistic girls into biting their nails off, and beat some poor woman in the street.

My body shakes with fear. I feel so helpless to deal with everything that is happening to me. What if tomorrow they break my arm? Or beat me? I am at the mercy of the Laves. I don't care what Sam and those stupid girls said, the Laves cannot be innocents trying to study us for the sake of peace. They are anything but innocent.

CHAPTER 6

THE MORNING COMES WITH THE sound of an alarm blaring into life. I reach around to stop the noise and ignore its demand that I must get up. Deep down I know that I should be launching into a frenzy to get ready, but I don't have it in me to care right now. Instead, I just lie on my bed with my arms spread out as I try to process everything that has happened to me. I think half of me still expected to wake up this morning back in my own bed, and now that it hasn't happened, I don't know what to do.

My life was so simple and ordinary just a few days ago—yes, maybe a bit boring, but this was not what I wanted. Otherworldly creatures that have horrible taste in food and whose hobbies include kidnapping a bunch of people and forcing them to live in cabins like some kind of messed-up camp? Never in my wildest dreams would I have thought that one up.

I think back to what the Laves look like and shudder, and I remember what they did last night to that poor woman. What did she do to deserve that? How am I supposed to live in a world that scares me so much? Before, when I complained that I wanted a more exciting life, I didn't mean that I wanted my life to turn into some sort of bad horror movie.

Unwillingly, my thoughts go back to my regular life; my subconscious wants to go home. Right now, at this time back home, I would be walking to school with Matt, most likely complaining about the long day ahead. That would go on for a while, but then Matt would make some cheesy joke, and I would forget all about my troubles and just throw my head back and laugh.

I am suddenly reminded that I will never see Matt again. The thought doesn't seem real. I have been seeing Matt's frizzy curls and goofy grin every day for eight years, and now I'm just supposed to let him go? I can't do that.

Is this karma playing some cruel joke? When I said my life was so boring, I just meant that I wanted to get my driver's license. Another pang hits when I realize that my driver's license is something I will never get now. Wow, karma really is a bitch.

I think about my family once more, as it all seems to sink in that I won't see them again. That I am stuck in a world where I hate everyone and the food sucks.

I blink away more tears that slide down my cheeks and dampen my hair. I am usually not a girl who cries this much, but as more and more thoughts of despair come, I can't seem to help it. Besides, if there were ever a good time to cry, it would be now. Everything that I thought would be mine is gone. Goodbye, college. Goodbye, twenty-first birthday. Goodbye, being walked down the aisle by my father on my wedding day. Goodbye, all hopes and dreams I ever had.

I roll over onto my side and curl into a ball. I wish that I could go back five minutes to before all these thoughts came crashing down on me because, now that they have, it is really depressing. I hug my knees to my chest and decide that I deserve to cry, and then I start to let it all out in unladylike sobs.

I am so lost in my own head that I barely hear my name when it is spoken in a gasp. I decide to ignore it and go back to my dark thoughts when suddenly I am being yanked out of my bed and forced to stand up by strong hands that clasp my shoulders. Irritated that someone has interrupted my much-needed cry session, I shake my head so that my hair covers my face, as though I can show that I am closed for business. Unfortunately for me, whoever it is pushes my hair back again and gently slides the pad of a thumb against my cheeks, wiping away the tears.

"Haylyn! Don't do this, you're fine, everything will be fine," a voice pleads. I can now tell that it is Sam. I mean, no duh, he said he would be here at eight, so it's obviously him, but somehow I didn't really expect him to actually come. I try to break away; I'm never quite comfortable being comforted. But to my surprise, he pulls me into a hug. I've hugged Matt like a thousand times, but this couldn't be more different. I can feel his hard muscles, but they are handling me like I am as delicate as thin glass. I put my head on his chest and cry, too exhausted to hold on to any dignity. My mind screams to me, *What are you doing?* But I tell it to shut up.

I can feel Sam's heartbeat jumping out of his shirt. I gradually try to relax my clenched muscles and let myself breathe in his scent—a mixture of cinnamon, citrus, and something that I can't quite put my finger on that is noticeably masculine. Little by little my tears dry, and my breaths become less ragged. I take a deep breath and step back to look into his eyes. His pupils are dilated, and his touch is friendly and protective. I see myself in his eyes, as well as his own worry.

"I really don't think that I can go to that school thing today," I murmur quietly after a silent minute. I take him in—his beige sweater, jeans, and Converse shoes. His brown hair looks freshly brushed for the day ahead. His lips press together and his emotions swirl in his eyes like the clouds during a storm.

"I wouldn't think of sending you," he answers, his hands slightly out, as though he wants to reach for me again. "I had hoped that you would be one of the few that took to this place right away; I guess I was wrong."

"Yeah, you were," I say, giving the smallest of smiles and feeling my heart leap when Sam returns it. "So what now?"

"Therapy," Sam answers.

"Therapy!" I ask in astonishment. I am not about to go complain about my life to strangers while they tell me all the things wrong with me. Besides, the only reason I am having this embarrassing meltdown is because I am mourning my old life. If they want to cure me, then they will have to send me back home.

"Yes, therapy."

"That is the stupidest thing I have ever heard," I grumble angrily.

"It will help you to get over the human world and adjust here," Sam replies.

"But I don't want to get over the human world! I want to go back!" I say exasperatedly, sitting on my bed away from Sam. Gingerly, he sits next to me.

"Haylyn, there is life here, too. It may have not been what you pictured, but everything will be okay; life goes on here," he whispers, coaxing me to turn around. I can feel his warm breath on my ear, but I stay firm and refuse to turn to meet his steady gaze. I flinch as he stands up quickly.

"Someone will be here at three to begin your therapy," he says plainly. He heads for the door, then suddenly stops and turns to face me again. He stands there, hesitating, his hands clasping and unclasping as though he is struggling to grasp a thought, before his eyes slowly find mine.

"What?" I question, never liking a pair of eyes staying on me for too long.

"I don't want you to get bad again while I'm gone," he says. "Are you sure that you're going to be fine?"

"Yeah, I'll be fine," I whisper, wondering whether I am telling the truth.

"Are you sure?" he presses, being unnaturally caring. I nod, and after one last pained look in my direction, Sam is gone. Usually, when Sam leaves, I feel angry and annoyed; now I just feel conflicted. I fear that the darkness of my mind will come back again now that Sam has left me alone. I hope that I will be able to make it through this mess without losing my mind.

I try to force myself to get up. If I go somewhere, maybe I can distract myself from all of my memories threatening to pull me under. I shuffle into the bathroom and look at the mess that is my hair. I brush it out with the brush the Laves have provided and try to French braid it the way I like it. After numerous failed attempts, I get frustrated and slam my brush onto the counter, my hair coming undone as I stare at my reflection.

Of course I can't French braid my own hair. My mom always does it for me. Who is supposed to braid my hair now? I suppose that, being my age, I should be able to do it myself and that I will learn to do it, but that's not the point. The point is that my mom will never braid my hair again. That *I will never see her again.*

I crawl back into my bed as the memories reclaim me. I remember being four when a little jar of candy was kept on the top of my bookshelf, where I couldn't reach it. Every morning, my mom would wake me up with a sweet voice and open my curtains, letting in golden light. Then, after I was up and dressed, she would pull down the jar and give me one bite-sized Snickers, and I would run off to start my day, filled to the brim with happiness.

The smell of grass washes over me as I remember how, when Avery and I were little, my dad would mow the lawn and make huge piles of grass. Then Avery and I would run around and jump into them, or make forts out of them. I don't remember exactly when all the fun of my dad's lawn mowing ended, but for years now, my dad has been bagging the grass in garbage bags, and I never see it. I wish that I could go back in time and jump into the piles of grass with Avery every week that my dad mowed. It seems now as if every time I didn't do that, it was a wasted opportunity.

I remember being twelve and lying outside on the trampoline one night, with my father next to me. We lay there for hours as he pointed out all the constellations to me. I still remember his deep voice as he talked and pointed each one out. He seemed to know everything back then. I can still feel the cold plastic of the trampoline pressing against my back. I was so cold, but I didn't want to go inside and miss all the wonderful stories he was telling me about Greek heroes.

I angrily wipe the tears away from my cheeks. It's the happy memories that hurt the most because I have to face the fact that I may never have another happy memory with any of those people again.

I slowly open my eyes and gasp as I see Avery leaning over me. He looks at me with that troubled smile. I reach for him, but in a second, he is gone. Oh great, I'm hallucinating. Now I've really gone off the deep end.

"When are you coming home, Haylyn?" a voice calls, and I recognize it as Matt's. I whimper and close my eyes until I see stars. I stretch my fingers, feeling Foxy's rough coat under them. I ball my hands and shove them under my pillow. *Hello, Crazy Town? I've got your new mayor right here.*

Moments later, another voice comes. It is a man clearing his throat. Agitated, I put my pillow over my head, just wanting the visions to stop. A second later, the voice comes again. Now I know it is real. I peek my head out from under the soft cushion. In front of me stands a man with a balding head and a brown tweed suit. He smiles at me, a nice, kind smile that helps me relax. He has an aura that radiates calm and safety. He reminds me of my grandfather, and the deep lines around his eyes tell of the many people he has given the same comforting smile to.

"Hello, I'm Mr. McKulhan," this strange man announces. I stare blankly until I realize he has just addressed me and is waiting for my answer.

"I'm Haylyn Jones," I reply shakily.

He nods. "Very nice. I'm your 'therapist,' so to speak," he says, taking a seat on the chair in the corner of the room. "However, I prefer to call myself a counselor. I will listen to your fears and worries and give you my thoughts and ideas. So tell me anything you need to tell me."

I smile. He is already my favorite person in this world.

"Well, I don't know," I start hesitantly before it all comes rushing out of me. "What is there to say? I'm stuck in some messed-up world away from my family, trying to process the loss of my former life. I'm hallucinating, so now not only am I in a different world, but I'm losing my flipping mind! To top it all off, everyone here is annoying, and my captors look like something that walked straight out of a child's nightmare.

"I just want to go home, so if it's not too much trouble… Scratch that, I don't care if it troubles you, I need to go home now! I already missed a birthday party for one of my best friends, so I have to go back and apologize for that, and it's almost Christmas!"

By the end of my rant, the tears have started to fall again, and I try to hastily wipe them away before it becomes some big deal where he feels like he has to comfort me.

As I shove the water off my cheeks, I wonder what is wrong with me. Matt is one of my best friends and has *never* seen me cry! Now it's all I seem to be able to do. I pull myself together and say, "Sorry, I'm usually not like this. I hate crying. It's just that I don't even know how to handle this."

Mr. McKulhan sits patiently, soaking in my words, before answering. Then he calmly says, "It's a hard situation, and I am sorry that I don't have the power to get you home."

I deflate further but keep from crying another set of tears.

"But if this isn't what you're like," he asks, "then what *are* you like?"

I think for a second. His question catches me off guard.

"Well, I'm Haylyn Jones. I like reading, watching TV, and going to the movies with my friends. I love animals; my favorite is a wolf because they are fearless, but only when they have their friends to support them, which is like me because I need my friends, too. My favorite color is purple. I have two best friends named Matt and Cassie. They are so much better than they will ever know. And…" I falter when I see Mr. McKulhan's smile. I am rambling, but it is making me feel better.

"Haylyn, if that's who you are, then why are you acting like someone you're not? This is still you, just a 'you' who has been relocated."

Before I can respond, he gets up and declares, "You can be all of those things here, too." He walks with a slow gait toward the door and starts to turn the handle when I find my voice again.

"Mr. McKulhan!" I call. He stops and turns to face me. "Am I done?"

He chuckles. "We will meet at the same time tomorrow, but yes, we are done for today." He opens the door, leaving me feeling much better. I barely have five minutes to think about what Mr. McKulhan has said when another knock comes at my door. This time it's Natalie.

"Hey, Haylyn! I heard you've been having a rough day," she announces as she shoulders her way into my cabin. Before closing the door, I silently curse Sam for telling her

"Hey, Natalie," I reply with resignation.

"So I had been planning to take you out shopping," Natalie starts, "but since you were having a mental breakdown, I took it upon myself to go shopping for you!" She holds out several large bags as proof.

I eye the bags skeptically. If Natalie got me outfits that are anything like her clothes, I am in for a world of low-cut shirts and tight pants. "Um, thanks Natalie," I say with as much enthusiasm as I can muster while taking the bags from her.

"No problem. I had the cashier charge everything onto your account, so it didn't cost me a thing, and I love shopping for other people; it makes me feel like I'm a stylist for the stars!"

I give a small smile at this confession because Natalie is just so ridiculous. She lives in her own little world of sunshine and rainbows, and when I'm with her, for that brief moment, it's like I can feel the sun's rays on my cheeks. She makes me believe that maybe not *all* happiness dies here.

"Well, thanks anyway," I reply.

"But wait, there's more! I have decided to do something for you that always makes me feel better."

"And that is?"

"A makeover," she divulges with a manic gleam in her eye.

"A makeover?"

"Yes, a makeover! You know, I'll do your hair and makeup, fix you up all nice and pretty. It's hard to be upset when you know you look sexy."

I snort. "Yeah, I don't know about that, Natalie."

"Oh, come on! What's there to be afraid of? It'll be fun!"

I look at Natalie's pleading eyes and feel my heart melt a little bit. She reminds me of Cassie when she was twelve and just discovering the magic of eyeshadow. She was so excited about it that she needed to share it with the world; there were a lot of days in the seventh grade when I went to school with blue eyeshadow.

"Okay."

"Okay?"

"Yeah, do your worst," I say.

At this, Natalie squeals and pulls me into a hug. "You won't regret it, Haylyn!" she declares.

I try to resist as much as possible at first, but I learn quickly that it is easier just to give in. So I obey as she insists that I take a shower and use her favorite conditioner. Then she makes me sit in a chair for an hour as she does my hair and makeup. Let me tell you, this girl does makeup like it's her job.

Thanks to Natalie, when we are all done, I look gorgeous. My hair is curled perfectly, my makeup flawless. My eyes look huge and are surrounded by long black lashes. Natalie is definitely much better at makeovers than twelve-year-old Cassie.

When it comes to picking out an outfit, I am initially worried, but I quickly realize that Natalie found me a lot of cute things that are far more conservative (in a good way) than anything I've seen her wear. After perusing my newly stocked closet, I settle on black leggings and a long brown sweater with matching brown boots.

When Natalie finally finishes my makeover, she touches up her own makeup one last time before dragging me out the door. I momentarily worry about going outside for the first time since last night, when I saw that woman being attacked, but something about walking with a person as mundane as Natalie has me feeling safe from the otherworldly. She fusses over my curls the whole way there, conveying a motherly sense that comforts me and distracts me from how messed up this whole situation is. However, with Natalie acting motherly, it makes me think of my own mother.

It's funny how we think of everyday things differently after we've lost them. Suddenly, they go from ordinary to extraordinary. There is also the guilt of not appreciating them as we should have. I wish that I could go back and spend a day with my mom—more than I ever would have had I not been taken, and this thought makes me sad. Now she'll never get to know how much she really means to me.

When we finally make our way to the food court, I am stunned by the amount of people that are actually here. It's way more crowded than it was last night. The masses of people move back and forth in a diverse collage. The room is abuzz with their noise, all of them with their own agendas, thoughts, and worries. A person would almost think that this is a regular buffet upon seeing it as a whole. It's not until looking closer that it is clear something is wrong. A close look at each individual's pinched face and tight smile reveals a pain that cuts to the core.

Before I have any time to wallow in this revelation, Natalie is leaving me, saying she is going to find Tana and Emily. I sigh and scan the room until I find the counter with a line of people in front of it. I cut through the crowd and step in line. I wait for several minutes before arriving at the front. I smile as I notice that working the counter is the same nice man who served me before.

"What's it going to be today?" I ask, now knowing better than to try and order.

"Dough flats," he replies politely. I sigh, also knowing better this time around than to ask what the hell a dough flat is.

"Okay, serve me up," I say with resignation. The man smiles and hands me a plate of round, plain, cooked dough. I sniff it and shrug before taking a bite. It tastes sort of like plain pizza dough, except it leaves your mouth feeling dry as cotton. I ask the man for a glass of water and slurp down several gulps in order to get rid of the dry feeling. After all that, it is still better than mash, so I take another bite.

I turn around, hoping to find Natalie and the wannabes in a timely manner. I scrunch my eyes, ready to scan the room, but instead find myself face to face with Sam. He smiles charmingly; his teeth looking insanely bright under the lights. A brown jacket is thrown on top of the same outfit he wore earlier today. His eyes are clouded with thought, and I long to know what he is thinking. I would have guessed that Sam is in a great mood, but I can tell by the tense set of his shoulders that he is veiling his real emotions.

"Hello, Haylyn," he greets me, with his arms entwined in front of him and his gaze fluttering up and down my body. "Now, I must say, this is dressing to impress."

"Don't you have someone else you need to stalk?" I ask, shrugging off the compliment and trying to forget that the last time I saw him, I was crying and he was holding me through it.

"Nope," he replies flatly.

I narrow my eyes. "Oh?"

"Don't flatter yourself," he replies gravely. "As your guide, I have to keep a watch on you, and before you start to judge me, I don't like this anymore than you do. In fact, I probably hate it more."

"Well, I'm glad that's all clear. Next time, I'll try to avoid being kidnapped and forced away from my family, so I won't inconvenience you," I say sarcastically.

"That's all I ask," Sam replies placidly. I roll my eyes and try to step around him, only to have him step back in front of me.

"Stalking, actually, wasn't my only goal for tonight. I also have something to say," Sam elaborates.

"So, shoot."

"Will you eat with me?" he asks innocently. I tilt my head in surprise as Sam's expression remains serious.

I mull this over before deciding my answer. "No," I reply curtly. Hurt flashes across Sam's features.

"But … what? Why not?" he asks, utterly confused. I have no doubt that this is the first time a girl has turned him down.

"You can't just be a jerk to me and then expect me to eat with you," I declare exasperatedly. "One nice thing this morning does not make up for the fact that every other time I've talked to you, you have been a complete asshole."

Sam's eyes fill with an odd woe, so I look at my shoes. I start to nudge around him, but he catches my arm before I can get away.

He works his mouth for a second before speaking. "I'm sorry that this happened to you, despite how I've acted. I just wanted you to know that." His voice drops as if he is saying a farewell. I look back into his eyes in confusion, not quite sure how to react to this.

How am I supposed to stay mad at this boy? I want to be furious with him, but I can't. I sigh. I don't know if it is the fact that he actually has said he's sorry or that I can't stand the brokenhearted look he is giving me, but I have to give in. "Where do you want to eat?" I relent softly.

Sam's woeful eyes suddenly snap up, filling with a spark. "There are some tables outside," he replies with a hidden smile, acting far too mischievously for my comfort.

I follow Sam outside, staring at the back of his jacket. I feel the hate- and envy-filled glares of Natalie, Tana, and Emily, but somehow I just don't care. It's not like I'm following him because I want to … or maybe I do. Maybe I just want to figure him out. Or maybe I shouldn't even be going outside alone with him, considering he is practically the Laves' spokesman. However, we all know what killed the cat; he can be so mean most of the time, but there are flashes of something more, and now curiosity has gotten the best of me.

We make our way outside, and I shiver as the air touches my skin, even colder than it was on the walk over here. The darkness takes over the sky as the day surrenders to night, and I look up, hoping for the familiar glow of stars. But just as the night before, the sky is only an empty black void—no moon or anything. I have now figured out that the sky moves from black to white, with no other color involved. I never thought that I would ever miss the sunset.

I am lost in my memories of sunsets until Sam's voice brings me out of my nostalgic longing, like a candle giving light to a room.

"Are you okay, Haylyn?" he asks simply, his tone honest. It is one of the few times that he has spoken with no hint of sarcasm or mocking. If he is being honest, then I guess I should, too, I decide regrettably.

"I'm better than I was, but I've also been better than this," I answer. He nods, indicating that this is the best he could have expected. I stare at the ground as I am about to walk around the curve of the food building. I try to take the last step around but stop as Sam sticks his arm out to the side in front of me, stopping me from progressing.

"Are you ready?" he asks through a smile. I laugh at the big deal he is making of this.

"As ready as I'll ever be," I counter. Sam drops his hand and together we turn the corner. My eyes light up. It is an adorable little area that is covered by trellises and vines with old lights stringing across it all. I give a little noise of happiness.

"It's precious! How come nobody else eats here?"

"Reservation only," Sam responds, pleased at my reaction.

"And you made one for us?" I ask in surprise.

"I actually already had one made, but we needed to get to know each other, since I'm your mentor, so I figured that we could just talk here," Sam answers. I give him a measuring look, wondering whether this is a trick and he will report everything I say back to the Laves. For once, I feel like trusting him.

I feel a smile creeping onto my cheeks as I take a seat at one of the wooden tables. I begin to eat and watch Sam move into the seat across from me with his own dough flat in his hand. There are a few bites taken out of it, but he doesn't move to take any more. After a few minutes of silence, I long to talk to him. I don't know what I'll say, but I have this urge to make him laugh. Sam bites his lip, and before I can say anything, he does.

"So where are you from?" he queries.

"We're going right to the touchy questions already?" I ask with slight sarcasm.

"Okay, I'll start small then. What's your favorite number?" Sam asks with extra sweetness, humoring me.

"Nine," I reply shortly. "And I'm from Denver," I say, longing implicit in my voice. "Where are *you* from?"

"I lived just outside of Detroit, Michigan," Sam answers, his expression telling me that I am heading into a no-go conversation zone, which, of course, only makes me more curious. Especially since he has brought this topic up.

"So how did you get here?" he inquires next. I nearly choke on my food, not sure if I should be mad or wary that he isn't leaving the touchy subjects alone.

"Well, it was really weird. The day started out normal, except I kept seeing shadows, which I'm now assuming were the Laves." Sam nods, seeming to agree with my assumption, so I continue. "Anyway, I was taking my dog on a walk, where I walk her every week. Only this time, I thought I saw a shadow again in the trees, and I knew that I had to get out of there. When I looked ahead to grab Foxy, she was gone, and she's never run off before. I ignored my previous instinct to leave and went deep into the trees looking for her. After several minutes, I got a call from my little brother saying that she was at home. I was filled with relief and started to turn around to head home when I realized that I had wandered onto a frozen pond. Before I could react, I was thrown into the water, and I was drowning. The next thing I knew, I was waking up in a strange room, and you were there," I tell him.

Sam has been silent throughout my whole spiel, but now he looks as if he is biting his tongue. While waiting for his take on my story, I force myself to finish my dough flat and hastily drink down my water. I try to act casual, but I can't shake the feeling that Sam already knows how I got here.

Sam scratches his chin, and after several minutes of silence he says, "You knew something was wrong, but you still plowed ahead to save your dog? Disregarding your own safety?" he asks. I look at him with surprise because that is not what I would expect him to say about my story.

"Well, yeah. She's my dog, that's just what you do; anyone would have done it," I say, not knowing why he was being so weird about this.

"Not *anyone*," Sam says quietly, giving me an awe-filled look before looking back down at his hands. "The Laves must have taken your dog back to your house when they saw that you were close to one of their portals. They must have known you'd run ahead, right into their hands," he explains. I swallow, not feeling comfortable with the idea that I walked straight into a trap.

"So how did *you* get here?" I ask after a moment of silence. Sam's mouth turns tense so quickly that I immediately wish I hadn't asked it. "You don't have to tell me," I add hastily.

"Let's just say, some things will never be forgiven, nor forgotten," he growls, self-hatred ringing in his voice. Before I know what I am doing, I lean across the table so our faces are mere inches apart, and I look into his eyes. He has switched from looking lively to looking sullen and apprehensive. I feel guilty that I am the one who has done this to him.

"I don't know what happened, Sam, but I know that it wasn't your fault," I whisper with force. Sam looks deeply into my eyes for a flicker of a second before looking back down again, making his lashes shadow his cheeks.

"You don't know anything," he says roughly.

"I know how it feels to be taken and brought here. I know whatever happened was the Laves' fault and not yours," I say. "I know that you may be a complete jerk, but you're not a bad person."

Sam looks up at me as I sit back down, an odd emotion swirling behind his eyes. I wonder if he'll admit to what plagues him so, but he remains silent. He still isn't being his typical cocky self, but he does look at least a little bit lightened by my words. I hope he takes what I have said to heart, because I meant every word.

After a second longer, I stretch my open hand across the table and ask, "Walk me home?" like I used to do almost every day with Matt.

He replies by placing his hand in mine as a silent yes, causing electricity to pass between our fingers. Together we slide off the bench table and start walking into the cold, dark night. I vaguely worry again about Laves coming and beating us, the way they did to that woman, but for some reason I feel safe. I wonder what that says about me.

The only other time I have held a boy's hand for this long is when I have walked with Matt, but again I am struck by how different it feels. I try to tell myself, *Sam hates you, and that's why it feels different,* but every second of touching him makes this harder and harder to say.

His eyes watch me as we walk. Sam's walk is a graceful, fluid movement of limbs; mine is a fast but short stride. You would think that those two walks wouldn't mesh together, but we stay side by side the whole time. The walk remains silent, but I feel content just holding his hand.

When my cabin comes into sight, I am almost sad that our walk has come to an end. Sam walks me up the small path to my cabin before gently dropping my hand.

"'Bye, Haylyn," he whispers.

He begins walking away and I whisper, mostly to myself, "'Bye, Sam." I open the door and jump inside. I lean against the door once it is closed and slide down. I feel myself sway in a tizzy of emotions that I can't afford to think about right now.

"He hates you," I snap at myself out loud. "But do you hate him?"

CHAPTER 7

I BARELY GOT ANY SLEEP last night, with Sam's words echoing through my head and my reliving every word, trying to see if he meant something more between the so-casually-delivered words. Well, maybe not *casually*. At one point, Sam seemed truly distraught.

Now I sit all alone in my cabin. I have hours to kill before Mr. McKulhan arrives. I feel a creeping darkness in the back of my head. I know that I have to find something to do before I start going off the deep end again.

I crawl out of my bed in a dramatic fashion and open my shut curtains. The sharp white light spreads in, warming my face. I grab one of my new coats and shrug it on, enjoying the warmth it gives my arms. I open my front door and decide to get some food.

The chill in the air bites at my face, and I am thankful for my thick coat. The walk is very empty, of everything. I pass cabin after cabin, but all of them seem to be vacant. Usually the black gravel streets have plenty of humans, helping me not to feel so alone, but now nothing could stop the feeling of foreboding doom. There is no sound except the dragging of my feet and my ragged breath. I wish that I could just arrive at the food court and avoid having this troubled feeling any longer.

I am not too far from my cabin when a building partly separated from the rows of cabins, bearing a red cross and big windows, catches my eye: the infirmary. It's not the big red cross that catches my eye; it's something else, through the window, that's red. I quickly rush over and haul myself inside. My eyes scan the room until they land on the flaming red hair that caught my attention a couple nights ago. It's the girl that the Laves attacked that first night.

I rush over past the rows of beds to the one she lies in, ignoring the stares of all the nurses. Her hair is spread across the pillow in a flaming headdress, and she is hooked up to every machine imaginable. She is even younger than I originally thought, no older than twenty-two. Her face is covered in dark bruises and long scratches. My eyes wander down to her hands, and I feel like gagging when I see that every fingernail has been ripped off.

The Laves clearly tortured her ... but why?

A nurse clucks from behind me, interrupting my thoughts. I turn around to see a plump, middle-aged woman giving me a hard look.

"Excuse me, Miss, but only family are allowed to visit," she snaps, not sounding too sorry at all.

"Oh, sorry. I'm her friend and I haven't seen her in a couple of days, so when I saw her through the window, I had to check on her," I state, the lie coming easily.

"Well, now that you've seen her, you must be on your way again," she replies, starting to escort me out.

"What happened to her?" I ask as she pushes me from behind.

"We're not sure. Someone brought her in yesterday morning, said they found her in an alleyway like this. It was most likely an animal attack," she tells me. Lie! She's seen those hands. Anyone with a brain knows that animals don't go ripping the fingernails from people's hands. Why would she lie?

"Thanks!" I call out with attitude as she shoves me through the doorway and closes the door on me. "...For nothing," I add under my breath. Geez, these people are really strict about their family-only policy. It's like they don't want me there, like they have something to hide.

Why did she lie about what happened to the red-haired girl? She knows just as well as I do that an animal didn't hurt her. Did the Laves ask her to lie? What does the red-haired girl know that has the Laves' feathers so ruffled? I let out a long sigh. There are just too many questions.

I stand there on the small porch of the infirmary a moment before deciding that I am not going to solve these questions by just standing here. I continue on my way to the food court. My mind suddenly goes back to the infirmary's "family-only" policy. A rush of sadness greets me as I think more about it. If I were to get hurt, nobody would be able to see me; nobody would even be informed. Nobody would even care. I push those thoughts down and force myself to keep walking.

This is the fourth day I have been here, and what have I done with that time? I have done nothing but cry and feel sorry for myself. I need to get it together.

I am going back, I declare to myself. *I'll find a way; I have to. I'll wait until the red-haired girl gets better and then find out what the forbidden information she knows is.* My thoughts then unwillingly drift to Sam. "Well, until I escape, and I will, I just have to make the best of my time here and act normal," I think. Now, the only problem is, what is normal anymore?

Who am I without everything that I have ever known surrounding me? My parents, my friends, my little brother… They all make up who I am. So who am I without them? Before, I was a short smart-mouth on the fringe of popularity, never wanting to be a part of it or never thinking that I was good enough.

Either way, I don't know if this new me is strong enough—strong enough to face being in a place without my family. Strong enough to live on my own in a world that shouldn't exist, with demonic creatures planning my demise.

Who am I in this new world, and am I strong enough to survive it?

I start to create my new persona when I hit something hard. I yelp in surprise as I realize that I have just run right into someone. I look up to apologize and find myself staring at a hobbled and disturbed-looking man. His face has rough, leather-like skin; his nose is long and narrow, almost to a point. His hands are chillingly skinny. Bewilderment is spread clear across my face as he smiles his yellow teeth at me and squints his dark eyes.

"I'm sorry!" I blurt out after I soak in most of his frightening appearance. The worst part of it is that he looks eerily familiar.

"No problem," he responds, sticking his skeletal hand out for me to shake. "I'm Callock Mumbly." I tentatively take his narrow hand and am surprised by his steely grip.

"Haylyn Jones."

"Pleased to meet you, Haylyn," he greets me politely, his eyes sparkling with a devilish grin. This man looks like the kind of guy that would lurk around parks telling children that he has candy in his van. Under normal circumstances, I would run away, but these are not normal circumstances. I won't show any weakness, not here.

"I hope you don't mind me asking," Callock begins, "but shouldn't you be in Watching?" I wrack my brain, trying to remember again what that word means. *Oh yeah, the school thing!*

"Um, no, I'm new here, so right now I am in therapy," I answer, feeling weird about announcing my therapeutic necessity. Callock, however, looks tickled at my response.

"Splendid!" he purrs. "Well, I must be off, but I will see you soon enough!" he calls as he starts to turn away.

"What?" I say, taken aback.

"Sometimes it's better not to ask," he replies with a knowing look before turning on his heel and walking into the alleyway between two cabins and then turning onto another street on the other side of them, out of view.

CHAPTER 8

I STUDY THE CABIN THAT Callock disappeared behind, dumbfounded. There was something in his voice that tells me he wasn't lying; I *will* be seeing him again, sooner than I feel comfortable with. After several moments of standing awkwardly in awe of Callock's words, I collect my nerves and start to walk again. Luckily, I'm not too far away from the food building. If I were any farther, I would be too distracted to find it.

I open the door and the warm air from within blows out to greet me. My eyes adjust from the outside light and, to my surprise, the place is empty. The man behind the counter is still there, but there aren't any people at the tables. Everyone must be at Watching.

I walk up to the counter, hearing my boots tap gently against the hardwood floor. The man smiles, clearly happy with the surprise of having a customer at this time. I quickly flash a smile in return.

"What will it be today?" I ask.

"Do you really want to know?" he inquires dubiously with a kind smile.

"True. Just hand me whatever it is today, and a glass of water please," I say, smiling faintly.

"Sure thing," he says, turning away and returning with a bowl of things that look similar to pita chips and a tall glass of water.

"Thank you," I say, taking my food. I walk around absently before sitting down at an empty table next to one of the pillars that holds up the ceiling. I hesitantly reach for a chip, not wanting to be fooled by their familiar appearance. I bite into the chip, and it takes me several seconds until I finally manage to break a piece off. These things are hard as rocks! I slowly crunch it down in my mouth, not surprised at all by the bland flavor. I eat the whole basket simply so I can have the feeling of a full stomach, and soon find myself wishing I hadn't when I notice the terrible toothache they've left me with.

I finish off my glass and wave to the man at the counter before heading back outside, where a rush of fresh air hits me like a wall. Once outside, I meander aimlessly and wonder where the Laves get all their food. All the food I have been eating requires a lot of wheat. Do they grow it here, or take it from earth? The latter seems more likely, for two reasons: One, I can't picture the Laves farming, and I don't see any fields to prove that opinion wrong; and two, the Laves already have a history of taking things from earth that don't belong to them.

After several minutes of walking, I come up to a wall of trees. They aren't the hauntingly tall trees I saw on my first day, but these look nicer anyway. Next to the start of a trail that weaves through the trees is a sign that reads "Park." I smile. It sure doesn't compare to my Wash Park back home, but it is a nice attempt.

The morning light pours through the branches of the trees, casting patches of dancing shadows on the path. The ground beneath my feet has turned from gravel to dirt now that I've entered the park. It feels nice to walk on solid ground, giving me a break from the physical demands that the gravel places on my feet.

A soft breeze tickles my hair, and I let a sense of peace wash over me. I look vaguely around the park, and it strikes me that the trees don't show any sign of it being winter. The weather here is warmer than Denver's is currently, but still. If anything, it seems like early fall. The trees still rustle with all of their leaves, and the small groves of grass are tall and green.

I wonder if it ever snows here, I think. The idea of never seeing snow again makes me indescribably sad. I try to push the worry away and follow the twisting trails. Eventually, I start to grow tired from walking around and settle myself down on a patch of soft grass. I absently start pulling on the grass and making a pile of the blades I uproot. It is such a normal thing to do that it comforts me; I could be doing this same thing in my backyard at home.

The sharp and yet oh-so-familiar sense of sorrow grips me again. If I were doing this at home, it would result in a grass fight with Matt and

Cassie—Matt and I going after Cassie with everything we've got, making her squeal about her clothes and hair while running away.

I look around the trees. There is no one to have a grass fight with now. I lie down, listening to the green blades crunching as they accept my weight. I can picture the fight so vividly it almost seems real. I snap my eyes open, trying to focus on the present. I gaze at the blank, white sky above. There are no clouds, so I have to imagine my own fluffy shape-shifters. There is something very sad about having to imagine your own cloud shapes.

After an hour of cloud-creating, my thoughts go back to the two strange events that happened this morning. First, with the red-haired girl in the infirmary, then with that weird Callock fellow. I lay my head back onto the grass and just try to forget about everything for once. Within several minutes, my eyelids become increasingly heavy. I am in no mood to fight, so I surrender to the call of sleep.

In my dream, I instantly recognize the setting. I have only seen the movie like eight times, so I'd better know the setting. It is that of *The Wizard of Oz*, only this time, I am Dorothy walking on the picturesque yellow brick road. My dream then shifts to flashing pictures of how the movie plays out, and how Dorothy eventually gets home. Dorothy then says her famous words and clicks her heels, and she returns home.

The dream then starts a new chapter. It is my life portrayed as parallel to Dorothy's. A simple question then emerges in my thoughts: *Who will be my wizard?*

My eyelids flicker open and I slowly sit up, waiting for my eyes to adjust to bright light. Strange birds hop from tree to tree above me, their soothing calls calming my pounding head. I stretch my arms out, relieving the stiffness left over from sleeping on the ground. My dream leaves me with an unnerving thought: Will I be able to find my wizard? Then again, Dorothy discovers that she has had the power to go home all along—I don't think that the same thing will happen in my case. I already know that, unlike Dorothy, I am not dreaming this whole thing.

Maybe the dream means nothing; dreams usually are just a mish mash of nonsense. But there is something about this one that makes me think. I will have to keep my eyes open to make sure that I don't miss any opportunities.

I stand up and continue my walk through the park. For several minutes, I follow the snake-like trails until they grow wider and open out to a small square with benches. In the center of the square stands a long, old iron clock. The clock reads five minutes until three. Alarm shoots through me. I only have five minutes to get back to my cabin before Mr.McKulhan arrives!

I sprint through the park, churning up dust as my feet kick back up. The more I run, the more confused I get. This park is like a labyrinth! I turn from trail to trail searching for any break in the trees. My hair waves behind me like a banner as I push myself to go even faster. I am just about to give up when the exit to the park comes into view. I run as fast as I can, my heart racing in my ears.

I jog down the streets until my cabin finally pops into view. I scrunch my eyebrows together and make a beeline for it. When I finally touch the brass handle of my cabin's front door, I feel unusually fulfilled. I throw myself inside, and I am glad to see that I have beaten Mr. McKulhan. I rampage my way into the bathroom and fix my messy hair. I brush the grass from my clothes at a fevered rate until a knock announces the arrival of Mr. McKulhan.

"Come in!" I call, sitting on my bed as if I have been here all day. The door slowly opens, and I almost fall back in shock.

"You!" I screech as I realize that Mr. McKulhan is not the only one standing in my doorway. Beside him stands the amused-looking face of Callock, the strange man I ran into on the street.

"Why, Haylyn, you shouldn't screech like that," Callock snaps as though I am his own child. I pull my eyebrows together, my face filled with disbelief. *Who is this guy?* Mr. McKulhan seems just as confused as I am.

"You two know each other?" he asks.

"We met earlier this morning," I blurt out before Callock can address the question. "I ran into him. But I only know his name; I don't know anything else about him." Mr. McKulhan looks from me to a hurt-looking Callock.

"Oh, Haylyn, I would say that we are friends!" Callock argues. Mr. McKulhan glances over to me, and I shake my head in a vigorous no. Callock definitely isn't my friend.

"Well, anyway, Haylyn, this is Callock. We brought him here to help you adjust to the Laves. He is half Lave and half human," Mr. McKulhan explains, making my jaw drop.

"Half human, half Lave? That isn't possible!" I declare, my mind spinning.

Callock shoots me a menacing glare. "Who are you to say what is or isn't possible?" he asks in a threatening tone. "Besides, you're obviously wrong, I'm right here."

"How is that even possible?" I ask.

Callock scrunches his eyebrows at this. "I had a very stupid mother," he replies.

I again look Callock up and down, this time with new interest. The pointed nose, the thin, wrinkled skin, all together with eyes so dark you can barely make out the whites… I don't know how I didn't notice all of this before! This must have been why I found him familiar looking; he looks like the Laves. I feel a new fear for this oddity of a man. Before, when he was just a human, I simply thought he was sketchy. Now that I know he is half Lave—half of the very creature that I fear and hate so much—I feel a new wave of uncertainty about him.

"You see, this is exactly why I want to go home!" I declare, my voice ringing clearly throughout my cabin as I wait for their response.

"Haylyn, Callock also wanted to meet you. He is quite intrigued by your strong hatred of Die Andere Welt. He believes that he can help," Mr. McKulhan says in what I recognize as his soothing voice.

I roll my eyes. Everyone wants to help me get used to it here; don't they get that the only thing that will help me is going home? Don't they understand that trying to get me to adjust will never work? There is nothing especially wrong with this place, besides the Laves and the food, that is. But it's not necessarily the place that upsets me. It's the being away from my family that does this.

"Callock asked to speak to you alone, so I will be going," Mr. McKulhan announces, looking hesitantly over at Callock as if he doesn't fully trust him. The quick look makes me feel worse.

I watch as Mr. McKulhan turns for the door and then stops to add something. "Oh, and Haylyn, I will have Sam escort you to Watching tomorrow. I think you are ready. However, we will still continue with therapy. So now our sessions will start at four to accommodate Watching. Sound good?"

"Sure?" I reply uncomfortably. I don't like the fact that he is asking a question when I know that I can't say no.

Mr. McKulhan gives me one last worried glance before gathering his coat in his arms and walking out the door, leaving me alone with Callock. For several seconds there is silence as we shift our eyes about the room, avoiding each other. The awkwardness in the room is so thick you could cut it with a knife and serve it like cake.

"I will make this brief," Callock blurts out. I stare at him with trepidation at his sudden outburst. His calm and slightly off demeanor has become all business. "I have certain plans, about which I am not sure I can tell you yet. I will continue to watch you until you have proven yourself. Hopefully, this won't take long," Callock declares striding off to the door before stopping. "You will be seeing more of me, Haylyn Jones. Until then, try not to make things too interesting, and mention this to no one." With that final warning, Callock is gone, leaving me to sit blankly staring at my door, wondering what has just happened.

Like a zombie, I reach across my bed and set my alarm for tomorrow. I stiffly change into pajamas, even though it is only three-thirty, and lie down like a board on my bed. I lock my eyes on the ceiling and think that between the red-haired girl and Callock, my life has turned into one messed-up television show. I fall asleep with the fog of Callock's words still clogging my head.

CHAPTER 9

I WAKE UP IRRITATED BY the sound of my alarm. I throw an arm over to the accursed contraption, hitting it like a mad woman as I try to end the jarring noise. I finally manage to get the beeping to stop and lie still for a second, enjoying my last few seconds of rest. I really hate mornings.

I heave myself out of bed and gather my shattered consciousness. I hop into the shower, and the warm water heats up my dark thoughts, giving me a new strength. I emerge with a new rejuvenation for the day. I throw on some clothes and brush the damp waves in my hair until they are all straight again. I actually don't look half bad in my outfit, a deep-red, long-sleeved shirt and dark jeans. Cassie would be proud if she could see me now.

At exactly eight o'clock, a hand begins pounding on my door. I open it to find the ever dashing Sam, in a green flannel and jeans, smiling at me. The sight of him stops my usually steady heartbeat as the green in his shirt complements his green eyes. I feel dizzy and pull all my strength together so that I can talk, feeling horribly pathetic because of my reaction to seeing him.

"Hello," I say. *Oh God what is wrong with me? What kind of greeting is that? I sound like a complete idiot!* But, then again, I wonder why I should care. I don't think that he is the Laves' right-hand man anymore, based on what I saw the last time we talked, but he is certainly involved with them.

"Good morning," Sam flawlessly responds. Luckily, he doesn't seem to mind my idiotic greeting. "Are you ready to go?" he asks, his voice crisp as the morning air.

"Yeah," I say and join him outside, closing the door behind me.

"How are you?" he asks casually, running his fingers through his shining hair.

"Super good and getting better," I answer sarcastically, sporting a winning smile.

"Really? Feels like just the other day when you were lying in your bed like a psycho-ward patient. Oh wait, that *was* the other day," Sam says pointedly. "Now, how are you *really*?"

I sigh at his notion. "I don't know. I mean, how can I say 'good' when I know that I will never be able to see my family again?" I pause, then add, "However, I can safely say that I won't have a meltdown in the next sixty seconds. After that, though, I make no promises."

Sam fires me a sideways glance and raises an eyebrow. When I don't elaborate, he simply shakes his head and chuckles. "So, are you at least *starting* to like it here?" he questions hopefully.

"What do you think?" I reply. Sam looks at his feet, so I wrestle out a real answer. "No, I hate it, but like you said, there is nothing I can do. So I will get over it." It is half a lie and half the truth. I will probably have to get over it, eventually. The problem is that I really don't want to. I don't ever want to stop missing my family or friends. Because once you stop missing them, you start forgetting them.

"You'll like it better when you make some friends," Sam insists.

I snort. "Oh, please, I have *wonderful* friends already! Like the ones you so kindly introduced me to. Natalie and her wannabes make for *great* company. They may all be Barbie dolls, but we are so inseparable now that I am practically Ken!" Sarcasm runs thick in my voice as I go on my little spiel.

Sam gives me a smirk as his mind is undoubtedly flooded with images of me as Ken and Natalie as Barbie.

"Okay, perhaps that was a regrettable choice of words, but you know what I mean!"

Sam waggles his eyebrows. "Oh, I know what you mean."

"Get your head out of the gutter!" I snap, moving to punch his arm.

Sam dodges my hit and throws his head back to laugh. My breath catches as the golden noise fills my ears. It is so perfect, a flawless hitting of notes that explodes with happiness. I watch as the morning glow of the white sky makes a halo around his laughing form. He looks so beautiful that I forget every other rude comment he has ever made. The light turns his long lashes into streaking ribbons on his cheekbones, and his pine green eyes stand out vibrantly. I am entranced … until he opens his mouth again.

"Touchy. How you ever wondered why the Laves chose you for your temper is a mystery to me."

And the moment's gone.

Grumbling to myself, I rip my gaze away from Sam and look around to see where we are heading. We moved past the food court a couple of minutes ago, leaving the collection of cabins behind. We are heading to a part of Die Andere Welt that I have never been to before, and this worries me. The ground has changed from volcanic gravel to compact red dirt, the kind you would find in a desert. My irritation fades as trepidation swells within me; I'm not ready to see the Laves.

"Sam, where do the Laves live?" I inquire, since there are no Laves around the cabins, in the daytime at least.

"Their city is behind the Watching building. Don't worry, we aren't going there. They won't let us anyway," he answers. I swallow hard. It is a relief knowing that I won't be overrun by the monsters holding me captive. However, I know that the Laves are going to be at Watching, and that they are going to study me like a lab rat, do all these tests on me, and fill my brain with their horrible ways.

What if I don't come back to my cabin as the same person? What if they change me? The questions fill me with new fear. I never had to worry about this before. I was always myself; nobody could change me, despite the fact that many have tried. But now I am powerless. I see that I took everything for granted before.

"Are you sure that Watching is safe?" I ask with a shaky urgency. Sam's head snaps up to look over at me. He scratches his eyebrow, looking uncomfortable.

"Safe? I wouldn't exactly use that word to describe anything here," he answers.

"Well, that's just what I wanted to hear," I mutter exasperatedly.

"Haylyn, in order to be safe here, you would have to follow the Laves' every order, which goes completely against the humans' way of life. We don't like to be controlled by anything, especially in this day and age. Even worse, you are a teenager, the synonym for defiance. So the Laves punish us, thinking that they can train us into submission. Sometimes it works, but I doubt that you will just sit passively while the Laves boss you around," Sam explains.

I nod. He's right, I won't let the Laves push me around. If I'm going to be stuck here, I'm going to be stuck here on my own terms.

"So being safe is nearly impossible," he confirms.

"Oh," I mumble, hanging my head down. This is not going to be a fun time for me.

"Haylyn?" Sam whispers. I lift my head to see his gorgeous eyes locked on mine. "I'm not going to let anything bad happen to you, you know that, right?" I bite my lip hard. The promise fills me with mixed emotions, mainly the warmth of Sam caring for me. However, a smaller part knows that it can't be true. Sam can't protect me from myself.

The walk remains silent for a long while after that. It is as if something has shifted between us. I try to ignore the fire that the left half of my body is caging—the side that Sam is on. It is like I can feel him next to me, even though we aren't touching.

We continue to walk in the same direction until something catches my attention. It is a giant gorge in the ground with heat rising from it. Even from here, where I am at least twenty feet away, I can feel the raging fire that it holds. The trail we are on curves, so we are going to have to walk closer to it. I tug on Sam's sleeve to get his attention and point to the canyon.

"What is that?" I ask. Sam shifts uncomfortably, like he doesn't want to tell me, which only makes me want to know more.

"That is the only known way to the human world," he admits, finally caving to my request. I look at it with new awe. I am about to ask why we don't jump in right now, when we get even closer. I grab hold of Sam's sturdy shoulders for balance and peer inside.

The heat hits my face like a wall. Inside, the gorge contains hot water running clear as a mountain river. The smell of sulfur hits my nose and I back away, gagging. The water is too hot to get anywhere near it. The worst thing is that at the bottom of the river, slightly disfigured by the water running over it, is a glittering, moving circle. It is the portal. I now understand why you can't jump through it. The water would boil you alive, and you would be dead before you hit the bottom and reached the portal.

"That looks like…bait," I declare in disgust.

"That's what it is; they are daring you to jump in," Sam says as he pulls my arm, leading me away from the edge.

We continue to walk in silence. I notice that more and more people are starting to walk next to us, heads forward with glazed eyes, like they are off to work. We walk a few more feet when a giant building comes into view, its looming shadow blanketing us in darkness. The building reads, "The Watch Center." Numerous people are scrambling inside of its front doors. The building looks like a school combined with a skyscraper. It is massive, both tall and long, and built from strange gray bricks. The thing screams danger and foreignness.

I watch as all the people blindly walk into it, sheep willingly walking to their own slaughter. All of us are so helpless to the Laves. They say "jump" and we say "How high?" simply out of fear of what will happen if we don't. We are stuck here in their world, so we're stuck with their rules.

I clench my hands. I can't live like this, constantly in fear. I have to face them. I muster up all of my courage and start forward to the doors when an arm swings out and stops me.

"Haylyn, a few heads-up before you go inside," Sam says.

"I'm listening."

"Well, one heads-up, really. Don't piss off the Laves."

I make a face at Sam. "Okay…?" I add, wondering where this is going.

"I'm serious; the Laves won't take an attitude like yours lightly," Sam stresses. I feel myself growing tired of this conversation; this is like a new school year already.

"Fine, I'll try. But if they provoke me first," I shrug, "it's not my fault." Sam gives me a worried look, which I ignore, and I stride ahead into the building before I lose my newfound confidence.

Inside, the place reminds me of a hospital. White linoleum floors glow under the bright ceiling lights. The air is stale and hard to breathe, permeated with the pungent scent of cleaning supplies. There are hallways leading left and right with a staircase sitting in the middle.

"This way," Sam calls as he turns right.

I follow him vacantly as he leads me through a series of hallways. I grow dizzy from the bright lights stinging my eyes, and I can't tell one hallway from another. Finally, Sam stops walking and faces a big metal door that reads, "Ages 15-18."

"This is us," Sam explains as his hand hovers over the handle. "Are you ready?"

I look at him pointedly. "Do you think that I'm not?"

"Well…" he says, trailing off.

"Thanks for that vote of confidence," I remark. Before Sam can say anything else and before I lose my nerve, I turn around and heave the thick metal door open.

The room behind the door looks like the shell of a classroom. It has desks in rows, like a classroom, and cubbies in the back, like a classroom. But the walls are bare—no maps or encouraging posters.

I look around the room at the class, and I instantly recognize Natalie, Tana, and Emily among the students. All of them are smiling, but not at me, at Sam. They fix their hair at a feverish rate and bat their mascara-covered lashes at him.

The rest of the class has around fifty kids. About twenty-five of them are boys who look bored or nervous; a couple of them wave at Sam, who nods calmly back. *They must be his friends*, I think to myself. It should be expected, since he is a teenage boy, but it still feels weird.

The other twenty-five are girls, all of whom are eagerly staring up at Sam. I look over at Sam, who doesn't seem to notice them at all. He just keeps walking until he sits down at a desk with his name on it. Sam's eyes then fixate on something behind me. I turn around to see what he is staring at and yelp. It is a Lave. It appears to be a female. Her lip curls over her rotting teeth, and her greasy, thin hair is pulled tightly into a bun. In her boney hands she clasps a yardstick, but she holds it like a weapon.

"Good morning, Sam and Haylyn," she hisses. I shudder; hearing my name coming from her mouth makes it sound like a curse. "Sit down," she adds to me. I gaze around the room until I see an empty desk with my name on it. I sit down awkwardly, but I am happy that my seat is diagonal to Sam's. To my right sits Emily and to my left is some boy that I don't know. I am feeling pretty good about this seating arrangement.

My original trepidation of Watching soon dwindles into nothing. It turns out that today is a teaching day instead of a testing day, meaning that the only difference between it and regular school is that Watching is even more boring. I didn't even know that it was possible. I thought that the Laves would have human sacrifices and such going on, but so far things are really normal. Almost too normal.

I eventually give up on trying to pay attention and zone out while the teacher goes on and on about the history of the Laves. Sam shoots me nervous glances every five minutes, as though he can tell that I am starting to grow impatient with all of this. But can he really blame me? Nobody cares about the stupid Laves' independence day, or whatever it is that she is rambling on about.

"Okay, pupils, take out your textbooks, and we will start some geometry," the Lave teacher announces.

Oh, great, geometry's reign of terror continues to harass me, I think as I pull out a thick book from under my desk and the teacher starts to drone on. Why are we even learning geometry? If we didn't need it in the other world, we really don't need it in this one.

After thirty minutes of watching the Lave flutter around the board with a piece of chalk, I come to the conclusion that the Lave teacher is, in short, worse at teaching than a pile of dirt. She just silently does problem after problem on the board and expects us to learn this way. I am utterly confused. After twenty minutes of this, the Lave teacher sets down her chalk and turns to face the class, her dark eyes scanning the room. I give her a face filled with menace, daring her to call on me. But she doesn't. Her eyes focus on Emily, who looks terrified.

"Emily, what is the answer to this problem?" the Lave demands, pointing to the board where a mess of a problem sits. She stalks closer to Emily, using her yardstick like a cane. Emily resembles a deer caught in the headlights. I feel so sorry for her; the Lave should have called on me.

"Um, ninety-seven degrees?" Emily mumbles. The Lave bares her ugly teeth in response.

"Wrong!" she yells. The Lave lifts back the yardstick, and I realize with horror what she plans to do. Air whistles past the wood as it heads straight for Emily's face. Before I realize what I am doing, I stand up and stick my hand out to catch the stick before it can hit Emily. I barely notice the sting in my hand as gasps sound all around the room and the Lave teacher's face turns red with anger.

"Intolerable!" she screeches.

"Haylyn!" Sam calls with alarm.

The Lave teacher grabs my wrist, her nails digging in until blood drips down my hand and spatters onto the floor. Pain travels up my arm, and she begins dragging me toward one of the closed doors. Sam is desperately calling my name, but one of his friends is holding him down. I try to dig my heels into the floor to free my wrist, but the Lave is too strong. Despite my best efforts, she drags me into the dark room and closes the door behind us.

I grunt as she shoves me down into an unseen chair. I try to process everything that has just happened and prepare myself for the worst. Everything is black and still, the unknown making my heart race more. I feel like I will go mad in this silence until the Lave's voice curls into my ear from behind me.

"Stupid, ungrateful rat," she snaps. "How dare you stop me from giving another student her well-deserved punishment!"

As I listen to her voice, my mind rages in a battle of fear and defiance. I want to argue, but fear holds my tongue. Based on Sam's reaction, I know that I should be terrified, but there is still that spark of will in me that won't let me break down.

"Aren't you going to plead your case to me? Tell me that you didn't mean to? Come on now, don't be shy, I want to hear you beg," she croaks.

"I did what was right, and I would do it again," I state simply.

"Very well, but let's see how smart-mouthed you are after you see what has been going on back in Denver while you have been acting out here," she says hotly as a glowing screen begins to sweep out in front of me.

The screen starts to form a picture, and I recognize my house. I see my parents clinging to each other, weeping. The image changes and I see Avery walking home from school, alone, silent tears making trails down his face. The image changes again, and now I am seeing Matt hanging missing-girl posters all over our neighborhood. He looks at the picture of me on the paper and starts to cry. "Haylyn, where are you?" he asks my picture.

"Please, I get it! Just stop already!" I scream, throwing my hands over my eyes, losing every ounce of defiance I showed just moments before. The Lave's boney hands catch my wrists, and she snaps at me to open my eyes again. The screen now shows Cassie. She sits in front of a pile of presents, sobbing. "I don't want any of these!" she screams at her parents. "I just want my best friend back!" The image changes yet again. It is my dad, standing in the police station. I can tell that he is about to cry, and it is awful.

"Why haven't you found her yet?" he screams at the man behind the desk.

"Sir, we are doing the best we can," the other man explains.

"Where is she?" he cries, falling to his knees. "Where is my baby girl?" he yells to no one in particular.

My family's voices and words thunder through my mind. I don't want them to go through all of this pain, to keep looking for me when I will never be found. Tears spill into my mouth and my breathing turns ragged and short.

This is worse than feeling hollow; now all of my family's pain and loss fill me to the brim and threaten to spill over. All of my hopes for success, dreams, and plans vaporize as if they never existed; they are irretrievable because of the Laves. Worse than that, all of my family's plans for the future are ruined. Avery will never be the same. Nobody will ever treat him the same again. He will always be the brother of the girl that went missing. My parents will always be pitied because they had the daughter that never came home.

"Stop!" I cry. The Lave teacher tries to grab me again, but I jump up. Acting in that last bit of life someone has before a crash, I force my way up until I am standing. Anger and hurt rush through me, controlling my actions. I push the Lave to the ground and tumble back into the classroom.

Every pair of eyes is locked on me, but the tears just keep falling. I stand there for a second, just staring at everyone, knowing that I must look like a wild animal. The Laves have broken me.

"Oh, Haylyn," Sam breathes. I feel a flash of embarrassment to be seen like this in front of Sam. Not that he matters anymore. Nothing matters anymore. My family and friends are going out of their minds for me, and I'm just supposed to sit here and learn geometry? No. I won't take it; I am going home one way or another. I rush out the door, my fluttering hair gluing itself to my damp face.

I run uncomprehendingly through the twisting halls. My vision is a blurry mess from all my tears. My family's voices echo through the halls, chasing after me. Their heartbroken calls are leading me somewhere, and I know where. I know what I am supposed to do there, and I am willing to do it.

By some miracle, I manage to find the front doors and break free of the Watching building. I choke on my own hair as it sticks to my cheeks and tumbles down my throat with my spasmodic breaths. I don't care, though; it will be over soon enough. I run toward the canyon where my only escape lies. I know that I will be dead by the time I reach the portal, but at least I can say that I tried to get back to my family.

Dust floats into my already-irritated eyes from my feet kicking up the ground. The closer I get to the canyon, the louder and more devastating my family's voices grow. They are calling for me desperately, begging for me to end their suffering. I have to do something.

When I finally reach the canyon, the heat hits me in waves, but I ignore it as I get closer. I look down and see my family inside of the portal. My mom, whose face was usually smiling her soft smile, now has tears dripping from her chin. My proud dad looks so crumpled and broken it devastates me. I remember looking up at him when I was little. I would barely reach his hip back then, and he seemed like the tallest, strongest person alive. Now he looks like a shell of what he used to be.

Avery just stands there, searching my eyes for any hope that I will be coming home, any hope that he can be happy again, that things will go back to normal. Beside Avery stand Matt and Cassie, the two of them looking hollow now that their friend has been tragically severed from the trio.

I remember when I first met Matt. We were seven, and he was about to be beat up by three older boys. I intervened and made those boys wish that they had never been born. I helped him then, and I have to help him now. I can see in their eyes what this has done to them. The whispers that they have to suffer through every time they walk down the halls. The haunting glare of the empty chair that sits next to them in math, where I used to sit.

All of them are saying how everything will be good again if I just jump off. Cassie promises that she will never let Mrs. Lyde, our math teacher, bother me again, that she will never let anything bother me again. I believe them, too. Everything would be better if I could just take one more step.

Just one more step. How could such a simple action carry such importance? I want to take it, I do. I want to see my family and friends again more than anything. The want—or, more accurately, the *need*—to see them is drowning me. One person is not meant to need something this much and be kept from it. I want this, so why can't I just take that last step?

It's because the last part of my sane mind is screaming at me not to jump, that these people calling to me are only hallucinations. They look so much like my family, though, and they need me. I inch a little bit forward, feeling the heat warm my toes. I am about to take the final step when someone calls to me.

"Haylyn, stop!" the ragged voice yells. I glance back to see who it is, not wanting to turn away from my family. But there, ten feet away, is Sam. His hair is messy from running, and it nearly covers his piercing eyes. Those eyes that carry so much beauty now have this dejected look in them. His jaw is painfully tight, and he just stands there, not moving at all, as if any sudden movement will frighten me and make me jump. Like I'm a scared animal.

"Haylyn, don't jump," he pleads. I just look at him as he carefully inches closer. I turn around again and start to lift my foot to take that final step. The heated air blows my hair back and I close my eyes. "At least I died trying," I whisper to myself. I move my foot forward and start to fall when Sam catches me and drags me backward.

"Haylyn, no! They're tricking you! They want you to jump!" Sam cries.

"Let me go! You didn't see them, Sam! My family needs me!" I yell, struggling within his grasp.

"I *do* know, Haylyn! But you have to think. Your family is worried because they think that you're dead. If you jump, you're just confirming that worry; you wouldn't be making them feel any better," Sam argues desperately.

"Let go of me!" I growl, not helping my already-animalistic look and not listening to his words of reason at all.

"No, I'm not going to let you throw your life away!" he cries, tightening his grip on my arms as he pins them behind my back.

"Why not? What's my life to you? Just let me jump!" I scream. Sam stills for a second, not answering. The only way that I am sure he has heard me is by the way he tenses and his breathing picks up.

Suddenly I pause, now realizing that something I have said has severely affected Sam. I gently turn myself around in his arms so that I am facing him again. His eyes find mine with a troubled look, all of his bravado gone. I don't know what it is that has suddenly gotten him so conflicted; it can't be because of the question I yelled at him in a blind rage, can it?

As I watch Sam, all of my family's calls quiet down, as if they too want to hear Sam's answer. Now, everything in the world seems to go still. It is just Sam and me, nothing else. No air passes my parted lips as I hold my breath. I am amazed at how calm I suddenly feel compared to how I was just a minute ago.

"I don't know, Haylyn," he whispers suddenly after the achingly long minutes of silence. He shakes his head sullenly, his pupils growing huge and innocent with emotion. My heart slows until I am sure that it has stopped entirely, just so I can hear Sam speak.

I stare at Sam in confusion. What is he getting at? My family's calls are almost silent as I am riveted to Sam. I bore my eyes into his, urging him to continue, letting him know that I want more information than that.

Sam shudders. "You make me…," he starts cautiously before suddenly stopping, snapping his head up and turning frigid again. In one second, all openness is gone and I am left in the cold. "Promise me that you won't jump off the cliff," he growls aggressively, catching me off guard and scaring me a little.

I open my mouth and shut it again, my frazzled emotions all over the map now. Sam grips my arms harder and shakes me.

"Promise me, Haylyn!" he demands loudly.

"I promise," I say meekly, knowing that I have given up on my blind hope of trying to get home.

Sam nods curtly before releasing my arms and walking back toward the Watching building at a brisk pace. As he leaves, I can physically feel what his absence does to me. I cringe inwardly, realizing that I would normally think this was a cheesy thing to say, but every step he is taking away from me hurts, and I have no idea why. I have to say something. He just saved my life; I owe him that much.

"Sam!" I call. He stops and slowly turns around with an eyebrow raised. "Thank you," I say softly.

Relief radiates around him. A timid smile plays at his lips, as though it is afraid to show itself, but it is still secretly there. I think he is going to say something, or maybe I just wish that he would. Instead, he turns back around and continues to walk away.

Sam's shrinking figure is disappearing fast, but not before I see a Lave standing a little farther up the road, where Sam looked earlier before freezing up. Has he been standing there the whole time? If so, then what does that mean?

Chapter 10

I stand there, stunned, unsure of what to think—did any of that really happen or have I just hallucinated again? How did everything turn to shit so fast? I give a small chuckle as I think back to Sam's one instruction: Do not make the Laves mad. It is a little too late for that now.

After everything that has happened, I feel completely empty and exhausted. I watch Sam's shrinking figure until I can't see it anymore. I let out a long sigh, my mangled thoughts floating around my head. I want to get home, but what about Sam? Would he be upset if I leave, or is that just my blind hope talking? He could have just been just being nice earlier. But even if he doesn't care, do I not care enough, after everything that just happened, to fling myself over this cliff without a second thought?

I chew on my cheek. I didn't think that this place could get any more complicated, but Sam takes the gold for conflicted feelings. He may not care about me, but I can't say the same about him.

Where do I stand now? The Laves had broken me, but then Sam and Mr. McKulhan came along with a box of Band-Aids. Sure, my family hasn't left my mind, but their message is coming in differently now. It no longer sounds like a plea to have me at least try; it is a pep talk telling me that I can ease their suffering by having a long happy life here. It's time to get my act together.

I stand there staring for about twenty minutes at the spot where Sam left my vision. All I have really decided is that all this thinking is giving me a headache. I slowly start to make my way back to my cabin. My legs seem to be moving impossibly slowly, but it can't be helped, so I push on. The compact dirt eventually starts to crunch its way back to gravel. It is strange to feel relief being back here. At least this part of Die Andere Welt is familiar.

After what seems like hours, I finally make it back to my cabin. I rub the winter chill from my arms as I walk inside. Crossing over to the window, I shut the curtains to keep out the harsh, bright light. Tiredness rolls over me like traffic, crushing me beneath its weight. I crawl into bed, ignoring the fact that I am still fully dressed. I quickly fall asleep and dream blank dreams, as dark as the Laves' shadowed eyes.

I fly back into consciousness at the sound of scratchy laughing.

"Look at her, all tired from her fight with the Laves! You know, Arnold, I have to give her props, this one has some guts!" a ragged voice says. I realize that the voice belongs to Callock. When the next voice responds, I recognize it as Mr. McKulhan, whose first name must be Arnold.

"Callock, don't encourage her, she could have been beaten or killed for her defiance of the Laves," Mr. McKulhan scolds. I don't know what it is about the conversation that bothers me, but something makes me not want them to know I'm awake.

"She could have taken them," Callock grumbles and then pauses. "Oh, don't give me that look! Someone needs to put the Laves in their place, and I think Haylyn might be just the one to do it." Loud footsteps then follow the outburst.

"Where are you going?" Mr. McKulhan demands.

"I will talk to her…later. I'm sure that the last thing she wants to see right now is a Lave, even if it's just half of one," he answers. With that I hear a door close loudly, and I know that Callock is gone.

Mr. McKulhan and Callock must not have noticed that I have been awake during their conversation. So I pretend that it's the slam of the door that jars me awake.

"Huh? What's going on?" I mumble, yawning. Mr. McKulhan smiles down at me.

"It's four o'clock, time for therapy," he informs me, looking down at me, and when I don't respond, he continues. "Remember the time change? We used to talk at three. Now we talk at four," he explains, even though I remembered.

"Oh, yeah, time change. That is good, I guess," I ramble, playing dumb.

"However, we could have met at three today, considering you left early," he says, frowning down at me as I stare back at him. *This is not my fault. The stupid Laves were about to hit a poor girl, and I should feel ashamed for helping her? Yeah, I don't think so.* I regret having to see my family's broken hearts and how I reacted after seeing them, but I don't regret stopping the Laves from hitting Emily.

"It isn't my fault! The Laves are stick-wielding maniacs! That awful teacher was about to hit this poor girl! I couldn't just stand by and watch!" I screech while glaring at Mr. McKulhan. He pauses, thinking for a moment. I smirk; it is hard to argue with someone when he is right.

"Haylyn, back on earth, what you did would have been very nice. But this is not the same situation. To the Laves, what you did was considered an act of defiance. They don't like that, at all," he explains after a moment of thought.

I take a minute to process what he has just told me. It is like being under a dictatorship. Everything the Laves want me to do is totally unfair, putting me on the bottom and them at the top of this strange new social ladder. Do they really expect me to sit back and do whatever they say while they hurt innocent people? Because that's not happening.

"Don't we have any rights?" I complain aloud, even though I know the hopeless answer. He sadly shakes his head, confirming my thought.

"When you're kidnapped, you don't exactly have the luxury. You are sort of like a prisoner of war right now. The Laves are studying the humans to see if there is a way that they can keep us from making our deadly weapons. They worry that if the humans discover the Laves, they will aim those weapons at them. So they study the humans, to get to know their enemy," he informs me. I bite my lip. *Oh, great, now I am in a war between the humans and the Laves—one that the humans don't even know of yet.* I give Mr. McKulhan a glare.

"Haylyn!" he exclaims accusingly.

"What?"

"Don't give me that look, this is serious. You don't even know how lucky you are that Sam stopped you!"

"Lucky?" I muse to myself. Is that what I am? Is that all that passed between Sam and me today by the canyon? Am I just lucky that Sam felt sorry for me and did the right thing? I feel disappointment bloom in my heart. I want it to be something more than that. However, that is probably what everyone thinks, that I am just lucky. It is probably what Sam thinks, too. But surely he had something more to say when he stopped me from jumping. I mean, Sam has never exactly been an open person, but that moment between us when I had every intention of jumping and Sam seemed desperate to stop me was breathtaking, magical enough to cover up all other thoughts and stop me from jumping.

Mr. McKulhan notices my conundrum of thoughts and smiles one of his warmest smiles.

"Do you not want to go to Watching tomorrow?" he asks. I nod innocently. "Very well, I will inform Sam."

"Thank you," I say.

"Now, do you have any other questions before I leave?" he inquires.

"Yes, actually," I say, remembering how something has been nagging at the back of my mind ever since coming to Watching and seeing how different it was from what I've experienced before. "How come Watching is so terrible, but outside of it things are almost too normal?"

"Ah, very perceptive," he comments. "It is so you don't shut down. If things were too terrible, you wouldn't be regular humans, you would be shell-shocked robots. A shell-shocked robot is no good for studying, so they try to keep things as normal as possible outside of Watching," he answers.

"Oh, yeah, I'm totally mentally stable. I've only had two complete meltdowns this week! The Laves have really got this whole making-humans-happy thing down to a science," I respond sarcastically. Mr. McKulhan gives me another look and I let out a sheepish smile. "Sorry," I mutter.

"It's all right, just remember to keep that tongue in check around the Laves," he says in a stern, grandfatherly way. "I'll see you tomorrow at three again, since you aren't going to Watching tomorrow. I'll see you then, Haylyn." He slowly stands back up and leaves my cabin. I wait until I see him walk past my window and down the street before letting out a sigh.

I feel bad about lying to Mr. McKulhan, but I am going to Watching. I can't let the Lave teacher have the victory of knowing she broke me. I need to act like nothing happened, like I am just as strong as ever. She has already broken me once; the only thing that would be even more gut wrenching is letting her know that fact.

But I told Mr. McKulhan that I didn't want Sam to pick me up because I'm not ready. I can't face what happened between Sam and me just yet. I may be acting like a coward, but I don't care. I'm just doing whatever I can to keep myself sane. Besides, I don't know how I feel about what happened between us just yet. So a long awkward walk, just the two of us, doesn't seem like the best idea. That is, until I can figure out my feelings for him.

I jump up from my bed and ready myself to go to dinner. I hope that by going this early I won't run into anyone. I brush my hair, throw on a jacket, and shut the door behind me as I leave. The night air bristles like a porcupine against my soft cheeks. I pull my hood up to protect my face from the cold.

Other than the cold, the walk to the food court is uneventful. Almost nobody is out walking. But, luckily, there are just enough people out here so that I don't feel like I am all alone. When I finally heave the door open to the food court, happiness swells within me. The entire place is decorated for Christmas! I feel a mixture of emotions: sadness over the fact that I won't be able to spend the holiday with my family, but also, mostly (and selfishly), I feel happy. I will still be able to celebrate Christmas; it may not be exactly the same, but it will still be something to look forward to. Two colors should not be able to make someone so happy, but the red and green that hang from the walls has me bursting at the seams! I skip to the counter, ignoring the strange looks from the few onlookers.

"Nice seeing you so happy!" the same friendly man greets me.

"I'm just excited about Christmas!" I explain. The man smiles at my statement.

"I agree. I may be old and in another world, but something about Christmas just lifts up your spirits! A couple of the adults here try to decorate every year. Luckily, the Laves don't seem to mind too much," he exclaims happily.

Of course they don't, I think, *because if we didn't have the holidays, then we wouldn't be normal humans.*

"So what will it be today?" I ask. Even if the food is totally disgusting, it's kind of like a game to see what it will be that day. I simply pray that it won't be mash again because I know that I would have to eat it. I have already started losing weight since coming here, weight that I am sure I don't need to lose. I know that I have to keep eating.

"Cabbage soup," he replies earnestly. I sigh. I don't like cabbage or soup, so this should be fun.

"Well, I might as well get it over with," I say with a small smile. The man crinkles his eyes in response and hands me a large bowl that is hot to the touch. I look down into its contents and find myself thinking that this might rival mash for worst food ever.

First of all, the water is a gross pale-brown color, similar to the Laves' skin. Second, there are random chunks of yellow cabbage floating about. There is nothing else even to say after that. That's all there is, just scalding, nasty water and cabbage that isn't even ripe yet.

The counter man looks at me with expectation, so I take a bite just to please him. I force myself to swallow the spoonful, thinking how this "soup" is really just water and cabbage. I don't think the Laves are going to win *Top Chef* anytime soon.

"Boiled water, my favorite," I choke out as I give a half smile to the server. The old man gives me one look before he begins to crack up. I stare at him a few moments before joining him in his fervent laughing. It feels good to laugh again.

"Well, thank you anyway, I can't really blame you for the quality of the food," I say after both of our laughing dies down.

"You're welcome! Have a nice night! And thank you for that nice laugh, it's been too long since I laughed like that," the man calls after me.

I smile in response and turn around to start looking for a table. However, when I begin looking, my appetite is gone in a second. Sitting at a table that just moments ago was empty is Callock. He smiles unnervingly at me and waves his hand, motioning for me to sit across from him. Warily, I make my way over to his table and gingerly sit down.

"Evening, Miss Haylyn," he greets me.

"Hello, Callock," I reply, gnawing at the corner of my lip. Luckily, Callock keeps the conversation going.

"You must be wondering why I am pestering you on this fine night," he suggests. I feel my eyebrow rise sharply.

"Um, sure."

"Well, if you must know, I have a proposition for you."

"And that would be…?" I ask, now genuinely intrigued.

"I want you to help me break out of this place," he declares in a whisper, not wasting any time on pleasantries. I stare at him, confused. "What I mean is, to leave Die Andere Welt, go back to earth."

My eyes go round with shock as I soak in his words. "It's impossible!" I growl, not letting the hope flare up inside me, since I know that it would only die again.

"I have my ideas," he replies.

"You're a mad man!" I declare, jumping out of my chair. I try to turn around and leave, but Callock catches my wrist. I try to yank it back, but he presses something into my hand.

"What's this?" I demand.

"My phone number, in case you have a change of heart," he answers. I angrily shove the paper deep into my pocket, wishing that I could throw it at his face. I turn on my heel and storm over to the exit.

"Do think it over!" Callock calls as I open the door.

"I won't."

CHAPTER 11

I STORM OUT OF THE food court like Freddy Krueger himself is chasing me. Who does Callock think he is, trying to make me believe some stupid story, to fill me with hope again, only to squash it like a bug? Or, maybe if I had said yes, he would have turned me in to the Laves. How dare he prey on the weakest of people living here! Not that I like to admit that I am probably one of the weakest in the bunch here. I hate Callock, I really do. His very existence irks me to the core.

I kick rocks all the way back to my cabin. The cold air is starting to cool down my heated temper. Now I actually start to think. Could Callock be serious? I shake my head. He couldn't be. But then again, he is half Lave. Who knows what he has up his sleeve?

I bite down on my cheek. *Callock knows that I am trying to move on,* I think as I walk up to my cabin. As soon as my fingertips hit the metal of my door handle, instant drowsiness captures me. I heave myself inside and sprawl out onto my bed. I close my eyes and simply let the sweetness of dreams bury me in their delusions.

I wake up to harsh, pale light stinging my eyes. I feel like nothing—the way you feel on the Wednesday of a finals week, when you have had days of testing and know that there are only more days to come. The way you feel when you have nothing to look forward to, but you have to buckle down and keep going. When every day is a struggle.

I drag myself out of bed and amble into the bathroom to take a shower. The warm beads provide me with a certain exhilarating feeling that helps a little. I have always been a strong believer in the healing powers of a good shower. I dress myself in a comfortable outfit and pin my bangs away from my face. By the time I am all ready to go, I look almost normal, like I am heading to school instead of Watching. However, I am late. Oh well, better to arrive late then arrive ugly, as the saying goes.

I quickly grab the coat I wore last night and run out my door. I sprint down the street, enjoying the heated, alive feeling that comes with running. The cold air slaps my face and stings my lungs, but I push myself to go faster. The streets are empty since everyone is already in Watching, so I don't have the problem of running into some poor pedestrian. I run as fast as my feet can take me, running past the canyon that holds the portal without a second glance.

I throw myself into the doors of the Watching building and spin into the hallway Sam led me through the day before. However, after that first turn, I can't remember any of the other turns he took. My shoes squeak against the floor and the lights nearly blind me. I have no idea where I am going as I turn randomly into new hallways. Bad memories are digging at the edges of my mind, but if the Laves are considering this a war, I intend to win it. Therefore, I ignore them and push on.

It seems like hours before I finally locate the metal door carefully labeled with my age group. I take in a gulp of air and mentally prepare myself for the onslaught I am about to face. I grab the handle and swing the door open.

Everyone's eyes shoot over to me as I take the first step inside. I risk a glance over at Sam. He looks surprised, which I am happy with. However, he also has another emotion, one that could be described as anger, or maybe even worry. I look back over to the Lave teacher; her eyes dig into me like she is aiming a gun at my heart. She seems royally pissed that her plan to break me didn't work—not that she knows of, at least. I do my best to ignore her and sit down at my desk.

"I'm so glad that you could join us, Miss Jones," she hisses. I roll my eyes. *Yeah, right. She would probably prefer for me to be dead at the bottom of the chasm right about now.* "Next time, I might be able to greet you on time, though?" she asks with a demanding undertone.

"Of course," I force myself to say in the same peppy yet hateful tone. "I'm still getting used to the hang of things around here, but don't worry. I am confident that I will get used to it soon. I just got a little lost today." I hear Sam cough in exasperation behind me. I would turn around to look at him, but I have to keep all of my focus on returning the glare the Lave teacher is giving me.

The Lave's eyes drill into mine with a demonic gleam, but I stare right back. I can't let her win at something as easy as a stare down. Call me crazy, but experts say that when a dog stares you down, it is challenging your authority. If it looks away first, then it agrees that you are its master. If you look away first, well then, congratulations, a dog thinks that it is in charge of you.

I may not be a dog, but I am not giving this monster more power over me than she already has. After several seconds, she clears her throat and glances away to look at something on her desk that has suddenly caught her interest. I am trying as hard as I can to hide my emotions, but I can't help it when I let out a little smirk.

Today is a testing day, which means additional Lave scientists come in and study us. With today being my first day, it is just about the basics. They take my height, weight, and skin color, writing all the information down in a little file with my name on it. They yank a strand of hair out of my head and put it in a sealed vial. They then take a skin sample, by scraping a little off of my heel, and, much to my horror, a blood sample.

After the needle is gone, I start to breathe a little easier, and the tests aren't as hard as I feared they would be. They just calculate how long it takes me to solve puzzles. It is really easy and boring. As more and more tests are put in front of me, the angrier I get. I am fed up with all of these stupid problem-solving things! Luckily, right before I am about to snap, the Lave teacher asks for our attention before we leave for lunch.

"All right, class, we will be doing a history project," the Lave teacher starts. "The history project will be a presentation and an essay. It can be on any historical figure that you felt made an impact on human culture. For this project, I will be giving you assigned partners."

The class mumbles several different responses to this. I am mostly indifferent; as long as I don't get stuck with some idiot that makes me do all the work, I will be fine. "First up is our newest student, Haylyn Jones." I look up at the mention of my name. "You will be paired with Sam Eveland."

I turn to look at Sam as he groans out loud. I give him a disbelieving look that says, "What is your problem?" He simply looks back at me with an expression that in unreadable. Whatever it means, it irritates me.

The rest of the partners' names are read off, and the class leaves to go to lunch. I don't want to be stuck in the hallway with Sam, so I wait for everyone to leave before heading for the door. I am almost out when a chilling voice stops me.

"Don't ever try leaving again," the Lave growls, her hot breath spraying over my face. I back up in disgust. "You can't escape, and if you do, we will find you!" she spits, before stalking out of the classroom and down the hall.

I stay still for a second, trying to process what has just happened. The Lave's intensity should have scared me half to death. However, I recognize her outburst. It is the kind where your anger gets the best of you and you snap. This helps me because usually, in the heat of the moment, you can say some stupid things when you're angry. No one knows this better than me. I have gotten in trouble too many times for my quick temper.

Ideas are starting to form quickly in my head, so I run out the door and turn into the hallway, going the opposite direction of the Lave. I run through the corridor, past all the metal doors, until I find one that is labeled "supplies." I double check that I am wearing the same coat that I wore last night and smile.

I look both ways to make sure that no one is looking before I slip inside of the closet. I scramble around for a switch to turn on the light before finding a metal cord in the middle of the room. I yank it, and the small closet is flooded with light. I pull my phone out of my jeans pocket, happy that I still take it everywhere with me.

I then dig my hand into my coat pocket to retrieve the slip of paper with Callock's number on it that I shoved into the pocket last night. I peel open the paper and dial the number, praying that it will work. Somehow, I know that it will. And I am right. After several seconds, the phone starts to ring, and then Callock picks up.

"Callock," I say, adrenaline rushing through my body, "I'm in."

"Lovely! What changed your mind?" he exclaims, seeming genuinely delighted and, curiously, not surprised.

"The Lave teacher herself hinted that it was possible. She said 'You can't escape, and if you do, we'll find you!'" I say almost gleefully.

"Ha!" he cackles. "Well, I'm happy to have you on board!"

I let out a nervous smile. It feels great to have a purpose again.

"I'm grateful to join, if it works, that is..."

"It will work," he says quickly, then pauses before adding, "if all goes according to plan." Everything we say has the hint of failure at the end, I realize—the thorn sitting upon the beauty of a rose. Normally, this would scare me, but these are not normal circumstances, and I can't let the idea of failure hold me back from the possibility of success.

"I'm up for the challenge," I say honestly.

"Glad to hear it, because it will be a challenge," Callock declares, making sure that I won't back down. He waits for a second for me to back out, but when I don't, he continues. "I have a plan, but I can't explain it over the phone."

"Okay, when should we meet? I could leave Watching right now if you'd like," I suggest, half hoping that he will say yes. In all honesty, though, I don't want to leave to start planning; I just want to leave because all of these tests are starting to drive me crazy.

"No, we don't want to do anything suspicious that the Laves might notice. We can try meeting tomorrow after your therapy, before you go to dinner. The time will most likely vary though," he answers.

"Sounds good. Anything else that I need to know before I see you then?"

"Yes, don't mention this to anyone, especially Sam," Callock instructs. I get a pang of shock. Why is Sam being singled out? Does Callock know something that I don't? Or is he just crazy? I'm betting on the crazy part.

"Why would I tell Sam?" I defend myself.

"Well, it's not so much that you would tell him about the plans as you would tell him how you still want to go back home, which would make him suspicious."

"So what? I would still want to go back, even if I didn't join up with you," I point out. Which is true—some part of me will always belong in Denver.

"That may be true, but we don't need to have any reason for Sam to be extra cautious of what you are doing. You need to be more aware of your actions now. Don't give the Laves any reason to look into what you are doing. And whether it seems like it or not, Sam could blow your cover if he felt like he would be protecting you by doing so."

I soak in what all of Callock's words might mean. Would he really be protecting me? Or just protecting the poor girl he has to keep an eye on? Callock seems pretty sure of himself in this statement, but then again, what does Callock know? Maybe Sam did feel something. Then again, he could only be worried about a friend. Just because Callock says Sam would try to protect me doesn't mean he would protect me for the reasons I want him to.

I swallow my confusion, bringing myself back to reality. I am an agent now. I have a mission to complete; I can't let my feelings get in the way. What is wrong with me? Back in Denver, I wouldn't spend more than a minute fussing over guys. Now just this one has me in a tizzy. True, he is gorgeous and funny, and his mood swings give me a rush like no other. But he is still just a normal guy. Right?

"Okay, I will keep it together around Sam," I say, determined to focus on the task at hand and ignore Sam. "Lighthearted talk only."

"Good. See you after therapy tomorrow. Don't mess this up," Callock insists. With that vote of confidence, he hangs up, and I am alone in the closet.

Well, thanks for that ego boost, I think, hitting "end" and returning my phone to my pocket. I wiggle out my limbs, trying to loosen myself up. I now have a whole new world of challenges ahead of me, but these are welcome compared to the despairing thought of living here forever. I am entirely scared and excited at what lies before me.

I may be trusting him too early, but I'm desperate. I can't let a possible opportunity for escape go just because I'm scared. If this does come back to bite me in the butt, at least I can know that I tried.

I crack open the door, making sure that there are no Laves in sight. With the coast clear, I slip out and begin walking down the hall like nothing has happened. At first, I don't know where I should go, but the sounds of teenagers are distinctive enough. I follow the sound of laughing and inappropriate jokes down the hall until I come to a small courtyard. My class is spread around picnic tables in small clumps of friend groups. It is just like real lunchtime back home.

I pull open the door and walk outside, the cool breeze fluttering my hair and rustling the leaves in the trees planted in round enclosures. I spot Natalie and the others sitting at a table in the light and move to join them when a body jumps out in front of me, blocking my path. It is Sam. The sight of him sends my thoughts spinning. I do my best to maintain an indifferent composure.

"So you got lost on your way here this morning, huh? The Laves should really assign a mentor to show a newbie like you around," he says.

My cheeks grow hot from the sarcasm, and I get the familiar switch that I associate with Sam, from starstruck to annoyance. "Sorry about that. Maybe the Laves have a suggestion box that you could put that thought into," I retort.

"Maybe if you don't like getting lost, you could just walk with me, like you were supposed to in the first place!" he parries back.

"I felt like walking alone. Not everything is about you, Sam. I can do things on my own."

"Well, obviously, you can't, considering you got lost on your way here," he points out in that superior tone of his. I clench my fists in anger.

"You don't have to babysit me!" I exclaim.

Sam's eyes flash as he tilts his head. "Seems like I do! Every time I leave you alone, you do the most idiotic thing that you can think of. Every time I leave you alone, you almost die. So yes, I do have to babysit you."

"So don't bother," I suggest.

"Don't bother?" he asks, incredulously.

"You know, if it's such a bother, just move on. If I die, oh well. It would be my fault. Just don't get involved," I say. His eyes fill with that same unidentifiable expression, and I suddenly feel like Sam and I are on completely different pages for this argument.

"You don't get it, do you?" Sam asks, sadly shaking his head. He runs his fingers through his hair with distress and fatigue. He asks the question mostly to himself, so I am unsure whether I should say something. His words are surprising and give me a weird curiosity. I need to know what he means.

"Don't get what?" I question, but it is clear that Sam isn't going to elaborate. Sam just shakes his hair, letting the silky brown strands fall into his eyes.

"Never mind that," he says, switching tones again. "Why were you so late to lunch?"

"Why do you always dodge my questions?" I reply back quickly. Sam glares at me, so I search my brain for a good lie. Why is it so hard to lie to Sam?

"The teacher pulled me aside after class and let me know how they grade things around here. By the time she was done, all of the class had left, so I didn't know which direction to go, and I definitely wasn't going to ask a Lave for help. So it took me a minute to find where everybody was eating," I explain. There, that wasn't so bad. I think it is actually pretty convincing. Sam gazes into my eyes, sending electricity to my toes. But I hold my ground, and after a moment, he seems to finally buy my story.

"Oh, yeah, the grading actually isn't too hard here," he responds. I nod as if I understand that fact since my "talk" with the Lave teacher.

"So you're not going to make me do all of the work on this project, are you?" I ask, teasingly. Sam flashes one of his brilliant smiles.

"Of course not, as long as you don't expect me to do all of the work for you," he says with a wink.

I mock a hurt expression. "Me? A freeloader? I resent that accusation!" I exclaim. Sam shrugs and sits down on a bench next to me. After a few seconds of staring at him, I sit down, too. "I seriously won't, though. History is one of the few subjects I actually enjoy," I add.

"Eh, it's okay. My real favorite subject is math," he informs me. I stare at him, open mouthed.

"What kind of person likes math?" I exclaim.

"What kind of person likes history?" he replies, a small smile hovering at his full lips.

"Touché," I admit bitterly. Sam starts laughing at my annoyance. I glare at him for a little, but soon find myself laughing, too. Sam just has such a strong presence that I always find myself falling into it. I know that he can do this with every girl, that maybe I'm not special. I don't want to listen to that part of me anymore, though—not when Sam makes me laugh so hard I forget every other reason that I should be upset.

"Knock knock," Sam says, after he is done laughing. I look over at him with exasperation.

"Who's there?" I ask, wondering why he thinks that now is the best time for a knock-knock joke.

"Albet," he replies. I roll my eyes. Are we really doing this right now?

"Albet who?"

"I'll bet that you are too chicken to come over to my cabin after Watching today to work on the project," he says, finishing with a smile. I laugh, all previous annoyances at the cliché joke forgotten. I glare at him with a devilish smirk on my mouth.

"Bet accepted," I say, hoping that Mr. McKulhan won't mind too much when I don't show for therapy today. Sam replies with the same mischievous smile back at me.

"Does that mean you're coming over later?"

"Why, yes, sir, it does."

CHAPTER 12

THE REST OF LUNCH IS a blur. Sam leaves to go back to his friends, and I walk over to Natalie's table. I snack on some of Natalie's pita chip-type things, the same kind I first tried the other night, as she, Tana, and Emily discuss their favorite stores and why. They discover that they all have the same favorite—shocker.

I hurry down the hall, determined to keep up with Natalie and her friends as we walk back to the classroom. I do not want to wander around these halls again. Who knows what I could stumble upon? Luckily, though, I am able to keep up. Usually, girls who are taller than me walk faster because of their longer legs. This time, however, all three of them are slowed down by their very high heels. How they manage to walk in those things through the gravel without sinking into the ground is a mystery to me.

I rush back into class and take my seat. The Laves immediately begin testing us again. The Laves are now testing my reactions: the time it takes me to react, how I react, and whether I will react the same way if they do it again. It is exhausting to have them constantly hitting my knee with that little hammer, blowing air into my eyes, and randomly throwing things at me. I think I am doing pretty well, but the Laves' cruel expressions are impossible to read.

In between tests, I look around the classroom to see what everyone else is up to. I want to know how they are doing compared to me and what they are working on. It seems like their tests are similar, but more complex. I know that if I were to stay here, I would be building up to that. The thought sends shivers down my spine. I will get home. I will.

After observing everyone else, I give in to temptation and sneak a glance at Sam. He is moving like a cat, in swift, decisive movements. I watch him in awe as the Laves gave him more and more tests. All of them he passes with ease. His tests have to do with strength and intelligence. They are combined so that every time he has a new test, he has to figure out whether he needs to use his strength or his mind. I love watching him move. Sam has lean muscles and is a quick "street-smart" thinker. He passes every test with efficiency. After every test that he passes, the Laves studying him grow angrier. Their hairless eyebrows furrow with impatience.

They want him to fail, I realize as I watch him. They anxiously await the test that he will fail. I feel unnerved by this new piece of information. I want to tell Sam. I want to warn him that the Laves want to push him until he fails, but I can't just launch out of my seat now and tell him. It will have to wait.

I huff in exasperation and power through the rest of my tests. On one of the tests, the Laves try to scare me. Since fright can often result in flailing your hands around, I see this as an opportunity. On the test where something pops out at me, I hit one of the Lave scientists directly in the face, and then tell them it was an accident. It wasn't.

When the researchers exit, we have ten minutes left in class. I take my seat, and the Lave teacher begins explaining the details for the history project. I listen vaguely and try to ignore the steady thrum of energy that comes from the fact that I am going to Sam's cabin after this.

When the bell rings, I collect the school materials provided for me at Watching. I shove my new binders into my new backpack. It's weird; all of these things feel alien to me. I let go of the uneasy feelings and continue to zip up my backpack when I feel a strong hand on my shoulder. I freeze, turning around slowly, and smile when I see Sam looking down at me.

"Hey, are you ready to go?" he inquires. I nod, smiling, trying not to make this awkward.

"Yeah, sure," I answer. We stand there for a few silent seconds, just staring at each other. "So, it's your cabin. Lead the way," I prompt him. Sam shakes his head, as though he is clearing it, and starts forward. When he holds the door open for me, I nearly collapse into a heap of overly flustered teenage girl.

I follow him through the hallways until we are back outside. They air is warmer now than it was in the morning. I take a deep breath of the dry air, enjoying the feeling of the heat on my cheeks. Sam walks more slowly now than he did the first time he was showing me around. Then, he seemed to be trying to shake me off his trail. Now, I notice how he slows his pace, the way he did when he walked me home the other night, so that he can walk next to me. I gently smile at the small gesture. I am content just walking in silence until I remember how I noticed that the Laves were trying to push him to his breaking point. I know that I have to warn Sam, even if he thinks I am crazy for it.

"You are really good at the tests that the Laves give you," I start. Sam raises an eyebrow and smiles.

"I guess you could say that. I am pretty awesome."

"But I noticed something," I venture, easing my way into what I want to tell him.

"And?"

"The Laves are trying to make you fail." At that, Sam starts to laugh. I pinch my lips together and cross my arms over my chest. "What's so funny?" I demand.

"I *know* they want me to fail," he explains. I glance at him curiously. "But joke's on them. It won't work. I am invincible."

"No one is invincible, Sam," I warn him. "The Laves are trying to make you fail, and one day they will succeed, and I can't see it being pretty. Humans are only capable of so much."

"I like to think that I am setting new standards for the human race," he drawls.

I roll my eyes. "Fine, you've been warned. When you fall on your face and all of the Laves laugh at you, don't come crying to me," I reply, turning my head away from him.

"Haylyn," Sam calls slowly, turning my head gently so that I am staring into those incredible eyes "I will be fine; I can handle myself."

"I know you can. It's just that the Laves are on a whole other level," I say. I don't want him to get hurt.

Sam's face softens at my words. "I will be fine. *You're* the one with the real problems. You provoke the Laves into bullying you," he says.

"Maybe they provoked me first," I declare, smiling again as he frowns at my words. I watch as Sam leads me to a section of older cabins where

I have never been before. These must be the upgrade cabins. They have a similar build to the other ones, but they are made out of wood instead of the sturdy, plain walls that make up my cabin.

When we stop at one cabin and Sam starts to go up its path, I know this must be his. I look around, trying to soak in every detail about it. The flower bed is empty, except for a few rocks. This doesn't come as a surprise; I can't see Sam gardening. There are vines growing along the porch, and Sam ducks underneath them. I follow him under as he opens his front door.

Sam holds out his arm, gesturing that I should go in first. I step inside tentatively and try to take in everything. The first thing that hits me is the smell. It is a mixture of sweet spices, the same smell that follows Sam around. I suddenly become acutely aware of the fact that I am alone, with a boy, in his house. A boy that is not only gorgeous but also has no parents to stop us from doing anything when they get home.

My heart pounds loudly with embarrassment and anxiety. I rub my sweaty palms against my jeans and try to keep my cool as I look around the rest of the cabin. The walls are painted brown and blue, and a couple of t-shirts are strewn across the room. Other than that, his place is nearly spotless.

His cabin is much bigger than mine, with a small kitchen and a living room. I guess that saving up for an upgraded cabin has its perks; it's almost like an apartment. The thought only makes me feel even more awkward. Sam steps forward and plops down onto the couch.

"You like?" he asks casually. I stand there, unsure whether I should sit down next to him or continue to stand.

"Um, yeah. It's nice," I say in return, deciding to sit on the chair beside the couch. "Bigger than mine, though."

"Are you jealous?" Sam asks, taunting me.

"No, I like my cabin. It's small and simple," I pause, "unlike yours. Overcompensating much?" I smirk.

Sam's eyes widen a fraction and a big grin spreads across his face, making his perfect dimples appear. "Never."

"Sure about that?" I question, my voice full of mischief.

"Positive. Want to check?" he inquires, returning my smirk, then getting up and moving to unbutton his pants.

I throw my head back and laugh, covering my eyes. "Stop! Stop!" I yell through my laughs, my eyes watering.

"You questioned my manhood. I had to defend myself," Sam says, sitting back down, his eyes glowing as he smiles.

"I blame myself. I initiated this."

"Yup, we both know that this was just a ploy to get into my pants."

I choke on my own laugh. "Someone needs to take your ego down a notch."

Sam shrugs. "Probably."

I roll my eyes.

"So, what should we do our project on?" he asks, now getting down to business. I sigh, wiping thoughts of Sam undressing from my mind. I have always liked history, surprisingly, so this shouldn't be too hard.

"How about Peter the Great of Russia? He forced westernization upon Russian society and really changed their culture," I suggest.

Sam presses his lips before shrugging again. "Sure, why not? I don't have any better ideas. I have some encyclopedias over there, if you want to start looking up information."

"What kind of teenager living on his own has a set of encyclopedias?" I ask curiously.

"The kind of teenager who doesn't want to get punished by the Laves when his project sucks. In case you haven't noticed, there isn't any Internet here, so this is the best we've got," Sam declares.

"Okay, okay. I'll get the encyclopedia," I say in surrender before walking across the room to his bookcase and snagging the correct encyclopedia off the bookshelf.

"We have to present our project for the class, so do you want to do a poster board with pictures and facts, and then we'll both take turns reading them off and talking about the pictures?" Sam offers.

"Okay, that's sounds good. Do you have a poster board?"

"I can get one tomorrow. We can just glue all the pictures and facts on once we're done with those," Sam says with conviction. "I'll draw all the pictures if you write out all the facts."

I give him a weird look. I have never known any guys my age to be very good artists, let alone to volunteer for the ridicule their art would bring upon them. If I let him do all the pictures, we will probably end up with a bunch of stick figures. But who knows? Maybe Sam will actually be good. He can't be much worse than I am, at least.

"Okay, sounds good." I flip through the encyclopedia until I find Peter the Great. I find a picture of Peter's palace, Peterhof. I point it out to Sam. "Can you draw this?"

"Yeah," Sam says almost quietly. I give him a doubtful look and lie down on the floor, propping myself up on my elbows. I snatch another book to use as a table and start taking notes on the passage. Sam gets up from the couch and grabs a piece of paper and a pencil before lying down on the other side of the book.

I watch in awe as his slender fingers start to curve out beautiful lines, his practiced hand never making a mistake. I can already see the outline of the palace forming through the graphite. He holds the pencil so delicately, yet also with an air of confidence. His face almost has a certain sadness about it as he watches the lines taking shape. He is fascinating.

I wish I could watch him forever, but if he finishes and sees that I don't have anything written down, I will die of embarrassment. I pry my eyes away from Sam and start to take detailed notes, underlining the important facts, pouring myself into the book so that I can try to forget about the boy beside me.

I take notes for about half an hour when Sam starts to get up from next to me. I look up and see him staring down at his picture with a nostalgic look.

"I'm done," he says, seeming not to be here fully with me. I sit up from the floor to join him standing.

"Can I see?" I inquire. Sam gives me a quick look, and I watch with awe as something seems to unlock within him. Slowly, he hands over the picture, and my heart catches at the sight. It is perfect; every detail is there, every dimension perfectly displayed. It almost looks better than the real picture of it.

"Sam, this is amazing," I say. I look up and Sam is biting his lip, almost looking shy about me seeing his work. Sam, who has never once been shy about anything.

"Do you really think so?" he asks, sounding like a child.

I nod. "Yeah, this is the best drawing I've ever seen. Where did you learn how to do this?"

"Well, both my parents were really artistic. My dad was an architect, and I always wanted to be one, too. We used to draw buildings up all the time," Sam admits. This is the first time I have ever heard Sam talk about his family. I wonder what sort of significance this has for him to be telling me right now.

"You would have been a really good architect, Sam," I tell him. Sam looks at my eyes for the first time since handing me the picture. One look tells me that this was the best compliment he could have heard. I wonder why it means so much to him just to hear this.

"Thank you," he finally gets out, something warm in his eyes that wasn't there before starting to glow to life.

"You're welcome. Now come on! We still have tons of stuff to finish, so let's get going!" I announce, trying to get us pumped back up. Sam gives me a wholehearted smile, and together we get back down and start working again.

Before, we had been working in silence, but now, after our little moment, we joke and talk constantly. I'm not quite sure what has changed in Sam, but something definitely has, and not being able to figure it out is driving me crazy. I wish Cassie were here. Usually, when I can't place my finger on something, she knows exactly what it is.

As more time passes, he becomes more at ease with his pictures and starts making even more amazing ones. I should never have doubted his art skills. Normally, a school project like this would have me clawing my own eyes out, even if it were about history, but Sam always seems to find new ways to make me laugh. Eventually, the trepidation I felt about being here fades away, and I grow comfortable on the floor of the cabin. I love how the smell of Sam permeates everything—how wherever I go, I can breathe him in. I would be quite content staying in this cabin with Sam forever. If only this cabin could be in Denver.

When it starts to get late, I desperately don't want to go, but when I start to fall asleep while holding a pair of scissors, Sam insists that I go and get some rest. I try not to resist as Sam helps me off the floor and walks me to his door.

"I'll walk you home," he says, reaching for his jacket when we reach the door.

"Oh, it's fine, I can walk myself back," I argue, not wanting him to come. It's not that I don't want to spend more time with him, because I want to so badly it almost scares me. It's just that I worry that walking in the dark with Sam, with him being all nice for once, will make me want to spill everything to him—which includes my plans with Callock. I don't see why telling Sam would be such a problem, but if Callock says no, then I have to trust him.

"No, it's dark, and you could get lost," Sam protests sternly.

"You didn't seem to care about that my first day here when I had to walk back alone in the dark, not even sure where my cabin was," I say with a smirk, making Sam look uncomfortable. "Besides, I'm stopping by Natalie's on my way back to pick up a coat." Sam seems to weigh this for a second. I can almost see him flinching at the thought of talking to Natalie, and I smile, knowing that my lie is working.

"Text me as soon as you get back then," he declares.

"Um, okay. What's your number?" I ask, confused by his sudden intense interest in my wellbeing. Sam quickly gives me his number and I put it into my phone. I send him a quick text so that he has my number as well. When I return my phone to my pocket, Sam is smiling down at me.

"Thank you. I don't know if you've noticed, but your phone will still work within this dimension. Unfortunately, your 4G plan won't go interdimensional. Phone companies are letting me down so much these days," he says, making me laugh again.

"I'll be sure to complain about that the next time I have a phone upgrade," I say, feeling awed as Sam again flashes his perfect teeth.

"Glad to hear it! Someone needs to let them know of this outrage," he exclaims.

I laugh and start to turn toward the door when I hear Sam groan.

"'Is this just a ploy to get into my pants'?" he reads my text aloud with an amused glare.

I give him a coy look and shrug innocently. "Just wondering."

He laughs. "Goodnight, Haylyn. Remember to text me."

"Will do. Thanks for having me over!" I call as I start to head out the door.

"The pleasure was all mine," Sam replies with a wink, then slowly closes the door.

My smile remains on my face even after I hear the door click shut behind me. I sigh as the cinnamon-sweet smell of Sam falls away from me. I want to go back inside, but I know that I can't.

The walk away from Sam's is a lonely one. I hunch my shoulders and decide quickly to go grab some food, even though it's way past dinner time. I head to the food court as the night breeze ruffles my air, surprisingly warm for winter time, since I am used to Denver. Here, it seems like mid-fall. Just one more reminder of how I'm not at home.

I pick up my pace and make it to the food court in pretty good time. The warm air blows out from within and, not surprisingly, there is barely anyone there. I quickly grab my food and start to look for a table when a familiar flash of red catches my eye. The red-haired girl who was attacked by the Laves! Maybe I can find out what she holds over them.

I quickly make my way over to where she is sitting; my eyes take her in as I walk. She still has severe bruising around her throat and scratches down her face, but she looks way better than she did when she was unconscious in the hospital. I stop right in front of her table and smile when her sharp blue eyes flick up to me.

"May I please sit here?" I ask, motioning to the chair across from her. She shrugs and I take my opportunity and sit.

I scoot my chair in and take a bite of my food as an awkward silence begins. I have no idea how to make small talk here. I can just see myself being all, "Oh my God, aren't the Laves so annoying?" and then from out of nowhere a Lave would swoop in and drag me off to who knows where. Yeah, I definitely have to take this slowly.

"So, how about this weather? It's pretty nice," I say, choosing the lamest default topic.

The red-haired girl flicks up a golden eyebrow at me. "I suppose so."

"I'm Haylyn," I offer, since my last topic hasn't gotten us too far.

"Kat," she replies quickly.

"Nice to meet you," I say politely, to which Kat doesn't reply. I have lost her attention, and now she stares into a far corner like it holds the answers to all of life's problems. Screw this; polite talk isn't getting me anywhere. "I know that the Laves were the ones that attacked you. I saw you that night."

Her eyes flash up to mine in sudden interest. Her mouth opens slightly in shock before she closes it again and displays a small smirk. She leans forward onto the table. I definitely have her full attention now.

"Yes, well, are you really surprised by their behavior?" she inquires.

"Well, when I saw it happen, it was my first night, so I was. But now, not so much. What I'm really curious about is why no one else seems to think the Laves did this?" I ask. Kat narrows her eyes.

"Maybe people don't want to believe the truth?" she offers, like she already knows the answer, and what she is saying definitely isn't it.

"Maybe," I reply in the same suspicious tone that she is using. "It could just be me, but I would rather know the truth than be living a lie."

"Are you sure? Sometimes the truth can be brutal."

"I'm positive."

"Well, Haylyn, I think that we might get along very well," Kat admits. "So where are you from originally?"

"Denver, Colorado. You?"

"Los Angeles, California."

"Nice. I've been there a few times to go to Disneyland," I reply, trying hard to block those painfully happy memories of my family and me.

"Yeah, L.A. is really nice. I love all the places to shop and having so many things going on, like award shows and such. The weather is really nice, too. I didn't even have to wear a jacket the other day, and here I'm forced to wear a coat. There is one thing that I don't ever miss, though, and that's the traffic!" she exclaims.

I laugh as a stray memory resurfaces, and I remember how upset my dad got when we were caught in two hours of traffic on our way to the theme park. He was yelling at every driver in front of us as though it were their fault that we weren't moving. Avery was barely four at the time, and we got stuck there for so long that he nearly peed his pants, and I was laughing so hard at the time that I nearly peed mine.

Kat seems to notice that I have drifted into the past and gives me a minute to compose myself again. I'm surprised that she isn't more distraught about being away from L.A. She can't be much older than twenty-two, yet she acts so chill about being stuck here.

"Sorry, I just remembered something about the first time I went to L.A.," I confess.

"It happens."

"Yeah, it's just hard to think that everyone else around the world is still going about their daily lives, unknowing that thousands of people are trapped in another dimension." I feel kind of weird telling her all of this, but she seems to be the first person who actually has an appropriate reaction to the Laves.

"It is very interesting," she says hesitantly.

"I just can't believe that the government knows nothing about this."

"Maybe they know more than we think?" she offers, suddenly looking very uncomfortable.

"I doubt it," I snort.

"Well, I'd better be going; it's getting late. I'll see you later," she says, standing up and gathering her food tray. She is almost to the doors before she stops and turns around. "And Haylyn? I wouldn't be so quick to put labels on who knows what, if I were you." And with that, she is gone.

I stare at the door where she was just standing. Did she just imply that the government knows something about Die Andere Welt? I stand up in a haze and shuffle out of the food court.

I replay our conversation over and over in my head as I walk back to my cabin. Maybe there is something that I've missed. I don't even know what I am supposed to be looking for, though. Am I looking for a hint to prove my theory right? Or am I looking for something else?

I shake my head with frustration. I bet she was just sharing her own blind hope that the government is going to save her. Maybe she didn't even mean anything by it at all and has no idea that she sounded like she was dropping a ton of hints. Or maybe she is just crazy, and I shouldn't have talked to her in the first place.

Well, she did succeed at one thing, and that was making me forget to ask her about what she holds over the Laves. I sigh. None of this is adding up. Did she know that I was going to ask her about it as soon as I told her that I saw her the night she was attacked? Was it her goal to distract me? Maybe that's what all of that government mumbo-jumbo was about—distracting me.

Which piece of information do I take more seriously: the mysterious information she holds, her hints that maybe the government knows something, or neither of them? Either way, there is something that is nagging me about that conversation. Ugh, I have to talk to Callock about this tomorrow.

When my cabin finally comes into view, I let out a big sigh of relief. It is starting to become my sanctuary here; I never thought that would happen. Stepping inside, I press my hands to my eyes and collapse on my bed. I lie there for a moment before remembering my promise to Sam. With a sigh, I pry my phone from my pocket.

"I'm at my cabin, and you never answered the question about whether or not this is a ploy to get into my pants," I text him. I wait a few minutes for his reply, but when none comes, I turn my phone off.

Ugh! If you are going to bug me so much about texting you, the least you can do is text back! I think angrily. *What a typical boy. Is it so hard to reply "k"?*

My thoughts wander back to Kat. I run over in my head what she said about the government until I finally figure out what else struck me as odd. She hadn't talked about L.A. like she had once lived there. She talked about it like she still did.

CHAPTER 13

FOR THE FIRST TIME IN what feels like forever, despite my stressful end to last night's otherwise perfect evening, I have a good night's sleep. No nightmares, no tossing and turning, no waking up in the middle of the night calling for my family. It is nice to have dreamless, deep sleep for once. For the first time, this bed actually feels like my own.

Half of me is happy: I really did need that sleep. When I looked at myself in the mirror, I had come to expect the dark circles under my eyes. However, the other half of me feels bad, like I am cheating on my real bed back home. But it's more than just that. How can I be happy here while my friends and family are suffering back home? They are going out of their minds with worry, while I sit here fat and happy. Well, maybe not fat, or really happy either. More like, I'm sitting here at least having food and moderately okay-feeling.

I would torture myself with this thought all morning, but I know that no good will come from it. I have to keep moving forward if I ever want to get out of here, and something tells me that figuring out what Kat was talking about could play a big part in that. I want to keep thinking of reasons for why she talked like that and what that whole bit with the government meant, but I know that I will never figure it out on my own. I have to wait until I talk to Callock this afternoon. Who knows? Maybe I'm just overthinking this whole thing.

I sit up slowly and heave myself from the bed. I look over at the clock and sigh with relief; it's only six-thirty. I take a quick shower and get dressed, knowing that if I hurry, I will be able to eat breakfast this morning.

When I am done getting ready, I stare at myself in the mirror. The result is a welcoming one: my glossy hair flowing long and bright, and the dark circles under my eyes fading.

"Not half bad," I say to myself, smiling. I walk back into the main room of my cabin, clicking the bathroom light off after me. I grab my coat and head out the front door, my rumbling stomach providing good motivation for the cold walk ahead.

The air is indeed cold, as I predicted. It stings my cheeks and makes my breath come out in billowing clouds around me. I hum one of my favorite songs from back in Denver. I may not have heard it for a long time, but I still remember all the lyrics. It helps me to feel at peace, just walking and half dancing to a song in my head, doing my own thing. Not thinking about Kat's words to the point of madness.

The walk to the food court is a long one. I keep having to distract myself so my thoughts won't wander off again. Luckily, once I reach the food court, forgetting about everything becomes all too easy. A big grin attacks my face as I take everything in.

There are actually different food options laid out! There is oatmeal, plain bread, and even some bran muffins! It may not be much, but after what I have eaten all week, this is like winning the lottery!

I run over to the muffins and scoop one up into my mouth. I swallow it down without even chewing, which, unsurprisingly, ends with me almost choking to death. But even that can't ruin my mood after I discover that it actually isn't half bad!

"This is what I'm talking about!" I mumble with my mouth full of my second bite of muffin.

Over the next twenty minutes, I vacuum down several slices of bread and one more muffin. I am in food bliss! I am about to reach for another slice when my phone starts to ring from within my coat pocket. I set my food down and look at the caller ID. Sam. Oh, shoot.

When I pick up, Sam sounds so panicked I almost feel bad.

"Where are you?" he demands. "I came to your cabin and you weren't there!"

I laugh. "I know I'm not at my cabin! Chill! I'm just getting some breakfast."

Sam lets out a sound of relief. "Okay, I'll be there soon, stay there," he tells me before clicking off. Sam really needs to work on his phone manners.

I sigh and start to throw away my trash and all the crusts from the slices of bread. I try not to eat any more, but when Sam still isn't there after a few minutes, I give in to temptation and eat another muffin. The sad part is that they aren't even that tasty; they're just that much better than all the other food I have eaten here.

I am just starting to shove my face full of my latest muffin when I hear a door open and see Sam striding toward me in dark jeans and a blue, long-sleeved t-shirt.

"Hey," I mumble, my cheeks full of muffin.

"Hey," he replies, looking at me with amusement. "Going for that hamster look?"

I glare at him until I finish chewing and then declare, "I find hamsters to be the cutest of all rodents."

"Even cuter than bunnies?"

"Yes. Other rodents need love, too, Sam!"

Sam holds his hands up in mock surrender. "Okay, fine. Hamsters. I can get behind that."

"You better," I threaten jokingly. Sam laughs and grabs a muffin for himself before holding the door open for me as we leave.

"So how come today's breakfast is so much better than all the other meals? I mean, mash? That stuff is nastier than dog food!" I declare as we walk our leisurely pace. (Unfortunately, thanks to Avery, I knew what dog food tastes like.)

"It's for the holidays, ' Sam says, smiling as he takes another bite of his muffin.

"What?"

"Yeah, for the holidays the Laves give us more variety of food. They think that around the holidays, people are more likely to resist or try to escape. So, to distract us, they give us better food for a few weeks."

"What?" I repeat. "Why didn't you tell me before? I could have had something to look forward to!" I say, punching his arm, making him drop his unfinished muffin. Sam looks down at the muffin and then gives me a glare.

"What kinds of food are there going to be?" I ask.

"I don't know if I should tell you now, muffin killer."

"Sam, please!" I whine, stretching out the word. Sam gives a long, dramatic sigh.

"My muffin! It was so young," he says remorsefully.

"You were eating it!" I remind him. "Is that not killing?"

Sam starts laughing at my exasperation. "Okay, okay, calm down. It's nothing spectacular. It's pretty much just the same foods, except you can decide which ones you want to eat."

"How come they don't just give us this food year round?" I ask in wonderment.

"The Laves steal all this food," Sam starts. *Ha, I thought so.* "So, they don't want to take any more food than necessary simply to give us options. If they took this much food year round, the farmers would start to get suspicious." Then he adds, "But there is still no meat, at least for a little while."

"A little while? You mean that there will be meat in the future?" I ask, with a vision of a hamburger already popping into my mind.

"The Laves only have meat on the first six days of January. It's some huge Lave holiday. They force all of the males older than fourteen to go on this thing called 'The Hunt,' on the twenty-ninth of December. It's a giant hunting group, basically, like what royalty used to do. During the next five days after that, we get to enjoy all the meat killed during the hunt. On the sixth, the Laves present all the meat that we didn't finish to this big creature they worship as an offering." Sam informs me of all this as if it is the most normal thing in the world. I, however, find it anything but normal, and raise my eyebrow at him.

"Now that's just weird," I declare.

Sam just shrugs. "I guess I'm just used to it."

"They've corrupted you!" I exclaim, while making a pretend frightened face.

"Hey, this is your future!" Sam replies, striking a pose and making me laugh even more.

"I turn into a boy?" I question with surprise, making both Sam and me start cracking up.

Together we walk carelessly past the canyon—the only known way of escaping. I don't even give it a second look. When Sam is here with me, it's almost easy to ignore, as if his bravery and strength make me stronger, too, just by being near him. Besides, my job is to fool everyone into thinking that I'm starting to enjoy living here. But when I am with Sam, it becomes dangerously easy to make that statement true.

As we continue to walk closer, we are suddenly engulfed in the Watching building's shadow, and it's like a switch is flipped in Sam. The carefree teenage boy who was laughing only a minute ago is gone, and he's replaced by a soldier with a steely expression. He takes a step to the side, distancing himself from me, and looks straight ahead, as though I'm not even there. I try to keep the hurt I feel over that gesture from creeping into my expression.

Something about Watching has set him back on edge, so instead of asking him what's wrong, I copy him. Two can play at this game. I rid myself of all emotion and make my walk look stiff and uncomfortable. I push away the electricity that spreads from the side that Sam stands on and try to ignore him, as he is doing with me.

We walk silently into the Watching building, but I don't feel like we're walking together anymore. Now we are like complete strangers who happen to be going to the same place. The thought crushes me as I walk, but I ignore it, too. We walk straight past the few other people scurrying to their classes and turn into the first hallway that leads to our class.

The harsh light stings my eyes, and the squeaking of my shoes on the floor sounds deafening. I am almost looking forward to getting to class so I can escape the stark, uncaring feeling emanating from Sam.

However, despite my suffering, Sam seems indifferent. He just maneuvers expertly through the halls like a robot, not bothering to look back once to see if I am still following. I do follow, though. I think about just turning around and leaving, but I am all too conscious of the cameras that line the walls. I can hear them adjusting as they stay trained on our every move; I am constantly being studied. That is what makes me stay. If I leave now, I will only be confirming the Laves' suspicions that I am weak. But I won't be weak anymore; I will be strong, and I will show it.

Before long, we are at the metal door that leads to our classroom. I take a deep breath, readying myself for whatever horrors today's class might hold. Sam gives me a quick look before prying open the door. I follow him inside, trying to ignore how much I hate all of the girls whose eyes instantly fall on Sam.

Sam takes his seat, and I give the Lave teacher a weak glare before sitting in my own seat as well. I fidget around in my desk and the Lave teacher glares at the class while we wait for the last couple of kids to shuffle in before the bell rings. A few seats ahead of me, Natalie turns around in her chair and mouths to me, "How was last night?"

At first I have no idea what she is talking about, but then it clicks. She wants to know about how it was working with Sam. I almost laugh thinking about how jealous she must have been when she found out that we would be working together.

"Good," I mouth back. Natalie scowls before turning back around. I suddenly get the urge to turn around and see if Sam noticed what just went down, but before I can, the bell is ringing and it's time for class to begin.

Today we are doing creative writing. It doesn't sound too bad until more Laves pile in with a bunch of machines. It takes all my self-control not to start screaming as they attach numerous wires to my head. They explain to me that they are monitoring my brain-wave patterns, but I don't hear most of what they are saying. All my focus is going into calming myself down. I look around the class to see if anyone else looks as violated as I feel, but they all look calm, as if this happens all the time.

I take a deep breath. If Natalie isn't afraid, I'm sure as hell not going to complain. So I suffer in silence.

The rest of the morning I spend barely containing my irritation. I write some story that has to do with an ant named Gwendolyn. Unfortunately for her, my bad mood is bleeding into my story, and Gwendolyn does not survive the first shoe she meets.

I am so happy when they finally detach the electrodes from my head and release me for lunch that I literally jump for joy. I grab my food and wait for Sam to come over and walk with me, only he doesn't. He leaves the classroom with a mob of other boys, leaving me alone. I try to ignore how much that stings and walk out to lunch by myself. Now, I am forced to eat with Natalie, Tana, and Emily, all of whom nearly hassle me to death for information about last night. I am so ready for the day to be over already.

The rest of class goes by in a haze. I'm not going to relapse or anything; I'm just tired and really want to take a nap. I got like this sometimes in Denver, too, where I was just sick of school and wanted to stay home. When the bell finally rings, ending class, I give a small smile of relief, but the Lave teacher is not done yet.

"All right students, I'll see you in a few days. Enjoy your Christmas vacation," she announces, saying "Christmas" the same way I say "homework," which is really saying something about how much she must detest it.

I wait for any more last-minute announcements, then, when there are none, I start to pile all my books into my arms. Keeping the top one from sliding off, I smile at Emily's familiar face approaching me.

"Hello, Haylyn!" she greets me politely.

"Hey, Emily, what's up?" I reply.

"I was just wondering if you're busy tonight. Natalie, Tana, and I are going to have a girls' night, and I was just wondering if you would like to come?"

I smile brightly. "That sounds really fun, thank you. I would love to go," I respond, not even caring if this is just a ploy to keep me away from Sam.

"Sweet! I'll have Natalie pick you up and walk you there, since it's at my place, and you haven't been there yet," she says.

"Okay, that sounds great! Thank you so much!" I exclaim excitedly.

"No problem! I'll see you then!" she calls as she starts to walk away.

"See you!" I call after her.

I feel strangely excited for tonight. I haven't had a girls' night since Cassie came over and made cookies with me a couple days before I was taken. The thought sends remorse through me. It seems so long ago since I made those cookies. I can remember everything about that night. I remember how mad I was that my dad ruined my potatoes with a sneak attack of pepper, after teasing me endlessly to put some on. I would give anything for him to be able to ruin more of my food with pepper again because at least I would be able to see him happy again. I remember how exasperated I was with my plain and perfect neighborhood on my walk home with Avery. I would give anything to be able to see those white picket fences again.

I brush my hair back from my face and tuck it behind my ears, remembering how much my dad hated it when he couldn't see my eyes. I'm just about to leave the class when Sam strides up to me, blocking my exit. I give him an annoyed glare.

"Ready to go to my place to work on the project?" he asks. *Oh, so now he wants to hang out with me?*

"Can't, I'm busy," I reply, which is actually true. I am meeting with Callock, and then I am going over to Emily's. Sam looks taken aback, as if the last thing he expected me to say was that I am busy, which only irritates me more. *I have a life apart from him!*

"With what? It's not like you have any friends!" he exclaims. *God, he can be so unbelievable sometimes!*

"Yeah, well, maybe I have more friends than you think," I grumble angrily. Sam's eyes lock on mine.

"Oh really? Then what *are* you doing?" he asks.

"Wouldn't you like to know?" I reply, reveling in his confusion.

Sam now looks thoroughly taken aback, as if he doesn't know what to do now that I have rejected him. I bet he doesn't get rejected a lot. He looks so lost that I almost laugh. I am positive now that Sam has never been treated indifferently by a girl before me, and I'm enjoying the fact that I am the first one to do so, twice now.

"Well, okay, I'll see you later, I guess," Sam mumbles as he shuffles away. As soon as he is out the door, I start to crack up. I think I have just given Sam some kind of life crisis. He looks so confused, it's ridiculous.

At my sudden outburst, the Lave teacher spirals her head over to me, as though I should not be laughing in her presence. I happily return the evil glare with one of my own and walk gleefully out of the classroom.

CHAPTER 14

I WALK INTO MY CABIN and put all my Watching stuff down. Mr. McKulhan is coming over for therapy before Callock gets here. I almost sigh over the fact that I have to wait longer before I can start planning with Callock. Therapy used to be a refuge for me from this world, but now I don't need it. All that I need is hope, a purpose. And that is what Callock's mysterious plan provides me. It's something to believe in.

A knock sounds at the door and I open it happily, knowing that it will be Mr. McKulhan. As I open the door, Mr. McKulhan smiles brightly at me, deep creases lining his eyes, reminding me that he once lived in happier times. He wears the same brown tweed suit that he has worn every day. The very sight of him is enough to calm my raging nerves.

"Hello, Haylyn. How are you on this fine day?" he greets me.

"I'm good, really good, actually," I reply, making my mind swirl with images of the red-haired girl. Okay, so maybe I'm not *really* good, but I'm better than I was anyway, and I really do think it's time to let Mr. McKulhan go.

"I'm glad to hear it," he responds, giving me a certain look that makes me think he knows what's coming. I start to feel bad. What if this breaks his heart?

"In fact, I'm doing so good that I don't think I need therapy anymore," I announce carefully. Mr. McKulhan just smiles and nods; he is so kind that it makes me want to cry.

"I understand. I'm glad to hear it, actually," he says.

"Thank you for everything. You really did help," I add.

"I really am glad to hear it, Haylyn. I want you to move on and get better. I see this life in you; it burns in your eyes. All I wanted for you to do was find that inner strength, and I think you have at least started to discover it. You are the kind of person that needs tough situations to thrive because it is only then that people see just how amazing you really are. I am sad that I won't be able to see you grow anymore, but also happy. It is a bittersweet situation, but if you are going to go on to bigger things, like I suspect you will, I need to let you go," Mr. McKulhan explains.

I smile, trying to blink away tears of embarrassment from Mr. McKulhan's strong faith in me. "Thank you," I whisper as I give him a hug. Mr. McKulhan smiles one last time before leaving my cabin and leaving me to my own thoughts.

I walk slowly over to my bed and am about to sit down when a knock sounds at my door. I sigh. *You can't even get a moment of rest here!* I jog over and pull it open to see Callock grinning that disturbing smile at me.

"Hello, fellow rebel to the Laves," he greets me. God, he is weirder than I remember.

"Hello," I respond, letting him inside my cabin. "Have a seat." I gesture to a chair in the corner of my room. Callock sits down in it, and I take a seat on the edge of my bed.

"You're sure that you're committed to this? You won't betray me?" he asks.

I nod violently. "I want to go home more than anything," I reply.

Callock's thin lips pull into a smile. "Smashing," he purrs.

"So, pardon my frankness, but what exactly is your plan to escape from the Laves?" I ask. I have to make sure that this guy is for real and not just trying to cheat me out of something.

"Glad to see that you are motivated. So here it goes. I am half Lave, yes?" he starts.

"Yes?" I venture.

"And only the Laves possess the power to create portals between dimensions. The only problem is that every time I make a portal, it is only there for a few seconds before it vanishes because I am only half Lave. Now *that* is where you come in."

I stare at him with hesitation. "Okay...? So what do you need me to do?" I ask, feeling like James Bond.

"I need you to get me the Laves' power," he says.

"So, what? Kidnap a Lave?" I ask, confused.

"No, not exactly," he drawls, smiling with mischief. I feel myself slide as far away from Callock as my bed will allow. "I need you to take it from the very source."

"Which is…?" I say, hoping that he will elaborate.

"The Laves used to be a lot like humans. In fact, they used to live together on earth. The Laves lived in the Germanic area. However, neither species remembers that. Anyway, the Laves and the humans never got along. One day, the Laves and the humans were about to engage in a terrible war, one that would most likely have ended with the Laves dead, simply because they were outnumbered. However, a dark being intervened and rescued the Laves by taking them back to its home dimension. This being was so terrible that it corrupted the Laves, turning them into what they are today. Humans are only one-hundredth of one percent different from each other; Laves used to only be two hundredths. Now the Laves are too corrupted to find anything humanlike within them. The horrible creature is what gives them their power," Callock explains.

"What is this creature?" I ask, slightly afraid of the answer.

"To the Laves, it is called Retter. However, it is basically just a giant, ugly bird."

I give a small laugh at Callock's bluntness. "So, obviously, the Laves know about this bird?"

"Yes, they worship it. What they don't know is that they used to live with the humans and be a lot like them. The Laves just know that the bird saved them. They don't even know what from, but they still fall all over themselves for it," Callock snorts. "Idiots."

"So, then, how do you know all of this information when they don't?"

"There is this sacred library that the Laves refuse to go in, for fear of ruining its holiness or something. I, of course, do not follow the rules and broke in. The library holds records from the first Laves who were brought here, and they explain everything."

"So now I have to bring you this bird?" I ask. Callock's words are finally starting to come together in my head.

"Well, you have to kill it," he states bluntly. I flinch. I want to go home more than anything, but I don't want to have to kill anything. *You are not backing out of this!* I snap at myself. I have to do this; I can't just let my weakness keep me from seeing my family again. I won't let it. I just have to become stronger.

"Okay, and after I kill it?"

"You bring me its heart," he responds. I make a disgusted face. This has just gone from cruel to gruesome. I mean, cutting a squishy, bloody organ from a still-warm body? How am I supposed to do that? I couldn't even handle dissecting a chicken's wing in the seventh grade!

"Oh, relax, the heart isn't going to be like the heart of any animal you know. It will basically look like a rock. It's too evil to have the warmth of a beating heart," Callock explains. I still don't like the idea of it.

"Okay, I'm not backing out of this," I state to reassure Callock, but also to reassure myself.

"Good. And you must know, this thing is no chicken. It will be huge."

"Like an ostrich?" I ask.

"It dwarfs the ostrich," he replies. I bite my lip with anxiety and rub my palms down the front of my jeans.

"Then how, pray tell, am I supposed to be able to kill it? Last time I checked, I was not a huge body builder, and I doubt I'll be able to become one in the next few days!" I exclaim.

"Don't worry, you can do it. I believe in you," Callock responds.

I stare at him, dumbfounded. "Well, what if I don't believe in myself? I mean, maybe I could do it if I had a gun, but I doubt you're hiding one under that blazer!" I argue.

"No, I don't have a gun. But don't worry, I will give you the weapon you need. And beating it will be tough, but you just have to beat it with intelligence. When it sees you, it will go into a frenzy. It's so bloodthirsty that it won't think of any way to trap you or fight you, it will just think about eating you." I feel a shiver crawl down my spine. Humans are not used to being hunted.

"So when does this all go down?" I'm wondering how much time I will have to mentally prepare myself. "And how come you can't do it?"

"I can't do it because Laves are physically unable to hurt this creature. Our bodies will stop working if we even try. If I were to raise a weapon against it, the corrupted part of me that comes from the bird would act against me. The bird can control all the corrupted parts of the Lave, which is the majority of the Lave. The only reason that I am able to plan its demise is because I'm half human, but I would still turn helpless against it when the time came."

I nod understanding, and Callock moves on to my next question. "This will all go down sometime before the sixth. That is when the Laves bring the bird all these offerings, and they actually see it."

"Okay, so any day between now and the sixth?"

"Well, it also needs to be a day when Sam can't stop you."

I look up to Callock with shock. "What? I really think you overestimate his feelings for me," I say.

Sure, Sam may be a little closer to me now, but I really don't think he'll be that much of a problem when the time comes.

"Maybe I am, but I don't think so. It will not be a safe mission; you could get hurt. I fear that Sam might try to stop you from getting hurt, which would stop you from completing the mission," he concludes.

I feel a blush creep up into my cheeks. Whatever is going on between Sam and me, Callock has picked up on it. That has to mean that something is there, right? The thought sends bundles of emotion throughout me, but I push them all back down. I need to focus. Now, when would Sam be busy and not suspicious of me if I were absent? I wrack my brain when... *That's it!*

"The Hunt!" I exclaim. Callock looks at me wildly from my sudden outburst.

"Excuse me?" he says, bewildered.

"Sam will be gone for a whole day, with all the other guys, on the Hunt, right?"

"Yes, that's perfect! But," he says, his thought interrupted.

"But what?" I prompt.

"I have to go on the Hunt, too, so I won't be able to assist you like I hoped I'd be able to."

I snort. "Oh please! Standing on the sidelines, being my cheerleader and unable to assist with any of the fighting wouldn't have been that much help to me, anyway."

"Well, then, this will be perfect!" he exclaims, hopping up from his chair and heading for the door. "I will be here two days after Christmas to confirm our plan!" He begins turning the door handle to leave.

"Callock, one more thing," I call to him. "When I first got here, I saw this girl being beaten by the Laves because they think she has some kind of information that they want, and last night I talked to her again and she was behaving really weird. She kept acting like she still lived in L.A., and she hinted that the U.S. government knows more than we think. Do you think she knows something that could help us escape? Should I look into it?"

"That's all that happened?" Callock asks.

I nod my reply.

"Well, I would say that she is just crazy; it happens sometimes with the people here, and the Laves think everyone is plotting against them, which is why it wouldn't be worth the risk to talk to her more. My plan is our best bet," he says, seeming honest. I nod; she did seem a little cuckoo. I probably should listen to him and just stay away from her.

Callock starts to open the door when another question pops into my mind. "Callock!" I call, stopping him. "Why me? Why choose me to help you, when you could have had anyone else?"

He pauses for a long second before replying. "Because you had a fire in your eyes that even the Laves couldn't extinguish."

I smile softly. With that, Callock is gone, leaving me in a whirlwind of emotions.

How will I be able to do this? How am I, a petite girl with a bad attitude, supposed to kill something that is so much bigger than I am? I think about this as I brush my hair and get ready to go to Emily's. The answer comes to me as I sit down to wait for Natalie: because I have to.

CHAPTER 15

CALLOCK'S WORDS GIVE ME A new purpose. I can do this. I can get home. The simple thought of home now strikes me with new feelings. Just a couple of days ago, it made me indescribably sad because it made me think of all the things that I would never be able to see again. Now, when I think of home, I mostly have longing. I *will* go home, so now I just have to stay strong and wait.

I sit on my bed thinking about all the things that could go wrong with Callock's plan. Should I trust his plan? Hell, should I even trust him? I am about to go into an argument with myself over whether or not I should trust him when an aggressive hand begins to pound on my door. I swing it open to find a steamed-looking Natalie.

"Are you ready?" she demands.

"Yeah?" I reply warily as I step outside to join her. Natalie seems appeased by my answer and is off before I even shut my door behind me. Bewildered, I chase after her. "Are you okay?" I call.

"What? Yeah, I'm fine. Why do you ask?" she snaps.

"Oh, no reason." I nervously chew my lip and struggle to keep up with her as she powers down the streets.

"Sorry I'm late, my blow dryer completely broke on me, and I had to go out and get a new one! It's so irritating. I think I'm going to sue the company that made it," she growls. I sigh and struggle to hold back a laugh. Typical girl problems. Of course this is what Natalie is so mad about.

"Well, I'm sorry about that," I say with a small smile.

"Thank you. It's just very distressing!" she cries, talking wildly with her hands. "Anyway, back to the juicy stuff. Now that it's just you and me, how is working with Sam?"

I look at her, wondering what would make her think I would keep things from the other two girls but not her.

"Like I said, it was pretty good. The only thing is that he can be so infuriating sometimes!" I say, allowing myself to get into girly drama with her for once.

"Funny you say that, actually. He's usually much worse. He used to sass the Laves so much in class and get beaten or shown videos of back home every day. Now there's not a peep. I wonder what made him change so suddenly?" she wonders. *That is interesting. What would make him change?*

"How weird," I mutter.

"I think that the Laves may have finally found something to give them the upper hand to keep him in control or something. You should have seen him before."

"Hmm, I wish I could have," I say, lost in thought about what could have sparked his sudden change.

After our conversation about Sam, there is no more talking, and I follow Natalie silently through the twisting streets as she keeps up her "burning daylight" walking speed. Luckily, Emily has been here the least amount of time of the three, so her cabin isn't too far away from mine. When Natalie and I arrive, she doesn't hesitate before barging through Emily's closed door.

I step in carefully, worried that Emily will be mad that Natalie has thrown her door open. However, when I get inside, I see the two others casually talking as if Natalie's abrupt entrance hasn't fazed them at all.

I look around, impressed. Emily's cabin may have not been much bigger than mine, but she has put the space to good use. She has a small couch with a little coffee table in front of it, and her bed is pushed back into the corner so it will take up as little space as possible.

"Unfortunately, we can't do some of the typical girls' night things, since there is, like, no technology here, but I did manage to find a few bottles of nail polish in the store today!" Emily announces. "Must be a present for the holidays!"

"Oh my God? Really? They haven't had nail polish here since August!" Natalie squeals, wiggling her plain nails in my face.

"This will be so great!" Tana agrees. "Have you tried going shopping yet, Haylyn?"

"Um, no. I'm still waiting to get money from the Laves," I reply.

"You don't have to wait for your money, silly, it's like having a checking balance," Natalie exclaims. "You go up to the cash register, tell them what your name is, and they charge it to your account. Every month, the Laves put the same amount of money in the account, and you can either spend it all or save it."

"Oh, then maybe I'll have to try it," I concede, not wanting to fight them on a topic that they are clearly all passionate about. "So, what's for dinner?" I nod at the boxes on the table. I didn't even know you could do takeout here.

"Only the best food ever to be introduced to Die Andere Welt," Tana replies with a smile.

"Which would be...?"

"Well, it's not that great, but compared to everything else around here, it is heavenly!" Natalie exclaims. "They only serve it around the holidays, too! I have been looking forward to this all year."

"Would you guys just tell me already?" I insist, getting hungry just thinking about the possibility of better-tasting food.

"Okay, okay. It's called 'slush,'" Natalie finally admits. I raise an eyebrow; no food should be called "slush."

"Slush?" I say with disgust.

"It sounds gross, but it's just like mashed potatoes!" Tana informs me. Now I'm starting to feel this whole slush thing.

"Okay, let me at it!" I announce. Natalie hands me a bowl, and its contents do look very similar to mashed potatoes. I take a bite just to make sure and nearly cry over how good it tastes in comparison to everything else. It *is* like mashed potatoes!

After a few hours, I have eaten five bowls of slush, and all ten of my digits have been painted by Natalie. Sure, they are bright pink, but it feels nice to see a bright color after being here for so long. Not to mention that Natalie calls the color "On Wednesdays we wear pink," making it ten times better.

After thirty minutes of digesting, I decide that I am hungry again and start to slide off Emily's bed to get another bowl of slush. I reach for the spoon when suddenly a sharp screech pierces my ears. I drop the spoon in surprise and fly away from the bowl.

"Haylyn! What are you doing? You can't have another serving!" Natalie exclaims.

"Why not?" I ask, placing my hands on my hips.

"If you have another bowlful, how do you expect to fit into your dress?" she snaps, as if it were the most obvious thing in the world. I stare, confused, back at her.

"What are you talking about?" I reply. Now it's Natalie's turn to be confused.

"Your dress for the dance?" she says, looking at me like I am the biggest idiot she has ever seen.

"What dance?" I am bewildered and irritated that they won't just tell me what's going on. Natalie rolls her overly lined eyes.

"The Christmas Eve dance, of course," she answers. I continue to stare at her with confusion, and suddenly she seems to understand. "You don't know about the dance? That means you must not have a dress!" It's as if this is the most horrible news she has ever heard.

"No?" I say cautiously, taking another step away from the bowl.

"Haylyn, it is the twenty-second. We need to get you a dress tomorrow!" she squeals.

"There probably won't be any good dresses," I argue. I am not really in the mood to go to a dance.

"Nonsense. I know a person," she answers. "Come on! We need to get you to bed. We have a big day tomorrow!" She catches my arms and starts to drag me toward the door. "Thanks, Em! See you, Tana!" she calls as she hauls me outside.

I try to right myself several times on our journey back to my cabin, but Natalie never gives me the chance. I call it a journey because for it to be a walk, both of us would have to be walking. But no, Natalie insists on dragging me, practically ripping my arm out of its socket. I have realized something about Natalie: She is a little manic.

"Natalie, let go of me! You're going to rip my arm out!" I cry for the sixth time. Natalie finally lets go, and I straighten myself out.

"Sorry," she mumbles.

"It's okay," I reply halfheartedly.

"I'm just so excited! I love dances. Every year, I hope that Sam will ask me, but he never does," she admits regrettably.

I suddenly feel a flash of hurt. I realize that I also wish Sam had asked me. Although, this close to it, it is obvious that he doesn't plan to.

"I mean, it hurts, but I'm not too upset. If you're going with a date, you have to tell the Laves who you're going with. So I just try to think about how Sam is doing me a favor by not making me talk to them," she says.

Natalie looks at me, waiting for my answer, but I can't bring myself to say anything. I am almost jealous. I don't like the thought that Natalie thinks about Sam, probably all day long. I don't know why it bothers me so much; I almost feel like I am the only one who should get to look at him.

When it's clear that I don't plan on answering, Natalie pushes on, and we arrive at my cabin a minute later.

"Thanks for taking me there and back again," I say.

"No problem! I will be here at nine o'clock, so be ready," she orders, making me smile at how seriously she is taking this. "You are so lucky that we get the next three days off for Christmas, or else we wouldn't have had any time to find you a dress!"

"I guess so, and I'll be ready," I say, giving her a quick hug and nearly choking at the amount of perfume that is trapped in her hair.

"See you tomorrow!" she calls as she walks away.

"See you!" I reply, waving back at her.

When she turns the corner, I take a huge gasp of fresh air. How does Natalie stand that chemical weapon all day long? After a few more gulps of air, I shuffle inside my cabin and go through my nightly routine.

I finish brushing my teeth and slip between the covers of my bed. As soon as I set my head down on my soft pillow, sleep comes quickly.

The next morning, I am awakened by the cacophonous symphony that is my alarm clock blaring into my ear. I really should get up and start getting ready, but it's just so warm under my blankets, and so cold outside of them. Why does Natalie have to take me dress shopping so early? There should really be a law against leaving the house before ten a.m. I would be a strong supporter of that law.

Twenty minutes later, I have finally pep-talked myself into some action, and I am rolling off my bed and onto the ground with a thud.

"Ow," I groan into the carpet.

Five more minutes after that, I heave myself off the ground and drag myself into the shower.

After I get out, I go about my morning ritual. I consider getting breakfast, but I am still full from all that slush last night. Maybe I shouldn't have eaten that last bowl, but I have no regrets.

As the time ticks away, I start to get more and more impatient. At first, I pass the time by tweaking little things about my makeup, but eventually I can't stand the sight of myself in the mirror anymore. When it's finally nine-thirty and Natalie still isn't here, I have had enough. Not to mention that my wet hair soaked through my shirt forty minutes ago. Giving in to temptation, I crawl back into bed.

"Haylyn!" a high-pitched voice rings, forcing me out of my blissful sleep.

I glance at my clock. It reads ten o'clock. I make a sound of disapproval. *If you're going to make me wake up early, at least be on time.*

Eventually, I shove the covers off my body and open up the door to the sight of Natalie holding a big dress bag in her arms. Oh God. She picked one out for me. I can only imagine the amount of sparkles on that thing. I have never truly known fear until now.

Natalie brushes past me and instantly hangs up the dress in my closet, still not opening the bag.

Natalie fixes her hair before launching into a speech. "Sorry I'm a little late. I know you were looking forward to going shopping." *I was?* "But the more I kept thinking about it, the less it seemed necessary for you to come! I mean, I already knew the perfect dress for you, so bringing you would have just taken more time. Besides, the seamstress I know doesn't take well to new people. So all and all, it just worked out for you not to come," she concludes.

I shrug. As long as the dress Natalie got me isn't too bad, I think that I have actually dodged a bullet by not having to go shopping.

"So are you ready to see it?" Natalie inquires.

I take a deep breath. "Okay, I'm ready," I reply, already flinching.

Natalie gives me a smile as she slowly unzips the bag, revealing the dress.

"It's full length with a plunging neckline and slits up the sides of the skirt that are covered by mesh, so it really only gives boys a sneak peek. The beading is what really makes this dress special, though," she informs me.

As she rambles, I realize that I should never have doubted Natalie's dress-shopping skills. "It's perfect," I announce.

CHAPTER 16

I SIT ON MY BED, staring at the most beautiful dress I have ever seen, as it hangs from the outside of my closet. It is two hours until the dance, and I still can't believe I am supposed to wear that dress. The rich fabric is an inky black that moves like liquid mercury, and that isn't even the best part. It's the beading that really ties it together. The entire thing is covered lightly in twining flowers and leaves with just the tiniest hint of silver that makes them stand out. Pair that with the scandalous dips and cuts covered in a see-through material that leaves nothing to the imagination, and this dress is incredible.

I can't believe that I will actually wear something so beautiful. I don't want to put it on for fear of ruining it or having my bland appearance drag it down. I sigh as I survey it. I could be content just staring at it forever. Natalie, however, does not share the same sentiments.

"Come on, Haylyn, strip already! We only have a couple of hours, and we haven't even done your hair and makeup yet!" Natalie huffs.

"But it's so pretty."

"So are flowers, but you don't see florists refusing to pick them. Now, you have to get in this dress at some point if you want to go to this dance," she declares.

"But I don't *want* to go to this dance," I remind her. This whole thing has been orchestrated by her, not me.

Natalie shakes her head with aggravation. "Haylyn, this dress is perfect for you, so you are going to put it on and go to this dance, whether you like it or not!"

I sigh, feeling my battle being lost, and make my way toward the dress. I grab a handful of the thick fabric, running my thumb over the texture of the beads. Without further thought, I throw the dress over my head and feel it slide down my body. I put my arms back down when I feel fabric brush the top of my feet. I can't see what I look like yet, but for the first time since hearing about this night, I am actually starting to get excited.

The dress clings to every part of my body before flowing out around my thighs. I look self-consciously down out my chest, cringing at how much is visible. The mesh only provides a sensual shadow against my skin. This is definitely not the kind of dress that you get to wear a bra with. I am about to share my concerns with Natalie and take it off when she zips it up behind me, making it cling even more.

"Natalie I don't know about this—" I start.

"Nonsense!" she cries as she takes my hand and drags me into the bathroom to work her magic, not even letting me see my reflection before getting to work. My eyes water as she applies mascara and eyeliner. However, the real problem doesn't come until Natalie starts to curl my hair. The girl waves the hot piece of metal around my face like it's a baton. We don't do much talking, mostly because Natalie won't allow it because I might mess up my lipstick.

When Natalie is done, she has truly worked a miracle. I don't know how she did it. My hair is done up in a mess of curls pinned to my head, with several of the ringlets hanging down and brushing my bare shoulders. Braids cross in the front of my head, and within the jungle of my hair are tiny crystals that match the beads in my dress. My eyes look huge and mysterious, like I am keeping an important secret from everyone. I am not usually one to appreciate my own looks, but I look like one of those girls from the James Bond movies—both striking and deadly.

"Natalie, you have some serious talent. I look great!" I exclaim.

"Well, I did have a good model to start with," she states. I smile to myself as I realize that she has just given me a compliment. I am about to say thank you when the sounds of voices fill my cabin.

"Knock, knock!" one of the voices calls. I smile as I recognize Tana's voice. She and Emily must have just gotten here.

"We're in here!" Natalie calls back to them. The girls walk in and their jaws drop.

"Haylyn, you're a babe!" Tana declares.

"You look so pretty!" Emily squeals right after. I feel a blush rise into my cheeks, and I suddenly become self-conscious, unsure of how I should respond.

"Thank you," I answer.

"Oh, please, I'm the one that you should be complimenting. Do you think she woke up looking like this?" Natalie says half-jokingly.

"Thank you, Natalie, you did a really good job," I tell her, knowing how much she wants to hear it. Natalie smiles and flicks her hair, practically patting her own shoulder.

All three girls are being so nice, but under their kind words I can hear the hints of jealousy. Knowing that they are jealous brings a smirk to my face. I don't know why, but having the "perfect girls" be jealous of me provides me with a sense of poetic justice.

I say thank you again to all of their compliments, even if underneath the pretty words they are planning to "accidentally" spill their punch all over the front of my dress. I quickly grab my equally beautiful high-heeled shoes and slip them onto my feet. I walk to the door, and I am about to follow Tana and Emily outside when Natalie ambushes me with perfume. She sprays me about ten times before finally putting the bottle down. I sneeze with surprise and glare at her. At least this perfume isn't the same one she wore two days ago, the one that threatened to choke me. This one is softer and smells like sugar.

"Natalie!" I say accusingly. Natalie shrugs in return and hops out the door after Tana. I stare angrily after her, but decide revenge isn't worth it and hurry after the three girls.

The white sky that signals daytime here is minutes from being devoured by shadows as the day grows late. My dress rustles behind me, and I try desperately to keep the fine fabric from touching the ground. I have no idea where the dance is going to be, so I just follow the other three girls faithfully. I sure hope that we are not going far, though; walking in heels on a sand-like ground is proving to be the most difficult thing since chemical reactions in chemistry class.

The three girls continue to lead me forward to wherever the dance is being held, keeping up a constant chatter the whole way there. Despite previously not wanting to go when Natalie first told me about it, I now find myself growing eager for a night of fun. The girls take a sharp left, and I now know where the dance is being held. It is the park.

I worry as we begin to walk through the trails that are nearly pitch black, with the foliage blocking out the little light left in the sky. I start to panic that the Laves are luring us into a trap, but the three girls seem so confident in where they are heading that I decide to go with it. Once I start to hear the music, I know that we are heading in the right direction after all. However, it is not the normal music I would expect at any dance back home.

At home, I would hear a deep bass, and the music would be pounding so loudly I'd have to yell at the person standing right next to me in order to be heard. There would be a mosh pit of people with their bodies all pressed together. A few strangers would try to start dancing against me, but I would just shoo them away without a second glance and with a few snarky comments made by my friends. However, I don't think a random person will start to grind with me at this dance.

As we round the corner, I realize that all my knowledge of dances from back home will do me no good here. This is the exact opposite of that. It is magnificent, but I am unprepared.

The dance reminds me of *Cinderella*. There is a huge wooden dance floor laid out in the meadow, and a full orchestra is playing to the side. Old-fashioned lights zigzag between tree branches, providing low light. People from ages fourteen to what could be fifty-eight are dancing to their hearts' desire, but not the kind of dancing that I am used to. This is real dancing, full-on ballroom waltzing. The very sight makes me smile as it whisks me back in time. Natalie is trying to tell me something, but the music it still loud enough that I can't hear her. No real complaints there, though. The best part is that there are no Laves in sight. I guess seeing humans being happy must be nauseating to them.

I am about to leap onto the dance floor, despite my lack of dancing partner, when I see him. My senses are unprepared for the sight of Sam looking immeasurably dashing in his tux. His shoulders look broad and strong in the jacket, and I literally have to force myself to breathe. My reaction only gets more humiliating when my gaze reaches his face. His eyes are nearly glowing green as they are set off by the black. The gold in his brown hair is shining with the glowing lights that hang above.

"Oh my God! He has never worn a tuxedo to one of these things before! He looks so hot!" Natalie squeals into my ear, but my eyes are still locked on Sam. His full lips are curved into a grin, and I worry that I have been staring for too long, but when I look up to his eyes again, I find that they are looking me up and down. I blush and suddenly feel self-conscious.

I try to turn away and talk to Natalie to act casual, but she and the other two girls have already left and are halfway to the punch bowl. I begin to head over to them when Sam starts to move. *Sweet Jesus, he is coming over here! What do I do?*

"You look beautiful, Haylyn," he announces when he reaches me. The look in his eyes is so deep that I feel like I'm drowning in them. I need to get it together.

"Why, thank you. You don't look half bad yourself," I reply coyly, even though he looks way better than half bad. Sam smirks, seeming to read my mind, and holds his hand out to me as a new song begins to play.

"May I have this dance?" he asks. I raise an eyebrow, skeptical.

"Really?" I inquire.

"Of course, anything to see you smile," he says with a wink. I feel the same smile that he is referring to begin to show itself. Sam can be quite charming when he wants to be.

I nod a yes to Sam's request and let him pull me onto the dance floor, loving the feeling of how my hand fits perfectly in his. I probably would have fallen over by now if Sam weren't holding on.

"You really do look stunning tonight, Haylyn. Prettier than every other girl," Sam says, leaning down to whisper in my ear.

I eye him, not sure if I believe him, or any of this, at all. "Have you been taking any illegal substances tonight?" I question, half serious and half joking because I asked him that a lot when we first met. Sam's eyes snap to mine with a funny look in them that I can't name.

"Why is it that every time I tell you the truth, you can't believe me? You have to make up some excuse that I'm crazy or on drugs," he exclaims with exasperation.

"Well, you are talking crazy."

"I'm talking honestly," Sam responds. I bite my lip and feel myself almost subconsciously snuggle closer into Sam's side as we walk.

A minute later, we make it to the center of the dance floor. I look to see what the other girls are doing and then slide my arms around Sam's neck, mimicking them. I smile when he does the same to my waist. Together, we slowly sway back and forth while I try my best not to turn this into something horribly awkward. I feel the warmth of Sam's hands resting above my hips as it seeps through my dress, heating me to the core.

Sam's eyes remain steady on mine, sending shivers to my toes. We are so close that for the first time I am able to see that Sam's eyes have flecks of gold spiraling around the irises, the way sunlight filters through leaves. It's simply beautiful.

As we sway, Sam seems to get lost in the music, humming it to himself as his chest vibrates with the deep, resonant sound. "You know this song?" I ask in surprise. Since all the music is classical, I wouldn't expect him to like it, let alone know it already.

"Yeah," Sam says nodding with distant eyes, his hands clasping my waist tighter.

"Where do you know it from?" I ask. Maybe they played it at a previous dance.

"My mother used to play this song all the time when I was little. She was a violinist," he answers softly. "I used to only come to these things to listen to the music because it reminded me of her."

I smile tentatively at this. I love when Sam shares a piece of his past because it's a piece of him. Our past makes us who we are, whether we like it or not. I nestle my head against his chest; his heart beat is strong and steady behind my ears. The very sound fills me with a feeling of safety and happiness. I let the song wash over me and try to picture Sam as a child listening to his mother play while his bare feet padded all over the house. I wish I could save that Sam from the future that awaited him.

As we dance, I can't believe how much fun I am having in the worst place in the worlds (since, apparently, there is more than one). Sam delicately twirls me out and lifts his hand for me to spin under his arm. Every time I pirouette, my hair and dress spin out around me and the ground lurches, making it even more exhilarating when Sam catches me and holds me safe and steady in his arms.

After several songs, I try to stop and pull away. We have been dancing for ages, and Sam probably has other girls he wants to dance with and just doesn't know how to tell me. However, when I try to move, Sam's arms remain locked in place, holding me still. I arch an eyebrow and look into his eyes questioningly.

"If you wanted to dance with me this much, you should have asked me to be your date," I say playfully. Sam lowers his long eyelashes over his eyes so I can only see a sliver of green.

"I couldn't," he says quietly. I continue to stare with my eyebrows raised at him, hoping for a further explanation. When he continues to stand there with his gaze lowered, I know that I have to prompt him on.

"You probably have other girls you want to dance with, though."

At this, Sam's gaze flicks back up, his eyes flashing at me. "Haylyn, if you want to get rid of me that badly, you could just say so," he replies.

I give him an exasperated look. "I'm not trying to get rid of you; I was just trying to give you a way out if you needed one."

Sam looks at me. "I don't need a way out."

I smile at this, and before I can respond, Sam starts to lean in. My heart flitters erratically. *Is he going to kiss me?* I start to close my eyes and lean in, too, but at the last second, Sam pulls away, looking worried.

Hurt, I gaze at him in confusion.

"I should probably give you a break from dancing," Sam says.

"What?"

"I'm sorry," he whispers, already slinking away.

"I thought you said you didn't need a way out!" I call.

Sam doesn't turn to look back at me, doesn't even stop at all. Somewhere inside me, disappointment blooms, but I won't let myself go chasing after him as I watch his figure slip away.

In a daze, I walk over to Natalie and the girls, who immediately begin hassling me for details about what it was like to dance with Sam. I shake my head, dumbfounded. Natalie, seeming, for once in her life, to pick up on my mood, changes the subject and suggests that we all dance together. So for the rest of the night I dance with them—careless, sweet, fun dancing that makes some of the older folks look at us with smiles in their eyes.

After a while, the dance starts to die down. The number of people starts to dwindle, the orchestra starts to pack up, and thanks to my "friends," who I really am starting to think of as friends, my night has not been completely ruined by Sam.

When the other girls and I are finally ready to leave, I see him standing on the fringe of the forest. We meet each other's gazes, and Sam starts to move. His eyes seem to be filled with a thousand words, but when he reaches me, all he says is, "Can I walk you back?"

"I don't think that's a good idea," I reply, wringing my hands.

"Haylyn… I'm sorry about before. Just please let me do this."

The please makes me pause. I want to say no, but I find myself nodding. "Okay."

I hear Natalie, Tana, and Emily exchanging whispered words to each other behind me, but I ignore them as I walk to Sam's side and follow him into the trees.

Our stroll is a silent one, filled with bitten tongues and empty hands that hang limply at our sides. When we finally reach my cabin, I turn around to face him with my fists on my hips and questions in my eyes. I am about to ask him what exactly he hopes to accomplish by toying with me when he blurts, "I shouldn't have walked you home, but I just can't pretend anymore."

"Pretend what?"

"That you mean nothing to me."

I open my mouth to say something, anything, to this confession, but instead, as soon as my lips open, I find his pressed hard against them. At first, we are frozen against each other, but when it's clear that I don't want to push him away, all of Sam's restraint shatters. Our lips crash together, moving like waves, toppling and receding, giving and taking. I urge him on by shamelessly running my hands up his chest and then behind his neck, twining my fingers into his soft hair. Sam tugs me closer so that there is no more space in between us and deepens the kiss. I have never felt anything like this before.

We pull away together, both flushed and out of breath.

"I'm never going to be able to convince them again," Sam whispers under his breath, looking both awed and troubled.

"What?" I question, confused.

Sam shakes his head. "You know how I said I used to go to the dances for the music?"

"Yeah?"

"This time I went for you."

With that, Sam gives me one last look before turning to walk back into the night. I watch the shadows envelope him before I head into my cabin and fall to the ground in a heap, my dress making a cupcake around me. I can still feel Sam's lips on mine. Tonight, I go to sleep wearing a smile.

CHAPTER 17

I WAKE UP AND INSTANTLY wonder if all of it really happened. Did I really kiss Sam? I look at my dress, which is slung over a chair, and know that it is true. I let out a girlish squeal. Immediately, I think how I have to call Cassie and tell her everything. I turn on my phone and hit the speed dial for her number and hold the phone to my face, only to hear no ringing.

Suddenly, I feel hollow as I remember that I can't call Cassie; I can't go over to her house, and I might not be able to ever again. Numbly, I lower the phone from my face and turn it off. Sometimes I can forget what is really happening, and other times it hits me full force.

As I return my phone to my nightstand, another thought hits me. Today is Christmas. I think back to that carol, "I'll Be Home for Christmas." I guess I won't be home this year.

Flooded with memories, I think that if I were home right now, Avery would be shaking me awake, and then together we would run downstairs and into the living room to investigate the contents of our stockings. Here I have no brother to wake me up, no stocking to poke through, and no monkey bread to munch on with my parents.

I shove the thoughts away. I will be able to have a late Christmas with my parents when I get back in a couple of days. The portal will work. I just have to be patient and wait a little longer for Christmas this year.

I sit up and free myself from the cocoon of blankets that I have wrapped myself into overnight. I stand up and walk into the bathroom and brush my teeth and hair. I am about to hop into the shower when someone knocks on my door. I leap from the bathroom and hurry to answer it.

When I open it, my heart is ambushed by the sight of Sam leaning against the doorway in a gray pea coat and jeans, looking somber. My heart flutters as his eyes glow for a second when they see me; then something passes behind them, and the spark is gone.

"Merry Christmas," he tells me.

"Merry Christmas," I reply, trying to look confident in my flannel pajama pants and t-shirt.

"May I come in?" he asks. I mentally face-palm myself for not already thinking of inviting him in. Everything seems more important since the kiss. Has he been thinking about it? Will he bring it up? Is it bad that I want him to do it again?

"Yeah, of course," I spit out, stepping to the side as he slides past me and into my cabin. I gently close the door, and when I turn around Sam surprises me by attacking my head with a Santa hat. I laugh as Sam looks sheepish.

"Nobody should have to go through Christmas without a Santa hat," he informs me with a small smile.

Before I can stop myself, I blurt out, "Nobody should have to go through Christmas without their family."

Sam's smile falls and is replaced with remorse. I shouldn't have said that. *Stupid brain, why can't you have a filter?*

"I'm sorry. You don't need your family to have a good Christmas, Sam," I amend. He nods vaguely, already miles away in a different city and time, back with his family on a different Christmas. "All you need is to believe," I add with a tentative smile.

"In Santa?" he questions, flashing back into this room with me.

"Yup."

"Do you think he can make it to other dimensions?" Sam asks, a small smile now starting to grow at his lips.

"Of course," I answer.

"I don't know if reindeer are really suited for interdimensional travel," he points out.

"Please, if Rudolph couldn't handle a little dimension change, he wouldn't have a whole freakin' song celebrating his glory," I retort. Sam's eyebrows fly up before he starts to crack up, wholeheartedly throwing his head back and laughing. I smile widely, happy to have finally rid him of the sadness that I brought up.

"Very true," Sam says as soon as he finishes laughing.

"I know," I say.

Sam chuckles again before reaching into his pocket and taking out a small velvet pouch.

"What's that?" I ask.

"Your present," he replies smoothly.

"Oh," I say, taken aback. Warm excitement bubbles up inside me as I stare at it and think of all the possible things that it could be, especially with all that happened between us last night.

"You know that in order to see the gift, you have to open it, not just stare at it," Sam says playfully.

"Yeah, I know," I assert, snatching the pouch from his hand. Sam smirks at me once before turning nervous. I slowly pull open the bag and pour its contents out. I stare in amazement at the delicate silver necklace in my hand. It's beautiful. A tightly woven chain with a pendant shaped like a small flower with five metal petals.

"It's beautiful," I whisper to Sam.

"Colorado is a pretty big mining state, and the silver from this necklace was mined from there," he admits.

My fingers run over the cool silver flower. "Really?" I question in awe.

"I wanted to give you a piece of home," he says quietly, shoving his hands into his pockets, but keeping his eyes on me the whole time.

My heart stops at those words. Suddenly, I am rushing over to Sam and throwing my arms around him. Sam slowly twines his around me until we're holding onto each other like we are all that we have left.

"Thank you so much, Sam. It's perfect and I love it," I whisper into his ear. "Thank you for the hat, too. It gave me a piece of Christmas spirit that I did not expect to feel here." In a rush of bravery, I turn my head and kiss his cheek before disentangling myself from him. I hear Sam emit a low sigh once we stop touching.

"I feel bad that I didn't get you anything," I add as I sit down on my bed.

Sam shrugs. "I have everything I want," he says looking at me with thought. I look down, trying to hide the pink in my cheeks. My heart leaps as Sam sits down next to me.

"You looked amazing last night," Sam whispers. My blush now moves to a bright red.

"So did you. Natalie said that you've never worn a tux to any of the dances before. You looked really good in it." Now it's Sam turn to blush.

"The last time I wore a tux before last night was when my family and I went to an island back in Michigan called Mackinac Island. We ate dinner at the lavish Grand Hotel there. My mother used to always tell me that if I ever wanted to impress a woman, I had to wear a tuxedo. So I wore it for you," he confesses bashfully, his voice thick with sadness.

Well, there goes any chance of my heart being able to function again. He is so sweet when he wants to be. I wonder if this is what he was like all the time before the Laves took him. I can't believe that they would crush something so pure.

"Do you want me to put your necklace on you?" he asks, surprising me.

"Um, sure," I turn around and hand him the necklace, sweeping my hair to the side. I feel Sam's warm hand hovering over me as he fiddles with the clasp. I want to turn around and have him kiss me again like he did last night, but I am too proud and too much of a wuss to initiate it.

"Thank you," I murmur when he's done. I turn back around to face Sam as he looks at the necklace with sad eyes. "Do you want to go do something?" I ask, hoping that we could have a whole fun day together or something.

Sam takes one more look at the necklace as if he is convincing himself of something before looking at me with soft eyes. "I can't, sorry."

"Okay, that's fine," I mutter, feeling deflated.

Sam nods and stands up to make his way for the door. I want to stop him, but my mouth won't cooperate. He can't hang out today, and I have to deal with that. I don't want to be one of those girls who always obsesses over what the boy she likes is doing.

He is almost at the door when he stops and exclaims, "Oh, I almost forgot!" I watch as Sam reaches into his coat and pulls out what look like several CDs and one of those Walkman CD players with headphones. "I wanted to give you these."

"Where did you get those?" I ask in shock. I had thought there wasn't any music here.

"Black market," he says with a wink. "You have to know the right people, but I wanted to make this day a little brighter for you."

I slowly reach out and take the CDs and player. I'm still not sure how Sam got these, but I am happy that he did. I can't imagine a Christmas without Christmas carols. I stare down at the covers, the familiar names bringing me small comfort. I look up to thank Sam again, but he is already gone.

Watching him go is like swallowing a big pill and having it get lodged in my throat. I don't understand why he is acting like this, so distant again. After the kiss last night, I thought we had both admitted that we liked each other. Now I don't know what's happening between us.

Pushing away thoughts of Sam, I perch on my bed and stare down at the CDs in my hands. Unwanted tears rush to my eyes, and I blink as they fall down my cheeks. I put one of my favorites in, slide the headphones over my ears, and hit "play." With the first familiar note hitting my ears, the tears start falling like heavy rain.

I don't want to be weak, but I don't want to be here, either. I don't want my life to be like this forever, quietly listening to Christmas carols every year by myself. Wondering what my family is doing. Wondering if they will still think of me on Christmas in ten years. If they will keep putting my stocking up even though my presence has long since left.

I think of my dark, empty room. The Christmas lights that I hung up in it as soon as Thanksgiving was over, lying cold. I think of the cheesy potatoes that I don't get to eat this year. One extra portion sitting in the pan after everyone has gotten their food because I'm not there to eat them.

Callock's plan has to work because if it doesn't, I don't know what I'm going to do. I can't imagine never going home. I refuse to accept that never going home is even a possibility. I *will* go home.

I spend the rest of the day lying in my bed listening to Christmas songs. I sing my favorites out loud, trying to pretend that Christmas could be the same, but it isn't. Occasionally, my mind wanders back to Sam. True, I think about the kiss, but mostly I think about how he must be feeling right now. Sam has spent at least several Christmases alone here. I can't imagine how that must feel—a wound so deep that eventually you turn numb.

At some point, Natalie comes by to see what I am bringing to the gift exchange. When I explain to her that I had no idea there was a gift exchange, she begins to screech in my ear.

"Of course there is a gift exchange! Every year on Christmas there is a big dinner at the food court and everyone brings a present to exchange! You better have one by dinner; it starts at six."

"At six?" I exclaim, still confused and flustered at the sudden turn of events.

"Yes, get ready! You have to go shopping!" she snaps. "Normally, I would want to come with you, but I want to be surprised! Don't forget to wear something cute to dinner!"

"Okay, but what sort of gifts do people usually bring?" I inquire.

"Oh, anything, usually something on the small side. See you then!" she calls as she heads out my door as quickly as she arrived.

I shake my head. What just happened? I guess I'd better get ready to go shopping. I turn my gaze to my closet and look over the clothes Natalie bought for me, wondering which would be most appropriate for this occasion. After several minutes of shuffling hangers from side to side, I settle on an outfit of leggings and a cute red sweater dress that hugs my sides. At least I look somewhat normal on the outside.

Feeling like a preprogrammed robot, I shuffle out my door, start down the street, and head to the row of small shops. I step inside the first store I come across, which has miscellaneous things ranging from clothing to American coins sold as mementoes. It takes me a second to be surprised that this store is even open on Christmas, but I guess when your family isn't here, it doesn't really matter anymore.

I peruse the store, having a difficult time finding anything because of the store's layout. Back home, all stores are nice and orderly, with everything clearly laid out on display. This store looks more like a confused antique store with modern things, old things, and weird things all grouped together.

I head into the clothing area when I am struck with an idea. I rush over to the sweater section and pick out the most hideous sweater I can find. I hold it up for inspection and giggle at the ugly knit snowman covered in bells. Score.

I take my awesome find to the woman at the counter, who looks like a hollow ornament—all dressed up for Christmas, but with no happiness inside. It feels weird to stand at the checkout counter and not be taking out any money, but just like Natalie said she would, the checkout lady subtracts the sweater from my monthly tab and informs me that I have 300 Kiesel left, whatever that means. She finishes the transaction by gift wrapping my sweater, and I thank her profusely, being as kind as I can to make her feel better, but there is only so much that you can do.

After that, it is nearly six, so I head over to the food court. I stroll inside and I am shocked by the amount of people there, all milling about in a buzz of noise. From far away, you might even think that they are happy. It's only when you look closer that you see the pain in their eyes, the forced smiles, and the clenched hands. Everyone is a carved-out pumpkin that has turned stale in the winter cold, but is still forced to wear a jack-o'-lantern's grin.

I turn around to look for refreshments when I run straight into Sam. He immediately steadies me. A grin almost makes it to his mouth before a conflict reaches it. Looking unsure, he slowly lowers his hands back to his sides.

"Hey, sorry about that," I say.

Sam looks at me, his eyes matching his green dress shirt. "It's okay," he replies. "Have you had an okay Christmas so far?"

"I guess so, thank you again for the necklace," I add, running my fingers over the pendant and feeling elated by it. "And for the music, too; I really liked listening to it."

Sam nods, looking lightened by this. "I'm glad. So what gift did you bring?"

I look down at my box and smile at the thought of the gift inside. "An ugly sweater."

"Why ugly?"

"Because, it's what you do. It's like a joke. People have ugly sweater parties all the time now; they even gave them a day during my school's spirit week. Ugly sweater day, and everyone wears a horrible, ugly sweater." Sam eyes me dubiously. "It's funny, I promise."

At this, Sam's lips finally crack into a smirk. "Okay, I'll believe you. Want me to take that?" he asks, gesturing to my gift.

"Um, sure," I say, handing it over to him and then following him to where the presents are being kept, where he sets it down. Once we do that, a lady announces over the speakers that it is time to eat. Sam flashes a small smile at me before gesturing for me to get in line first. I smile back, jump in line, and scoop up several servings of food. It's all the same foods that have been alternating since I got here, but at least it is kind of like a variety now.

Once my plate is full of a symphony of disgusting things, I find that all the tables have been moved into one big circle in the center of the room so that everyone can see each other while they eat. I take a seat and practically hum when Sam sits next to me.

Surprisingly, I don't feel too sad during dinner. Listening to other people's conversations allows me to ignore my own thoughts. Watching everyone animatedly talk, it's hard to imagine that, in reality, every single one of them is trapped here. Every single person here was ripped away from a family and is missing them as much as I am.

I think of the families back home who have empty seats at their dinner tables, which should be filled by all the people in this room. Everyone here is missed by someone back home. I think of all their prayers for us to be alive and well. I guess half of their prayers came true: We are alive, but I wouldn't say well.

As I work on my Christmas dinner, another thought strikes me: This is only a Christmas meal. What are all the Jewish people doing for Hanukkah? Do they get their own celebration? I hope so.

I force myself to finish my whole meal, knowing that, in light of recent events, I have practically turned into an anorexic. Feeling accomplished when I shovel in the last bite, I turn my attention to the conversation that Sam is having with two other boys sitting beside him.

"That's ridiculous," Sam snorts, looking amused.

"No, it's not! I didn't have to do my laundry on earth, why should I have to do it here? The Laves should at least compensate me in some way," replies a boy with dark brown hair wearing a Packers shirt.

"Of all the things to be concerned about," Sam announces.

"I'm sorry, bro, but I'm with Sam on this one," adds another boy with a baby face and red hair.

"Oh, come on, like little things about this place don't bug you," the dark-haired boy says to his ginger friend.

"Yeah, maybe like being beaten and having terrible food. Surprisingly, I'm not too bothered by the laundry situation," the red-haired boy retaliates.

"I can't even believe that you're really complaining about this," Sam exclaims, shaking his head and turning so that he sees me listening with a bemused expression.

Sam sighs. "Haylyn, this is Miles," he tells me, nodding to the red-haired boy. "And that's Percy." The dark-haired boy does a small wave.

"So, laundry, huh?" I question.

"I didn't have to do it back home!" Percy groans.

I snort. "Maybe being taken was good for you. Back home you were quickly becoming the thirty-year-old man in his mom's basement."

At this, both Sam and Miles begin cracking up.

"Burn, dude!" Miles cries.

"Shut up," Percy grumbles, shoving his friend before the two begin arguing.

Sam and I are about to step in and break them up when a loud voice comes over the speakers again, informing us that the gift exchange is now beginning. Sam and I stand up to go and retrieve our gifts, and when we come back, the tables have been moved out of the way so that there is a huge circle of only chairs.

We sit down again as the lady over the speakers begins to read off the instructions.

"I will be reading a story. Unfortunately, we couldn't find any Christmas stories, but on every 'and,' you will move the present that you are holding to the right. On every 'the,' you will move the present to the left. Everybody got it?" the motherly woman concludes.

I nod. It doesn't sound too hard.

Boy, was I wrong. After the first trigger word, everything becomes discombobulated. Hands are flying everywhere, rushing to grab things from left and right. At one point, I chuck a little gold box at Sam, who hands it right back to me a second later. Toward the end, I am laughing hysterically, not even caring anymore as I randomly shove gifts in different directions. Sam looks truly happy for the first time that night.

"'The end.' All right, everyone, open the gift in your hands and see what you got!" the woman tells us, ending the chaos of rogue limbs. For the first time since the beginning of the game, I look down at the small decorative bag in my lap and rip it open. I cry with glee when my searching hands find a bottle of bubbles.

"What did you get?" Sam asks me right before I blow bubbles in his face. "Hey!" he exclaims, his nose scrunching as he wipes his face, glowering at me with amusement.

"I got bubbles!" I announce proudly.

"I see that!"

"What did you get?" I ask, leaning over him to look into his box and seeing several tubes of lip gloss. "They're just your color!" I say, blowing more bubbles into his face as I laugh.

"You really think so?" Sam asks sarcastically, swatting trajectory bubbles from his face. "I was thinking that I'd give them to you."

"No! That peach one is perfect for your skin color! You have to keep them!"

Sam chuckles, and I look around the room for who got my sweater. When I see who got it, I immediately start to crack up. Natalie is holding the sweater by two fingers with such disgust that you'd think she was picking up a dead rat.

Sam quickly catches on and starts to laugh, too. Leaning into my ear, he whispers, "You know, I think that is really *her* color."

The temptation is too strong; both of us head over to Natalie.

"Hey, nice sweater!" I say.

"It's so you," Sam adds.

"Are you kidding me? This is the worst thing that I've ever seen!" she seethes. The sweater is quite a contrast to her pink dress, white tights, and boots.

"It's not that bad," I assure her, though I am still laughing inside. "Merry Christmas, Natalie."

"Merry Christmas," she grumbles, still pouting.

I shake my head, grinning as I turn to Sam. "Will you walk me back?" I ask, half because I want to be with him, and half because I want to see if I can figure out what is actually going on between us.

Sam looks at me hesitantly, then around the room, before something seems to cave within him. "Sure." I look at him strangely, but he distracts me by taking my hand.

Fingers interlaced, we make our way out of the food court and into the black abyss of night. The inky shroud covering the sky leaves Sam's face barely visible, only to be revealed again when we pass a street light. Something is going on with him, some kind of inner turmoil.

The walk is silent, like most of ours tend to be, but it is not filled with tension like last night's was. Instead, it is a comfortable silence. I like that about Sam. Even though he constantly keeps me on my toes, I don't feel like I have to impress him or force the conversation to keep going to keep him interested.

I am used to the disappointment that I feel when we approach my cabin by now, but it still hurts. Sam slowly leads me up my walkway until my back is against the door and he is in front of me. His face is all angles in the orange light from the street lamp a few yards away.

I look at him curiously, my heart thudding with anticipation as he slowly tilts my chin up. I think he is going to kiss me until he whispers something softly. "*Comment pourrais-je ne vous aime pas?*"

I can tell that he is speaking a different language, but I have no idea what it is or why Sam is suddenly using it. All I took in middle school was Spanish, which, despite what my parents told me, is not helping me for later in life. It's later now, and my Spanish knowledge is getting me nowhere.

"What does that mean?" I ask, using the same hushed tone that he is. Sam shakes his head, eyes moving all over my face before he closes them tightly and starts to move away.

"Merry Christmas, Haylyn," Sam says before turning and moving back down my walkway.

"Merry Christmas, Sam," I mutter back, breathless. I watch him for several moments before giving up and going inside. Moving slowly, I slide my clothes off and put on my pajamas. I crawl into bed and turn on my phone, staring at all the pictures of my friends and family.

"Merry Christmas, guys," I tell them before turning off my phone and falling into a fitful sleep.

Chapter 18

My eyes open slowly, and I have that remorseful feeling that can only come after everything you have been looking forward to is done. I basically have post-Christmas depression, when the sad realization comes that I will have to go through a whole year before it is Christmas again. I sit up from my bed and sigh. I have Watching today... Great. I fall back onto my bed, feeling more unmotivated than when I first woke up.

Eventually, the thought of seeing Sam lures me out of my bed. I throw my pajamas to the floor and climb into the shower. When I come back out, I dry off and continue on with the rest of my morning. I settle with an outfit of blue jeans and a purple sweater and tie my hair back into a haphazard French braid. When I am all done preparing myself, I take the necklace Sam gave me from my nightstand and put it on. Running my fingers over it, I am flooded with memories of when he gave it to me.

At exactly eight o'clock, Sam knocks politely on my door.

"Hey, are you ready?" he asks, looking down at the necklace and smiling slightly.

"As ready as I'll ever be," I reply, as I step out the door and we begin walking.

"Don't get too excited now," he warns me playfully. "Why aren't you happy?"

"Christmas is over," I answer. Sam looks at me with interest. "Something I look forward to so much throughout the year is gone again, meaning that I'll have to wait a whole other year for another one."

"But that's a good thing, too, right? It means that you had a fun time?" he questions. I ponder this. I guess I did have an okay time. Mostly because of Sam. There is something about a cute boy that you like giving you an amazing necklace that brightens your day. I still can't believe that Sam put so much thought into a gift for me.

"Yeah, surprisingly, it was okay. You're the one that made it bearable. Thank you so much Sam, for everything," I say. Sam smiles brightly and brushes a stray hair away from my eyes.

"You're welcome," he says, satisfied.

"But it does kind of suck because now we have nothing to look forward to," I remark. *Well, besides escaping, that is. But Sam doesn't need to know that right now.*

"Well, there is the big feast where you get to eat meat for six days," Sam contemplates.

"Oh, great, the biggest thing that I have to look forward to is the end of my forced vegetarianism," I retort. Sam laughs and opens the door for me as we enter the food court to grab some breakfast before Watching. We never really decided to go here; it was just a mutual thought.

Sam makes his way through the food and picks up an apple. I smile brightly at the fruit, surprised that the Laves are giving it to us. We must still be on the holiday diet. He tosses it in the air and catches it again before it hits the ground, then examines it for bruises. When he eventually seems satisfied that the apple will do, he looks at me and nods his head toward the door, signaling that we should go. I nod back and quickly grab an apple, too.

Sam bites into his apple and I do the same. Sam scowls at me, and I arch an eyebrow in question at his look.

"Copycat," he declares, referring to my choice of fruit.

"Copying is the biggest form of flattery," I reply.

Sam lips curve into a smirk. "Well, in that case, thank you very much. I'm so glad that someone has finally taken note of how awesome I am. I was beginning to wonder if everyone had gone blind," he says.

I snort and roll my eyes. "Wow, modest, too. You are almost too good to be true."

"Almost," he says before falling silent for a moment and then speaking up again in a much different tone. "Be careful in Watching today, Haylyn," he urges me, his eyes turning from lively to serious in a flash.

"Oh, not this again!" I complain. "I told you, I'll be fine."

"No, you don't get it. If you get into trouble, I won't be able to do anything. If I even wince, the Laves will use you against me. They're already suspicious of my feelings; I can't let one more hint slide," he pleads.

"What are your feelings?" I venture. Sam turns his head down so that I can no longer see his eyes.

"I couldn't bear it if you got hurt and there was nothing I could do but watch for fear of making it worse," he whispers. I frown at the fact that he hasn't really answered my question, but I decide not to press him on it.

We walk in silence from that moment forward, passing all the familiar landmarks that map the walk to Watching without a backward glance. As we round a corner and trudge up the hill, the Watching building is revealed to us yet again. I wonder what is behind that building. I know that it's where the Laves live. But would it be a city? Would it have cars, streets, mailboxes? What kinds of houses do the Laves live in? I bet they live underground. It seems to me that all things creepy live underground. Exhibit A: earwigs. Exhibit B: snakes.

As we get closer, I feel Sam move farther away from me and stiffen, just as he did last time we had class. I wonder if this is somehow related to him not wanting the Laves to know his feelings, whatever vague feelings they may be.

Despite his actions, I continue to follow Sam as he pushes through the doors and moves with precision through the hallways. I struggle to keep up with him as he shoves his way into our classroom and sits down at his seat. I give the Lave teacher a little wave, knowing that it will annoy her, and take my seat as well.

The Lave teacher begins the class as usual when another Lave wearing a lab coat enters the room. The teacher looks over at him, and the lab-coat-wearing Lave clears his throat.

"Do you have any students who have not yet been tested?" he asks in a deep, hissing voice. The Lave teacher glares at me.

"Why, yes, we do. Haylyn Jones, please accompany this man out of the classroom. You will not need any of your belongings for this trip," she says commandingly.

My eyes widen with alarm, and I shakily stand up. I quickly flash my eyes back at Sam to see how he feels about this. He nods at me with an impassive face. He isn't quite smiling, so I know that it can't really be good. But he also isn't so distressed looking that I should be worried. I take a big gulp of air and pretend that it's courage before I shuffle my way down the aisle of desks. When I reach the man at the front, he gives me one quick lookover and then walks out the hallway. I stare at him a moment before deciding to follow.

When I make my way out the door, two other Laves flank me, a few steps behind, in case I try to run. I may be able to move around freely most of the time, but this is a prison, there is no mistaking that. This incident reminds me of how trapped I actually am, and I don't like it.

I follow the Lave upstairs and through an unlabeled metal door. I haven't seen an unlabeled door since I've been here, and the fact scares me. I hesitate outside the door, but one of the Laves shoves me from behind, so I tumble into the room. When I regain my balance, I look around. There is a large window on one side of the room where other Laves sit with microphones attached to their heads. I try to shake the feeling of their eyes watching me and move my focus to the mass of machinery that takes up most of the room. I shiver involuntarily at the sight of it.

"What is it?" I ask in a small voice.

"It is a magnetic resonance imaging system to take pictures of your brain, more commonly known as an MRI," the Lave man wearing a lab coat informs me. I stand still as the Laves shove earplugs into my ears and tell me that it will be loud. They also inform me that the earplugs have a speaker so they will be able to hear me, and me them.

"Any concerns?" the Lave man asks as he forces me to lie down on the cold metal. I shiver with both the cold and fear but say nothing. The Lave stares at me for another second before sliding me into the machinery. I vaguely wonder if the Laves built this themselves or stole it from earth. I then wonder what the hospital thinks about its huge piece of expensive machinery disappearing into thin air.

All thoughts end when the machine starts. I can still hear it thrumming through my earplugs. I lie there for what seems like an endless amount of time. Just when I am about to start screaming and demanding that they free me from this contraption, they tell me that it's over. They roll me back out and help me get up. I can't rid myself of the feeling of their cold hands on my arms.

The same three Laves walk me back to my classroom in the same order, the scientist in front and the jockeys in back. The air seems uncomfortably quiet without the constant blare of the MRI machine. I walk quietly and soberly, more a death march than a walk, really.

The Laves' hard footsteps remind me yet again that am in a colorfully decorated cage. I long to run outside and frolic around in the grass at the park. I can only handle so much, and being treated like a high-security prisoner and having my mind violated all in the same morning are pushing my boundaries. I hate that I am weak.

How many more tests will I have to go through before I finally crack? It is only a matter of time now. Sometimes I feel fine, but other times, like right now, I feel myself slipping. My only hope is that I will be out of here before I completely lose it.

The Lave scientist drops me back off at my classroom. When I walk inside, everyone's eyes lock on mine, and I feel suddenly self-conscious. I give them all a small smile and hold my eyes a little longer on Sam's. He gives me a deep look that asks everything from, "Are you okay?" to "How did they treat you?" I simply stare at him with a straight face because I don't know what to do. I can't smile because I am not okay. I feel like a snail without its shell. I now understand how Gary felt in that *SpongeBob SquarePants* episode.

I take my seat quietly and return the worried smile that Emily gives me with a reassuring one. Sam may be strong enough to handle the truth, but I feel like I have to put on a brave face for Emily. I just want to curl up and go to sleep. Or maybe drink some tea while watching a good movie. Even doing math homework seems like a more appealing idea than being here the rest of the day. With that thought, I now know that I have reached rock bottom.

The Lave teacher starts to pick up the lesson she was teaching while I was away. It looks horribly stupid, and her monotone voice is driving me into a half-conscious state. As much as I want to, I know that I can't just get up and walk out of class. Callock said that I can't draw attention to myself or else the Laves will get suspicious of me. And that would ruin everything. I have to stay strong. I have to. But that doesn't mean I want to.

The Lave teacher drones on and on until something finally catches my interest. I perk up and tune into the conversation. The Lave teacher is explaining something about ancient China.

"The ancient Chinese claim to have worn armor made out of paper. We know that to be false because, well, there is no way that paper could be used as a legitimate protector against weapons," the Lave teacher explains.

I now know what is wrong with this statement. It isn't true.

"Actually, paper armor is possible, and the ancient Chinese really could have made it," I pipe up, shoving my hand into the air. Sam gapes at me, a warning look in his eyes. The Lave teacher deepens her scowl.

"Miss Jones, my facts are correct. Maybe next time you should make sure that you are actually right before getting so cocky," she hisses.

"No, it's possible. *Mythbusters* did it," I declare. The Lave lowers her solid black gaze and stares me right in the eyes. I suppress the urge to flinch.

"Last time I checked, paper isn't going to do squat against a sword. Someone's being a little slow today, now, aren't we? I guess we'll have to wait to see your scans to confirm that something is wrong up there." The Lave smirks, but I ignore the comment. She expects me to get embarrassed and keep my head down, but I will not be bullied!

"It wouldn't be regular paper, it would be layered and have a design. Are you sure that it isn't actually you who is feeling a little slow today?" I suggest, smiling.

The Lave teacher closes the remaining gap of space between us frighteningly quickly. She lifts her arm, the one that holds the yardstick, over her head. I know what is coming, but I'd rather be hit fifty times with that yardstick than admit that she is right.

"This is not your place to speak out!" she bellows as she cracks the yardstick against my face.

I wince but otherwise do not cry out. My face stings. I didn't know a ruler could hurt that much, but I hold my gaze in a defiant look as I stare down the Lave. She gives me a snarl of a smile before turning and marching back up to the front of the classroom.

My cheek is burning, but I feel better off than Sam looks. His face is scrunched up in barely controlled anger and pain. His hands are gripping the edges of the desk so hard that his knuckles are turning white. His jaw is clenched shut, and I can tell that he is grinding his teeth in an effort to keep from yelling out. Somehow his reaction fills me with butterflies, distracting me, if only for a second, from the pain darting up and down the side of my face.

I give Sam a reassuring look and try to pay attention for the last few minutes of class until we are released for lunch. Half of me hopes that she will mess up again, and that I can point it out to her. However, all of those thoughts go to waste when a drop of red falls to my paper. I look at it in shock and realize that it is from my cheek. I put my fingers up to the wound, and they come away soaking red. Renewed pain comes from the touch, and now I am covered in blood. It runs down my cheek and stains my hand. Several drops are on my paper and my shirt. I let out a series of curses under my breath when I see that my shirt is ruined. *Hit my face, whatever. Ruin my clothes? She has to die now.*

The Lave teacher smiles her crooked yellow teeth when she sees me. And I snarl in return. I turn helplessly back to Sam. His green eyes are filled with such anger and compassion that I have to turn away.

I sit there for the rest of class, trying to do damage control. I don't want to get any more blood on my pants or on my desk, so I have to keep it under control. I look at my shirt and sigh; it is already ruined. In defeat, I pull my shirt up, exposing my stomach, and hold it to my cheek. How the Lave has managed to do so much damage with a yardstick is a mystery to me.

When the bell finally rings, I let my shirt drop over my stomach again and stand up slowly. I drag myself out of the classroom and start to move down the hall. Once we are outside of the classroom, Sam practically attacks me as he rushes up behind me and grabs my wrist from my face so he can see my cheek. He winces once he gets a good look at me and works his mouth with sympathy.

"Are you okay?" he asks while slowly running his finger around the cut, soothing it.

"Yeah, I guess I deserved it. Nobody likes a know-it-all, no matter which world you're in," I say, giving him a slight smile until it starts to hurt my cheek. Sam's eyes flash when he sees that it pains me to smile.

"Like hell, you deserved it. If I could go in there and kill her right now, I would," he says savagely.

"I'll help," I snort, well aware of the fact that Laves are freakishly strong and could take the both of us. The extent of the damage to my cheek just from a yardstick is enough to prove it. Sam gives me a long look and then runs his fingers through his hair. I can tell that he is upset, but I don't know how to soothe him. *Hey, sorry I got hit in the face. Next time I'll wear football helmet.* No, I don't think Sam would appreciate that.

"I think that you should go home early," he says.

"No! Then she'll only be satisfied with herself!" I exclaim.

"You need to get that cut addressed, and maybe some pain meds. You might even need stitches. You can't just sit there, merrily taking a test with your face all cut open," he points out. I roll my eyes in exasperation.

"First of all, I wouldn't be 'merrily' taking a test. I would be grudgingly taking a test," I argue, making Sam smile. Then, in defeat, "Second, do you have to be right all the time?"

Sam relaxes now that I consent to going home. "Yes I do. It's a blessing and a curse. Besides, she would just give you more crap today, and I don't think you would take it well. I really don't need to see you get into a full-blown fight with a Lave," he declares.

"Yeah, it wouldn't be fair to her," I say, a devilish smirk on my mouth. Sam looks at me with worry. "Relax, Sam, it was a joke." Sam doesn't laugh. "So are we going to go?" I ask after Sam's silence starts to become uncomfortable.

"I can't go," he says.

I stare at him wide-eyed. "What? You tell me to go home, and then you don't leave?"

"The Laves would be suspicious," is all he says in reply.

I glower at him. "Suspicious of what?" I press.

"About the two of us," he says, standing awkwardly with his mouth pressed shut. I glare at him until it become obvious that he won't elaborate.

I angrily wipe my bloodied fingers on my pants, not caring anymore. Sam is stressing me out. I want—correction, *need*—to know what is going on with us, and he shies away every time we approach the subject. I feel like I am in middle school all over again: "Do you like me? Check yes or no."

"So I'll just go alone, then?" I ask in confirmation.

Sam lightly shakes his head. "No, someone should be there with you," he says and then, turning around, catches Natalie by the arm. He flashes her a swoon-worthy smile and his aura instantly changes from upset to confident.

"Hello, Sam!" Natalie exclaims. Her eyes run over me, but she keeps my greeting in her mouth. Though I doubt it was even there in the first place. Natalie does not like me when it comes to all matters of Sam.

"Hey," he replies coolly.

"What's up?" she asks, her voice oozing flirtation. I feel like I might be sick as I watch them.

"I was just wondering if you could ditch and help Haylyn get that cheek taken care of?"

She looks at me with new interest, and when she sees my cheek, her eyes widen.

"Oh my!" she exclaims, as if she hadn't noticed before.

"Idiot," I say under my breath. Sam chuckles as he hears the comment, but, luckily, Natalie is too absorbed with Sam to notice.

"Well, I'm sure I could. My mom was a nurse, and I used to help her with some patients. I also have a first-aid kit in my cabin," she explains. I am surprised; this is the first time I have ever heard her mention her life before she came here.

"That would be great, thank you," Sam says.

Natalie beams in return. "Oh, it's no problem. This day has been so bland anyway, I could use a break." Natalie agrees, all too happily, to oblige whatever Sam says. If Sam asked her to jump off a cliff, she would do it with no hesitation.

Sam smiles and turns his amazing eyes back to me. "I'll be over there as soon as Watching is over. Try to hang in there," he says. I can tell how much he wants to leave with me, the burning desire reflecting in his eyes. Sam leans in, presumably to give me a hug, but when he looks over his shoulder and sees the Lave teacher clicking over to us in her high-heeled shoes, he backs away again. Sam gives me one last anguished look before turning on his heel and striding off with the rest of the class.

I sigh as I watch him go before turning around to face Natalie. Her eyes linger on Sam as he walks down the hall, a little too long for my taste. Frankly, I don't like the thought of her eyes being on him at all. I shove aside that jealousy, knowing that it's stupid to be worrying about it when I have much bigger things to deal with.

"Sorry about having to babysit me," I blurt out, successfully pulling her eyes away from Sam.

"No probs! I was serious when I said that this day was getting totally snoozeville," Natalie says, flushing as she realizes that she has been caught watching Sam.

"Yeah," I say meekly. Today wasn't exactly what I would call boring. If anything, it was a little too eventful.

Natalie ignores my halfhearted comment and starts to lead me out of the Watching building, her sandals flopping loudly against the floor and echoing off the walls. I follow her out the doors, and there is a small breeze with a sharp coolness to the air. The walk remains relatively quiet, and I am perfectly fine with the silence.

"So, how did your first MRI go?" Natalie asks. I stare at her, commanding her telepathically that silence is okay. But Natalie just keeps staring at me with those blue, overly glittered eyes, and I know that she is not receiving my message.

"Okay, I guess. It was really loud, though. I felt like my head was going to split open," I say. Natalie nods like she actually understands.

"Yeah, the first time is the worst. It gets better, though," she encourages. I give her a small smile. Maybe there is something underneath the layers of foundation.

"Let's hope," I agree.

The rest of the walk continues in silence, and the bleeding from my cheek is starting to slow. We reach Natalie's cabin and she opens the door with no comment. Her cabin is bigger than both mine and Sam's. Then again, she probably cares about material things more than the both of us. Hers has a living room and a guest bathroom, with her bedroom and bathroom in the back. The whole place is decorated with purple and white.

Inside, I am greeted by the smell of lavender. I breathe in the sweet smell. It isn't as nice as Sam's smell, but it is still pleasant. I vaguely wonder what my cabin must smell like to other people. It always seems that other people's houses have smells, but you can never smell your own house. I hope it smells good.

I sit down on Natalie's couch and make a note to put some sort of candle in my cabin when I get back.

"I'm going to go grab my first-aid kit," Natalie tells me as she walks into another room. I nod even though she can't see me and wander into her bathroom. When my eyes reach the mirror, I can suddenly understand why Sam looked so upset. An angry blue and purple bruise runs down my face, four inches long and two inches wide. It hides a deep, bloody cut in the center of it. I make a horrified face as I gently prod the disfigured skin, grimacing as pain shoots to where my fingers touch it.

My shirt has blotches of dried blood on it, and I throw it in the trash, which leaves me in a tank top. I wash my hands vigorously, trying to rid the blood from them. When the last of the tinted red water goes down the drain, I wet a washcloth and start to wipe away the dried blood that has dripped down to my chin. I am too afraid to try cleaning the actual cut, so I just leave it alone. I don't want to force the pain to return by rubbing it when it has finally subsided to a dull throb.

I hobble back out to the living area and find Natalie setting up her first-aid things. She looks professional as she lays everything out, behaving as if she knows what all of them do. I sit down on the couch in front of her and can't help feeling impressed by how serious she is about this.

Natalie positions a lamp over my face so the bright light shines on my cut. She examines it carefully, being cautious not press too hard when she touches it. Her expression is thoughtful and concentrated, so unlike her usual one of blissful ignorance.

"Well, I don't think you're going to need stitches. It was a close call, though, so you are going to have to be careful," she instructs me. "Now I'm going to spray some antiseptic on the cut so it doesn't get infected; it may sting a little."

I nod and she sprays my face. I grimace in pain and clench my teeth until it subsides. Natalie goes into her small kitchen and comes back out with a glass of water and two pills. "These will help with the pain and swelling."

I nod and swallow the two pills, then say, "You're so good at this; how do you know so much?"

"My mother was a nurse, and she had to take me to work with her a lot, so I learned some things," she answers tensely.

"That must have been nice. My mom never took me to work with her," I say encouragingly. Then again, I remember, I would have never wanted to go. My mom is a realtor, so I would probably have died from boredom if she had ever tried.

"Yeah, my real dad skipped out on my mom and me when I was just a baby, so she couldn't afford daycare for a long time. Every day after school, I would have to go to the doctor's office with her," Natalie admits. My heart sinks as I realize that Natalie didn't have the perfect life that I've been imagining her having.

"Natalie, I am so sorry. That must have been tough."

"It was only for a little while. Once I turned ten, my mother married my rich stepfather, and even though he is a jerk to me, I never had to go back to the hospital again because I had my own nanny," she says.

I sigh. Now *this* is the life I've expected Natalie to have. But at least I know there is something real underneath all that makeup. My heart yearns to get closer to that girl.

"Well, thank you for helping me with my cheek," I eventually say.

"No problem. I'm going to pluck my eyebrows; just holler if you need anything." Natalie smiles and flounces her way back to her room, the down-to-earth side of her completely gone again. I shake my head at the new conundrum that is now Natalie.

I look around her perfectly decorated room for anything that could provide entertainment until Sam arrives. I settle on reading some small, cheesy teenage-life book that Natalie has displayed on her coffee table. The book is ridiculously dramatic, but it is all I have, so I keep reading.

I shake the spiderweb-like thoughts from my head and allow myself to melt into the book. I turn the pages with ease, and eventually I am reading the last page of the book. When I finish the book I close it, sighing, and look up for something else to do. I turn around and jump with surprise—sitting next to me on the couch is Sam. He watches me intently and smiles.

"How long have you been sitting there?" I ask, incredulous. How have I not noticed him?

Sam shrugs. "Not long. Sorry I didn't announce my presence, but I like watching you read. Your face is relaxed. I like seeing you happy." I smile brightly at this and Sam's face grows serious again. "How are you feeling?" he asks, brushing his fingers against my cheek and tucking my hair behind my ear for a better look.

"It's just a cut, Sam, I'm not dying." Sam glares at me. "I'm fine. Natalie gave me some pain pills, and it hasn't bothered me since."

Sam relaxes again and throws his arm over the back of the couch as he leans back. "Glad to hear it," he says sincerely. "I'm so sorry I couldn't leave with you, or do anything to stop the Lave. I wanted to, trust me. I…"

I hold up my hand to stop his blabbering. "It's fine! It's just a flesh wound." I laugh at my movie quote, and Sam looks bewildered by my outburst. I am coming to the realization that Sam has been practically living under a rock. Or, more accurately, in a different dimension.

"You shouldn't have talked back to the Lave like that. Don't you have any concern for your own safety?" he asks me, suddenly taking a dark tone.

"I'm not going to sit back and let the Lave give you all false information. Someone has to teach the youth of Die Andere Welt."

I mean it jokingly, but Sam doesn't laugh. Angrily, he says, "Well, you could have pointed it out more nicely, or let it drop after she told you that it was correct."

"I wasn't just going to let her bully me when it wasn't correct."

"Or better yet, next time, just don't open your mouth at all," Sam snaps.

Anger flashes through me as if I've swallowed hot water. "You're not the boss of me, Sam. I'm not going to let you or anyone else force me into submission."

Hurt fills Sam's eyes and he looks down. Guilt swells within me, eradicating the anger. "I won't do it again," I add halfheartedly

Sam gives me a thankful look but doesn't smile as he says, "Thank you. I don't think you know how much I fear that the Laves are going to hurt you, and today I had to see that nightmare come true." His words warm me to my toes. Natalie must have heard Sam's voice, for she comes running in as if a wall of flames has sprung up behind her.

"Oh, hey, Sam, how long have you been here?" she asks, maddeningly batting her eyelashes as she leans over the couch, giving both Sam and me an unwanted view down her shirt. Sam just rolls his eyes and gives me a look.

"Not long," he says to her, nonchalantly. Natalie beams and sits next to him on the couch, forcing me to get up and move to the chair. I plop myself down in my new seat and glare at her.

"Do you want a glass of water or anything?" Natalie asks as she leans heavily on Sam's shoulder. Sam gives her one look before scooting over a notch, causing Natalie to nearly fall over. I suppress a laugh and cover my curving lips with my hand to make as if I'm yawning.

"I'm good, thank you. So, what's the diagnosis for Haylyn's cheek?" he asks. Natalie frowns as though she has completely forgotten I am here and is not happy to be reminded of it.

"It's pretty deep, but I don't think she'll need stitches. The bruising should clear up in a few days, and the cut will be there for a week or two," Natalie informs him.

Sam smiles like this is great news. "Great, thank you so much, Natalie, you were a big help today."

Natalie's face looks like it is going to split in half, she is smiling so hard. I feel rather guilty for hoping that it does.

"No problem," she says. "Hey, this day is going so great, I don't want it to end. How about we play a card game or something and then go out to dinner?"

Sam and I shoot each other looks of dread, but Natalie doesn't seem to pick up on it. "I'll go grab my deck of cards," she announces and runs to go grab them.

"Kill me with a rock!" I groan as soon as she leaves the room. Sam laughs, and he looks as if he is dreading the next couple of hours as much as I am.

"Do you think if we both went to the bathroom and hopped out the window, she would get offended?" Sam asks innocently. I laugh out loud and move back to my previous seat on the couch so that now my shoulder brushes Sam's.

"She just might," I agree regrettably. Sam's lips curl into a smile, and I suddenly remember what it was like to kiss those lips. My fingers ache to touch them, and I start to subconsciously move forward. Sam looks at me in surprise and starts to lean forward, too. We are only inches apart when Natalie rushes back into the room, causing us both to shoot backward, away from each other. Natalie looks at our flushed cheeks suspiciously and then shrugs.

"So what game do we want to play?" she asks, shaking the deck of cards.

"Poker?" Sam suggests.

"I don't know that one," I admit.

"Me neither," Natalie sadly agrees.

"We could play blackjack!" I suggest, remembering how my grandfather taught me when I was little. Both Sam and Natalie shake their heads, say they don't know it, and veto my idea.

"We could play bridge," Sam says jokingly.

"That's for little old ladies!" I argue. Sam's eyes flash and he smiles broadly.

"That's why I thought it would be perfect for you!" he exclaims. I throw a pillow at his face, causing him to fall over. His laughter shakes the couch as he just lies there with the pillow over his face.

"We could play solitaire," Natalie suggests. I roll my eyes and Sam starts to laugh harder, the pillow muffling the sound.

"Natalie, you play solitaire by yourself. You can't play it with other people," I inform her. Natalie deflates and starts to busy herself by shuffling the cards.

A smile forms on my lips as I suddenly know what game all of us would most likely know. "We should play go fish!" I announce. Natalie's head snaps up.

"I know that one!" she cries excitedly.

"Me too!" Sam agrees as he removes the pillow from his face and sits up. I laugh, as his hair is a wild, static mess. I reach up and brush it down for him, loving the feeling of his soft hair under my fingers.

Natalie, who is surprisingly nimble with a deck of cards, starts to count out each person's cards. Sam tries to peek over my hands and see what cards I have, causing me to hit him over the head with the pillow again. Sam laughs and I banish him to go sit on the chair by himself to keep him from cheating. He complains all the way there, but otherwise obliges, leaving Natalie and me to share the couch. I peer over my hand, methodically eyeing my competition. Whom should I go after first, Natalie or Sam? Natalie is rather incompetent, so until I know how good Sam is at this game, it would be smarter to go after her first.

I smile, as I have my game plan in mind, and turn my attention toward Natalie. "Got any threes?" I ask, since I already have three of them. Natalie pouts and hands over one three. I grin as I put my first stack of four cards to the side.

Now it is Sam's turn. He grins like the devil and turns his flashing green eyes over to me.

"Got any sevens?" he asks. I scrunch my eyes; he only knows this because he cheated.

"Nope, go fish," I reply casually.

Sam's eyes fly wide open. "Yes you do!" he announces.

"Cheater!" I reply. Sam looks at me and then at Natalie's bewildered expression and starts to laugh. I stare at him a second, but soon my anger begins to fade, and I join him in laughing. Natalie stares at us both like we are crazy, but eventually all three of us are laughing hysterically. I never knew that go fish could be so much fun.

"Okay, it's a tie. You don't get my sevens, but I'll get a new hand and you can go again," I say as soon as I calm down again. Sam nods, still smiling, and Natalie looks like she's not exactly sure what just happened.

I rummage around our go-fish pile and get a new hand. I sit back down again and keep my cards high so Sam can't see over them. He watches me and smiles. I arch an eyebrow, challenging him to go.

"Do you have any eights?" he asks. I look at my cards and smile; this time I really don't.

"Go fish," I say, grinning. Sam gives me a questioning look to make sure I'm not lying to him. I hold my ground and watch as he reaches into the pile for a new card.

"Got any fours?" Natalie asks Sam.

"Nada, go fish," Sam replies. Natalie pouts as though that will sway Sam's decision, but soon she gives in and grabs another card. Now it is back to me.

"Do you have any fours, Natalie?" I ask, knowing she must have at least one four, since she just asked Sam for them.

Natalie frowns and, just as I suspected, hands over three fours, completing another stack of four for me.

The night goes on like this, with me asking Natalie, Sam asking me, and Natalie asking Sam. I am way ahead of everyone else, but I don't count this as the biggest accomplishment. Sam isn't even trying to play the game; he's just trying to irritate me, at which he is succeeding—he has already had five more pillows thrown at him since the game started. And Natalie has the brain capacity of a kiwi when it comes to logic.

Eventually the game starts to die down, and it is clear that no one is going to be able to catch up to me. Natalie excuses herself to go to the bathroom, and Sam leans over to show me his hand of cards. I look at the numbers curiously and see that he has at least five of the numbers that Natalie last called for. I shake my head, smiling.

"Cheater cheater pumpkin eater," I announce.

Sam laughs and sets his cards down. "Sorry, I'm not sorry," he replies. I glare at him and he continues. "What can I say, you were on a roll, and I couldn't just have Natalie win for sheer dumb luck when you were giving it so much thought."

I feel myself smile brightly again. "I still would have beaten her," I say.

"Sure, keep telling yourself that," Sam says, making me hit him with the pillow again.

"You're pretty good at keeping a straight face when you lie; you should join a poker group. You could start to make some big bucks," I suggest.

Sam flattens his hair back out from my pillow attack and smiles at me. "And you're pretty good with a pillow. I think we need to get you into some sort of militia; you could do some serious damage."

I laugh and look down at the decorative pillow in my hands. "Oh yeah, weapon of choice, the throw pillow," I reply.

"They could call you Haylyn, wielder of the great plush life-smotherer," Sam suggests.

"I like it. Maybe I should join the Army. Either that or get my own TV show with that title," I say, smiling brightly.

"I can see it now," Sam answers as Natalie comes back into the room.

"See what now?" she asks, a little too alertly.

"Nothing," we both say, in the most suspicious tone possible.

"Oh, okay," Natalie replies, completely ignorant.

Sam and I exchange a look and quickly bite our lips to keep ourselves from laughing. Natalie just continues to smile with a blank look on her face, unaware of the fact that she is the object of our laughter.

"Well, are you guys ready for dinner? I have some mash already and some dough flats, or we could eat out if you would prefer," Natalie says. I shake my head. *Stupid peppy people and their need to have food ready in case people come over.*

"I am so sorry, but I'm afraid I will have to decline that wonderful offer," Sam says, regaining his composure and brushing his long fingers through his surfer-style hair. "I unfortunately have to meet up with a friend to plan strategies for the Hunt."

Natalie frowns, and I suddenly realize that I need to come up with an excuse to get out of dinner as well.

"Sorry, Natalie, I'm behind on some of my work and I need to get it finished," I tell her. Natalie frowns more as she looks back and forth between Sam and me.

"Well, I'll see you guys later then," she mutters.

I slowly rise from my spot on the couch and stretch my muscles from their longtime sitting position. Sam stands up as well and crosses over to the door with Natalie hot on his heels. He swings open the door and marches out to the walkway without a second thought. I am about to join him when Natalie hands me one of her more plain coats.

"What's this?" I question.

"Your sweater got ruined, so I thought you might need a little more than just a tank top to go outside," she explains, instantly making me feel like a jerk for ditching her.

"Thank you," I say as I take the coat and shrug it on. "I'll give it back to you tomorrow."

Natalie swats her hand as though my words are flies. "It's fine, keep it. I outgrew it anyway."

"Oh, well, thank you, for the coat and for helping me with my cut. I really appreciate it."

"No problem, see you!" Natalie replies.

"See you!" I call back as I join Sam out on the walkway, and Natalie closes the door behind us with a click.

CHAPTER 19

I SHIVER AS THE COLD air touches my skin after hours of being inside. Suddenly I'm very grateful to Natalie. Sam starts to walk without another word, and I follow him in silence. The sky is fully black now, signaling the imminent night time. It spreads over the world, a vast sheet of black with no end and no beginning. I wonder for the first time since coming here, where are we in the universe? There are no stars in the sky, so could this world be in a dark corner of the universe, or an entirely new one where stars don't exist?

This thought brings a string of new thoughts with it. If there are no stars, what makes the sky change from black to white? What heats the atmosphere? There has to be something because this place is definitely warmer than Denver this time of the year. I guess these questions will just have to go unanswered. My goal is to leave this place, not to understand its astronomical location.

I turn my attention back toward Sam, who is thoughtfully watching the cabins as we pass them. I wonder if he really is going to meet a friend for strategy planning. I thought he was just using it as an excuse to escape Natalie, but I guess he really could need to go. The thought of him leaving fills me with a desperate ache to reach out and touch him. I am close enough; all I have to do is lift my arm up and... *Get a hold of yourself woman!* I snap at myself, ending the thought. *You will never be able to escape if you can't stop thinking about Sam every five seconds!*

"So do you really have to go meet up with a friend to plan strategy?" I ask, giving in to curiosity.

Sam looks over at me and smiles. "No, I was hoping you would grace me with your presence for dinner," he replies.

My cheeks heat up, and for once I am thankful for the dark sky that is hiding my blush. "Sure, that sounds great."

"Now I can show you all the different foods they serve around the holidays," Sam says, his eyes flashing in amusement, indicating that the selection really isn't that great at all.

"So what did you do in class after I left?" I ask, ignoring his previous comment.

"Not much, we just worked on the history project, mostly."

Oh yeah, I had almost forgotten about that stupid thing. With everything going on, it just doesn't seem important anymore. I know that I should probably be giving it more thought. I mean, who knows what the Laves do for punishment when you don't turn in a project? However, the majority of me doesn't give a crap anymore. I want the Laves to try to hit me again. This time I'll be ready.

"You're not planning on finishing it, are you?" Sam remarks, flashing me that smile that excites and infuriates me at the same time.

"I never said that," I protest.

"Yeah, but you were thinking it," he declares, continuing that infuriating grin.

I grumble something that might pass for "whatever." Sam just laughs and shakes his hair out of his eyes. The rest of the walk remains silent because I am too stubborn to admit that he is right.

When we reach the food court, Sam and I both order bowls of slush because, even with the holiday food, it is the only option here that doesn't make us want to eat our own toenails as an alternative. Sam then leads me to a small table for two by a window, and I feel practically giddy as I sit down in the stiff chair. I feel so grown up, like I'm on a real date. The only difference is that a real date would have better food.

"So what kind of music do you like?" I ask Sam, adding to the ambiance of a real date.

"I don't really know. I haven't heard radio-type music for a while, so I don't really know what's out there right now," he confesses, shrugging.

"You don't have any favorite artists?" I press on in amazement. Right now, I am currently in the 'music is my life' phase, much to my parents' annoyance.

"Nada. What about you? Who's your favorite artist? What kind of music do you like?" Sam asks with a sly smile.

"I like pretty much anything. I mean, Taylor Swift has a song for whatever you're feeling, but Arctic Monkeys have songs that make you want to move," I answer.

"I have no idea who either of those people are," Sam says, shaking his head with a lost expression.

"Oh, come on, Taylor Swift has been around for a long time, you've got to know her!"

"I have no idea who she is," he replies shortly, now starting to look uncomfortable.

"I bet you've heard at least one of her songs before; you probably just didn't know it was her," I say.

"I doubt it," Sam snorts, making me eye him with speculation. "Haylyn, she was probably just after my earth time."

"But she's been around for a while," I say, thinking back to singing her songs with my friends when I was around eleven years old.

"Well, it must not have been long enough," he mutters, looking down.

There is a moment of silence before I work up the nerve to ask the question. "How long have you been here, Sam?" I suddenly fear the answer, for his sake.

"A while," he replies flatly.

"Sam," I say sternly. He knows the answer I want.

"I was taken in the beginning of 2007," he finally admits, looking at his hands. An alarm fires in my head.

"But that's eight years!"

"Yup, I was taken when I was nine years old." Sam shrugs and continues to eat.

"You're seventeen?" I ask curiously. I never knew exactly how old he was.

"Yeah. Is this when you tell me that you're actually older than me?" he asks nervously. I give a quick smile despite the information I've just learned.

"No. I'm fifteen, almost sixteen," I reply, thinking how odd it is that we haven't known each other's real ages until now. Sam smiles slightly and takes another bite. I muster my courage and decide to press on.

"How did you get here, Sam?"

He lets his hand fall, and he snaps his gaze up to mine. Still, he sits there silently.

"You don't have to tell me if you don't want to," I say. "It's not my place, but…"

"It's not that, I just…," he says, breaking off with a lost expression before asking, "Do you want to hear about the failed attempts, or when they actually got me?"

"Failed attempts?" I blurt out in confusion.

"Yeah, it took the Laves several tries 'til they finally succeeded in getting me," he says flatly.

"But how did you dodge them?" I ask, remembering how I was taken. I had no chance of escaping from that.

"Portals didn't used to be a clever as they are now. They used to just be gaping holes in the ground that would pop up in front of you as you walked. I had quick reflexes and was able to jump out of the way before I fell in," Sam explains.

I stare at him blankly. This just didn't seem possible to me.

"Go on," I urge, curiosity driving me now. Sam sighs, and I can tell that he doesn't want to talk about this, but I need to know.

"Before the Laves took me, I had a great life. I grew up in a pretty house made of brick and went to a fancy private school. My father and mother were always nurturing, and they loved and supported me with anything I ever did. At least one of them watched every soccer game I had. My sister was a year older than me, and we got along great. My parents taught me how to draw and play piano; they were great at everything. I had great friends, always did well in school, and had the two best beagles in the world. My best friend, Connor, lived next door, and we would play at the park behind my house all the time. My parents were so proud of me," he says, for the first time really giving me a picture of what his life was like before.

"Everything started going downhill after I dodged the first portal when I was eight. I had no idea what it was, and I could see the Laves on the other side of it, willing me in. I tried to tell people about it, but no one ever believes a little kid, especially when he's screaming about holes in the ground.

"My parents took me to all sorts of counselors and therapists, but of course nothing worked. The hole in the ground had been real, and they didn't get that. I had somehow convinced myself that the creatures I saw were trying to hurt my family and that I had to stop it. I started to exercise like crazy and take all sorts of defense classes. My family and friends thought that I had turned mad."

I nod as he tells me this. It explains why he is so muscular and fast; he probably kept up those exercises. But that's the worst part—the fact that I understand. I wish I didn't understand how awful that must have been for Sam. I wish I didn't understand how all those looks from his family, who thought he was insane, must have felt. This is too terrible for any kid to have to go through, and I would do anything to protect Sam from all that's happened to him. But how do you protect someone from their past?

"I had just turned nine years old when I was able to avoid another one. Things had just started to die down since the first one, and I was starting to accept that maybe I just imagined it. But when the second one came, it threw me off my rocker. I went mad with crazy superstitions as I tried to protect my family. By now the Laves were in hysterical determination to get me. They couldn't let their secret get out just because of some kid. So a few months later, they lit my entire house on fire." I watch Sam in horror as his eyes grow hard with emotion.

"The heat was nearly unbearable, and I couldn't breathe. I fell to the floor from my bed and crawled to the one door that wasn't engulfed in flames. I tried to reach my sister along the way, but I couldn't see anything with all the smoke. I called for her and my parents and my dogs until I couldn't talk anymore and was barely clinging to consciousness. I had to assume they had gotten out already, so I started to crawl away. When I finally heaved myself out the one exit that I could find, a portal was waiting there, and it brought me here."

Sam puts his face in his hands. "I cost my family everything. The Laves only wanted me, and if I had just gone in that first portal, none of that would have happened."

I feel horrible and helpless as I watch him ripping himself apart right in front of me. "Sam, you thought you were protecting your family. That is the bravest thing I've ever heard, and you were only a kid," I say, trying to lift his spirits.

"Yeah, and where did my 'protection' get them?" he snaps bitterly, wrenching his hair with his fingers.

"Sam, it was only a house. I'm sure they had insurance and could get another one," I say softly. Sam's head snaps up, revealing an expression that could only be described as broken.

"Haylyn, my whole family burned to death in that fire."

CHAPTER 20

I WAKE UP. I TAKE a shower. I get dressed. I brush my hair. I do all the same things that I normally do. But now I feel hollow, the scraped-clean kind of hollow. The brutal kind where things keep chipping and chipping away and you're fine until one final blow is cast, and then you are broken.

Sam's story cuts me to the bone. I am a mash pot of mixed feelings. I am filled with sympathy for him and anger at the Laves. I know that Sam doesn't want my sympathy, but my heart can't help it. Nobody should have to go through that, especially Sam. Throughout that whole awful time, he was just trying to protect his family. He didn't even give a second thought about his safety. I always knew that he was gorgeous, funny, and occasionally kind. But now I know just how tortured he really is.

I try to go about my morning routine, but I can't; my thoughts keep returning to Sam. I want nothing more than to just make it all better for him, but I can't. There are no words that I could ever say to make that hurt go away. No action I could perform that would take back what the Laves did to him. However, I could get revenge for what they did. And trust me, I plan to.

After Sam told me, he just stood up and left. I knew that he wasn't mad at me for asking, even though part of me still worries he is, but that doesn't change the fact that I am mad at myself. I came along with my shovel and dug up every bad memory that he tried so hard to bury deep inside himself.

At eight o'clock, I sit on the edge of my bed, ready to go but unsure whether Sam will actually come. At a minute past eight, I am beginning to worry when there is a soft knock on the wood of my door. I leap to my feet and rush over to open the door. Sam stands outside, a ghost of a smile on his lips.

"Hey, you ready to go?" he asks in a fake pleasant voice. This time I see straight through that mask of confidence. I see the broken, delicate child that the Laves destroyed, and it crushes me as well. I don't want him to have to hide from me anymore. He will never heal if all he does is keep shoving it down.

Without any hesitation, I walk out the door and throw my arms around him. Sam just stands there for a second before deflating in my arms and hugging me back.

"They were such good people who didn't deserve to die," he mumbles softly. "All of them were such better people than me. So why did I live while they couldn't?"

"Sometimes good people die for no good reason, Sam, but you honor them in everything you do. You are a good person. They would have been proud of you," I say into his chest. I pull back, and Sam is nodding slightly. I can tell he is trying to wrap my words around himself like a blanket for comfort, but this is just too deep of a wound for a couple of my words to heal, and I see their comfort slipping away again.

"Are you ready?" I say slowly. Sam nods and we start to walk away from my cabin.

"I better not get hit in the face again," I say jokingly after a few minutes. My cheek is still carrying a raging bruise from the day before and the cut has scabbed over, leaving me to look like a hot mess.

Sam gives me a hard look.

"I'll hold my tongue, I promise," I say, crossing my heart. Sam calms down slightly and continues the walk in silence.

The rest of the way to Watching, neither of us says a word. I guess that it is because there is nothing left to say now. Sam has finally let me in, and I am tortured by what I have found. Underneath all that façade is just a boy who has lost everything. A boy who has had to grow up too quickly. I think that Sam is the bravest person I have ever met.

We are about to walk up to the doors when Sam catches my arm and pulls me off to the side. He drags me down the Watching building wall until we round the corner. I look at him questioningly as he looks up at the walls. I am about to ask him what on earth he thinks he's doing when I realize that he is situating us so that the security cameras can't see us. Genius.

"What are you doing?" I ask demandingly. Sam holds a finger up to his lips, gesturing that we should be quiet.

"I just want to make sure that you won't try to get picked on by the Laves again," he says, whispering harshly.

I glare at him. "I don't *try* to get the Laves to pick on me, and I already swore that I wouldn't say anything."

Sam lets out a huff of air. "I know you did, but I don't think you get it! I can't take watching the Laves hurt you anymore," he says desperately. "I try to stay away because I know that if they find out they'll only hurt you more to get to me." Sam wrenches his hands.

I watch dumbfounded, unsure of what to do. "Sam, I can handle myself against the Laves," I try to reassure him. "Besides, we won't have to deal with them much longer."

Sam's head snaps up, his eyes locking on mine. I realize with horror what I have just let slip out.

"What?" he says, pouncing on my words the way a cat does a mouse.

"I just mean that I will get used to them and learn the ropes for how to not piss them off," I respond quickly, trying to cover it up. Sam can't know, not yet.

"I hope so," he says, narrowing his eyes with suspicion.

I heave a sigh of relief that he's bought it. "I will. I'm just adjusting. And I'm not looking for trouble; the Laves are pushing me to it."

"Haylyn," Sam whines, warning and tension filling his voice.

"Sam," I reply softly in the same tone he's just used, trying to calm him again. Sam sucks in a painful breath and lowers his head until our foreheads are pressed together. I feel myself growing stronger under his touch. Sam, on the other hand, looks like he is breaking down.

"The Laves destroyed everything I cared about. But now, after all these years of not caring about anything, I care about you. I didn't know good could still exist in someone here, but you showed me goodness. The kind my parents had, the kind that died in me the day I got here. You showed me how to have the strength to still be good. Because of that, I tried so hard to convince them I felt nothing for you. But after that kiss… My God, after that kiss I knew that I was never going to be able to convince them again."

Sam breathes, shuddering against my forehead. "If one more Lave tries to hurt or touch you, I will have to kill it," he says flatly. His brutally honest words scare me to the core, but not for my sake—for his.

I take a second to grasp everything he has told me. My heart feels like soaring. *Sam does likes me!* I want to scream to the world. The more childish part of me wants to scream it in Natalie's face. But with knowing, at least partly, that Sam has some sort of feelings for me also comes the awful truth. Every one of my actions has been hurting Sam, and when I kill the bird, it will only hurt him more.

I don't want to be another sad story for Sam. If I die, what if that is the straw that breaks his back? There is nothing I can do to stop it. I have to try to get home, and I don't want Sam to get hurt. How do I accomplish both?

"Ego check: The Laves would beat you like scrambled eggs," I say after a moment of silence, letting some humor creep into my voice. Sam gives me a hard look, but the corners of his mouth creep up as he keeps his head pressed up against mine. He knows how strong the Laves are, probably better than anyone.

"At least you're honest," he says. I smile and Sam's arms wrap around my waist, pulling me closer. I sigh deeply and breathe him in, welcoming the familiar scent of citrus and cinnamon.

We stay entwined together for a long time. Even when the bell rings, signaling that we are now late for class, Sam doesn't even budge. When I am starting to grow content with the idea of standing here all day, Sam separates himself from me and takes my hand. He gently pulls me to the front doors until we are close enough for the security cameras to see us again, and then he lets my arm drop. I sadly return it to my own side, missing the feeling of his touch already.

We walk quickly through the halls, with little emotion. When we barge into the classroom, every pair of eyes glances over to us with surprise. Natalie's eyes take on a sparkle when she sees Sam, and I struggle to refrain from taking another step closer to Sam. I glance at the clock and see that we actually aren't *that* late. The Lave teacher, however, isn't as happy about the fact that we are only ten minutes late. She raises a gnarled eyebrow at us and bares her ugly teeth. I open my mouth to come up with some lame excuse, but Sam is already jumping on it.

"I'm sorry we're late," he starts, flashing one of his most dazzling smiles. The Lave teacher crosses her arms over her chest, remaining unfazed by his charm. "When I went to pick Haylyn up this morning, I found she had locked her door and overslept. I tried everything to get her to wake up and unlock the door, but nothing seemed to be working," he explains. I stare at him, amazed by his on-the-spot lie. Sam gives me a sharp look; I wipe my face clean of awe and nod along with his story.

"Then why didn't you just leave? It's better if one of you is late than both of you, is it not?" she hisses, finding the one flaw to Sam's seemingly perfect story.

Sam remains on his toes. "Well, Haylyn was sleeping so soundly that I worried that something was wrong with her," he states. I try not to gag as some girls literally sigh out loud at Sam's thoughtfulness. "So I had to go pick up her cabin key from the Living director, and there was this huge line. So when I finally made it to the front of the line, I grabbed the key and ran back to the cabin," he says, finishing his story. The Lave considers this a moment and then snarls her confirmation.

Sam heads to his chair first and I follow after. I sit down in the chair and cringe at the sharp creaking it makes. I place my elbows up on the table. I try to put an interested look on my face as though to say, "I'm so excited to learn more false information as I fight off narcolepsy from your monotone hissing!"

"Okay, students, now that all of you are present," the Lave teacher starts, pausing to glare at Sam and me, "I will be collecting your book reports."

Alarmed at not knowing anything about a book report, I look back to Sam, who mouths the words, "Before you got here." I let out a sigh of relief. Thank God. I slowly look around and see everyone shuffle out of their seats and turn their papers in to the Lave teacher. I continue to watch until I see that everyone is getting up except one. A boy with shaggy blonde hair sits at his desk with a very worried expression, and I quickly realize that he must have forgotten.

"Timothy," the Lave teacher asks, "where might your book report be?"

"I ... forgot ... I'll have it tomorrow," he stammers, his lips shaking as he talks. The Lave's lips spread into a grin, and I can almost hear her rotten skin cracking as it folds upward.

"I don't want to have to do this, Timothy, but you know the rules."

"But I'll have it tomorrow, I promise," he pleads.

"Yes, but I didn't want it tomorrow, I wanted it today. Everyone else got it in on time, so there are no excuses," she snaps as she grabs his arm and yanks him from his seat. Timothy hits the ground hard, and he lets out a small groan before she starts to drag him to the front of the classroom.

"Please, it will never happen again!" he calls as the Lave teacher leaves him in the front of the classroom while she stalks over to what looks like a phone on the wall.

"Late homework," she mutters quickly into the phone before clicking it down and striding back over to where she left Timothy on the floor. "Stand up, you pathetic baby, you had this coming," she spits as she forces Timothy to his feet.

Suddenly, in the middle of this, our class door flies open and three Laves come filing in. Timothy screams and doubles his flailing efforts, but the Lave teacher hands his arms over to two of the Laves, who grip him so hard that he can barely move. Not knowing what is going on, I look back at Sam, but all he does is shake his head with a sad look in his eyes.

Our teacher stands to the side as the final Lave that has just come barging in stands before Timothy. I watch in horror as the Lave pulls a knife from his coat and holds it out toward Timothy, who in return begins to thrash and scream even more. *Oh no. They can't possibly be going to do what I think they are. They aren't really going to stab a kid for not turning in his homework.* But they do.

Without any hesitation, the Lave pulls back the knife and drives it into Timothy's stomach. His screams fill the air, along with those of a girl who cries out, "Timmy!" I look over at who has screamed his name and see a sweet-looking girl, her eyes filled with horror. She opens her mouth to cry out again, but suddenly a wave seems to wash over us and her face goes blank. I shrug off a weird feeling that begins to creep over me and try to figure out what has just happened.

I look all around the room and everybody has the same blank expression, even Sam. I scream wildly as the Lave drives the blade back into Timothy's side, but besides my screams and his, the room is silent. Tears begin to fill my eyes, but I know that there is nothing I can do to help; there are just too many Laves around him.

I turn my attention back toward Sam, and I am horrified to see that he still looks frozen. "Sam!" I scream. No change. Another round of Timothy's cries pierce the room, and my desperation grows. "Sam!" I cry with everything I have left. Sam suddenly blinks and shakes his head as though to clear it from a daydream.

"Sam?" I call questioningly. Sam looks over at me with flashing eyes and runs over to my side, hugging me tightly.

"He's going to be okay, everything will be okay," he whispers to me. I shudder in his strong embrace and tuck my head into his shoulder, trying to block out the screams.

"Okay, I believe that he has learned his lesson," the teacher finally croaks out after what seems like an endless amount of time. The other Laves nod and carry Timothy out of the room. Sam gives me one last soothing look before heading back to his desk. Slowly, everyone seems to fall back out of their stupor, leaving me to wonder what the hell that was all about.

The Lave teacher eyes me with speculation, and I eye her with hatred right back. Everyone looks so unfazed by all of this that I wonder if it really happened. I glance back at Sam and with one look know that it really did. Geez, I thought getting docked twenty points for turning in homework late was bad, but this? This is on a whole other level.

After I calm back down, I curse myself for being weak again. Everyone else was able to keep a straight face, but I had to be the one to freak out and start crying. What is wrong with me? Timothy is going to be fine, and now I've just made myself into a fool in front of the Laves again!

"Okay, class," the Lave teacher starts, breaking into my thoughts, "today we will be separating based on gender."

Oh, great, the Laves are sexist, another fabulous item to add to the Laves' long list of charming qualities. It can go right up there with kidnapping people and stabbing children.

"The boys will stay here in the classroom to learn and practice techniques for the great Hunt. And pay attention; this is the last class we will have until January sixth," the Lave announces. I nod, now knowing that this is the Laves' holiday season. "Girls will be helping the cooks make bread for the boys to take along with them on the Hunt." I roll my eyes. *What is this, the 1800s?* "Girls follow me; boys, your instructor will be here shortly. Do behave yourselves or you will face the consequences," she adds with venom.

I sigh, seeing no way out of this. I slowly stand up and start to follow the rest of the girls out of the classroom. As I am about to walk out the door, I glance over my shoulder and find Sam's evergreen eyes locked on me. I suddenly remember this morning, how he told me that he hadn't cared for anyone but his family, and now he cares for me. I can still feel his warm forehead pressed against mine, how it seemed to fit perfectly there. He is probably even more worried about me after how I handled the whole Timothy thing. I give Sam a small smile, trying to reassure him as he gives me a worried look, and then I head out of the classroom.

I apparently suck at baking bread. I am so bad that the Lave teacher personally asks me to leave so that I won't mess up any more of the bread. Before I am kicked out, though, the main chef Lave, who is supervising us, has the nerve to ask me why I can't make bread. My response is, "Like your mash tastes any better!" The Lave gawks at me as I storm out. Whatever. I didn't want to bake their stupid bread, anyway.

I walk angrily past the food court, ignoring the calls of food from inside. I'm not hungry after the whole Timothy episode, and I have to get down to business. I send Callock a text, asking him to come to my cabin for planning. He messages back a "yes," not even asking why I am not in Watching.

I jog hurriedly back to my cabin, the slight breeze stirring my hair. We need to get the bird-killing plan all set. I don't even know where I am supposed to go to get this bird thing. For all I know, it could be in a zoo.

I rush inside my cabin and throw my jacket in a chair, readiness bubbling up inside of me. Before, I was hesitant about killing it; now, after what Sam told me and seeing how the Laves handle late homework, I am all too eager. The Laves have personally ruined thousands of lives and killed countless innocent people. Now I can't even remember what was holding me back before.

A sturdy hand knocks quietly on my door, and I know that it is Callock. I hurry across my cabin and swing the door open. Callock steps inside swiftly. Before I can even greet him, he blurts out a frank question that used to make me nervous. "You're sure that you want to do this?"

"I'm sure." I'm more than sure, actually.

"Okay, good. Now, why did you call me here, then, if you don't plan on backing out?" he asks, settling himself into my chair in the corner.

"Well, I have some questions about the plan. I just want to make sure I know everything from top to bottom so I can't mess anything up."

Callock nods that this is a good idea and smooths down his gray hair. "Then what do you want to know?"

"Okay, well, for starters, where is the giant bird thing?" I ask. "And won't I run into the Hunt if we're both in the same forest?"

"There are three forests in Die Andere Welt. The first one is the park, which I'm sure you've been in. The second one you have probably seen before, since you have a view of it from your window; it's the sacred forest of the beast." I nod, remembering threatening trees in the distance when I looked out my window on the day I arrived here. He continues, "The third one is about an hour's walk from here. It has the most life, and that is where the Hunt will be taking place."

I nod again. At least that's one less problem to deal with. However, there is something else that I'm concerned about. "How am I supposed to find one animal in a huge forest?" I ask. "What direction would I even go in?"

"Go left, right, north, or south. Go any direction you please. I give it an hour before it finds you."

I swallow hard. The idea of a larger animal stalking me for prey sends stabs of panic down my spine. But I am not backing down.

"So just go in whatever direction I want?" I muse for confirmation.

Callock nods. "Whatever tickles your fancy, as long as you remember what direction you came from; we can't have you getting lost now."

"Okay, well then, what am I supposed to wear, and what time should I leave, and where is this weapon that you're supposed to give me?" I blurt out, firing questions like bullets out of a machine gun. Callock chuckles at my eagerness.

"Wear light clothes, but something that will also keep you warm. You should leave around six a.m. The hunting party plans on leaving at five a.m., so hopefully this way you won't run into each other. And I have it." He reaches into his suit. I watch in trepidation as Callock pulls out a long, decorative dagger. My jaw drops open in shock.

The dagger's handle is made out of a thick, silver metal. Curving lines are etched into it, and I'm surprised that something so deadly can also be so beautiful. The blade of the dagger is hidden by a smooth sheath of jade green. I want to reach my hand out to touch the cool metal and run my fingers over its flawless surface.

"Dang Callock, you are officially sketchy!" I exclaim. Beauty aside, it is still a weapon that Callock has just pulled out of his coat like a pair of reading glasses. Callock raises a hairless eyebrow.

"Why is that?" he asks, confused.

I gape at him. "Because you're running around with knives in your pocket, ready to shank people!" I explain.

"My dear, the only one that will be using this knife for shanking is you." I stare at him dumbfounded until the reality of his words sink in. I stare at the piece of shiny metal in his hands. This is the object with which I will take another life. I am going to kill something with this blade. The thoughts won't sink in and I don't blame them; never before have I had to stare at something that will be the demise of one thing, but the savior of others. It seems too powerful to touch.

"Remind me again why this bird won't kill me before I can kill it?" I ask, my voice shaking.

"When the bird sees you, it will go into a frenzy. Humans are a rare and delectable treat for it." I shut my eyes nervously, and when I open them again, Callock's eyes are holding me in place. "That is when you use your smarts to trick it. Use its own power against it. Make it run into the blade instead of trying to stabbing it. Do whatever you have to do to kill it. Get the idea?" I nod stiffly. "Good. Now I won't be able to see you until after you have succeeded with the task. Then I will take the heart from you and begin the next part of the process," Callock explains.

"Sounds good," I say, the lie tasting sour in my mouth.

Callock walks briskly over to the door. When his hand reaches the handle, he hesitates and turns around, giving me a sad look.

"Good luck, Haylyn," he says softly, pressing the hilt of the dagger into my hand. I flinch as it touches my palm and close my fingers tightly over the metal. I give Callock a small smile and, without further pleasantries, he opens the door and strides outside, leaving me to my own thoughts.

I fall back against my bed, my body trembling. I can't believe the task I'm about to perform. The dagger feels unfamiliar and dangerous in my hand, only making my thoughts go crazier over what I said I could do.

I snort. If only my friends back home could see me now, talking to something that shouldn't exist about killing something that shouldn't exist, to escape from a place that shouldn't exist. What has my life come to?

I turn around quickly and lift up my mattress. I slide the dagger under it, praying that no one will look under my bed. It's a rather obvious place to hide something, but nobody has good reason to be looking under my bed, so it should be safe.

I can't believe that any of this is really happening. I am going to be able to leave this place! I can't wait to see my family. I can't wait to sleep over at Cassie's house again, or to hug Matt again. I can't wait to see if Cassie got a car from her parents for turning sixteen. All of it seems like a dream.

I take a deep breath, trying to cool the excited smile that threatened to break loose. I have to keep myself under control; otherwise, the Laves could get suspicious and ruin everything. Until I get home, I have to act as if I plan on spending the rest of my life here, and that I am adjusting to it.

Acting as if I am planning to spend the rest of my life here also includes going to dinner. Which, right about now, I am fine with. Now that the image of Timothy isn't so fresh in my mind, I am so hungry I could probably eat several bowls of mash. I grab my brown puffy coat and throw it on. I head over to the door and let out a noise of surprise when I open it. On the walkway, with his hand held up in a fist, only seconds away from knocking, stands Sam. His eyes light up when they see me standing there, and he flashes me a smile so bright I forget to breathe.

"Hey! Want to go get some dinner?" he asks. I swell with relief. For the first time since last night, I now know that I am fully forgiven for making him tell me how he got here.

"Yeah, that sounds great!" I exclaim, joining Sam as he begins to walk.

"So I hear that you were asked to leave the baking session today," he laughs.

I sigh. "You hear correctly," I admit bitterly.

Sam chuckles and flicks his hair out of his eyes. "Can you not cook anything, or is it just bread?"

"I can cook; I've just never made bread before," I snap.

"Cereal doesn't count," Sam says, a smirk on lips. Then his voice shifts to a mock macho voice and demands, "Make me a sandwich. Oh wait, you can't!" He laughs at his own joke, and I shoot him an evil glare.

"You want to go?" I demand, preparing my "Come at me, bro" fighting stance. Just because I like Sam doesn't mean I'll hold back while kicking his butt.

Sam eyes me with suspicion. "No, I think I'm good. Besides, it wouldn't be a fair fight to you anyway."

"I could totally take you," I growl, knowing that, in fact, I probably couldn't, but confidence is everything.

"Ha, okay, keep telling yourself that," Sam snorts.

I scrunch up my face and purse my lips angrily. I glare at Sam a second and then, angered, I start to stride away. I do my best fast walk until I leave Sam behind me. He quickly catches up.

"Are you trying to run away from me?" he inquires, a smile spreading across his cheeks.

"I'm not doing it for my sake; I'm doing it for yours. I could do some serious damage," I say pointedly.

Sam just rolls his bright eyes.

"If you could do serious damage to me, I would have to seriously rethink my life choices to see what went wrong," Sam declares, and then, pretending to be offended, he begins to quickly walk away, as I did to him a moment ago. The only difference is that I can't keep up.

"Sam, slow down. You're going way too fast!" I call out to him, after several minutes of struggling to catch up.

Sam turns around, a mischievous smile in his eyes. "That's what she said," he replies. At first my jaw drops, but then I burst out laughing, not expecting the stupid, cliché joke.

"Oh my God!" I cry, running to catch up with him. "Out of all the pop culture you've missed over the years, that's the *one* thing you know?"

Sam shrugs. "Blame Percy."

I try to mentally curse the boy, but end up laughing.

Still laughing, we fly into the food court, without a care weighing down our thoughts. Sam smiles down at me, but suddenly my eyes are locked on something else. The sight before me shouldn't be here. My mind radiates with sheer disbelief as I try to comprehend what I am seeing. My whole knowledge of the new world that I now find myself in is crumbling around me. I recognize the lady who stands in front of me—not because I've met her in this world, but because I knew her in the old one.

I rub my eyes to make sure I'm not hallucinating again. When I blink to clear my vision, I nearly choke because the image still stands before me, clear as day. Distantly, Sam calls my name, but all I can focus on is the woman's expression. Her shocked face when she sees me looks quite similar to the look I am giving her.

"This can't be happening," I murmur, ignoring Sam, who is now becoming worried about my statue-like stance. I take a step back and dash out of the building. Confused, Sam calls after me, but I don't care. I claw at my head, trying to keep the memories from resurfacing, but they tumble out anyway.

The woman was my neighbor, someone I lived next to my whole life. I thought everyone back home was safe, that I was the one in danger. I am fine with that. But what I can't bear is the new truth beginning to make itself clear: No one is safe.

I run away from the food court, trying to run away from my mess of a life. I run until my lungs burn and my legs sting. I need to get away from this, from everything. Eventually, I collapse to the ground not that far into the park.

The leaves rustling overhead help soothe my raging head. Once I am calm enough to make out that I actually know where I am in the park, I also notice that Sam is standing a respectful distance away, studying me. Probably trying to gauge what the heck just happened with me.

Resigned, I raise my head to meet his gaze. I feel embarrassed about how I reacted and guilty that I made Sam chase after me like a child. Sam, always understanding, comes over and joins me in the grass.

"What happened?" he finally asks.

I take a deep breath. Saying it aloud makes it real. "I saw my neighbor... my neighbor from Denver."

Sam's eyes cloud over with thought. "You're sure?"

"As sure as Percy thinks doing laundry is unfair."

He gives me a sad smile. "I know you don't want to hear this, but this is bad."

"Why? I mean, besides the fact that the Laves took someone I know."

"If the Laves took your neighbor, they're sending you a warning," he replies grimly.

"A warning? What did I do?" I haven't done anything that bad for a couple of days, I think. Well, at least, not that the Laves know of. Sudden panic grips me as I worry that maybe they found out about me being Callock's accomplice.

"Probably for speaking out in class," Sam replies.

I scoff, relief pouring through me. "They're still on that? These people have some serious grudge problems, not to mention that I've already been punished for that," I say, gesturing to my still-healing cheek. At least the Laves probably don't know about me and Callock. If they did find out, I would probably be locked away right now... or dead. Sam is right; this is probably about my smart mouth.

Sam gives me a sympathetic look as I point to my cheek, and I feel awful. I know Sam feels like it's all his fault, but it's not. This is my fault; everything is, from getting hit in the face to my neighbor being here. I've brought all this upon myself.

"Are you okay?" Sam suddenly asks, bringing me out of my reprieve. I look at him quizzically. "I mean, seeing your neighbor must have been hard to process."

"I thought *I* was the one in danger, not my friends. Clearly, I was wrong," I say remorsefully.

"No one is safe," Sam says, eerily echoing the realization that I made earlier. We sit in silence for a few moments, both of us unsure about where to go from here. I think about my neighbor again, and I suddenly make a decision.

"Do you think she's still there?"

"I don't know. We can check."

I nod, and together we pull ourselves off the ground and trek back to the food court. When we get there, we split up to search for my neighbor but have no success in finding her. Disappointed, we have a quiet dinner before Sam walks me back to my cabin.

"We can find her tomorrow, Haylyn. We have plenty of time," Sam consoles me.

I shake my head. "It's already too late."

Sam leans over and kisses my forehead, his lips lingering there as a goodbye; I try to wrap his affection around me like a blanket. But I'm not a little girl anymore. No blanket can protect me from the monsters that plague me.

CHAPTER 21

I WAKE UP CONFUSED. THE knocking comes again, and slowly my wits return to me. Realizing that the knocking is actually someone at the door, I leap up, only to experience a head rush and fall back down. When I finally make my way to the door to greet Sam, my pajama shirt is falling off one shoulder, and I am clutching my head.

"Get in a fight with the floor?" he asks, having heard my fall through the door.

I give him an unamused look and let him in. "Any particular reason that you're here at…" I check the clock, "seven in the morning?"

"Just thought you would be interested to know that, at this moment, your neighbor is having breakfast in the food court."

"What? Why didn't you just say that first?" I exclaim, running to my closet to throw a jacket on over my pajamas and shoving my feet into some tennis shoes.

"Come on!" I cry, grabbing his hand and hauling him out the door. "We have to catch her before she leaves!"

Once outside, Sam and I sprint the whole way to the food court, mania pushing my legs to the limit. I nearly cry with relief when we plow into the food court and find my elderly neighbor sitting quietly, gnawing on the Lave version of toast. I grin up at Sam, whose hair looks perfectly feathered from the wind. It's just unfair that after running his hair looks even more perfect, while mine looks more like a cat's hairball.

I look over at my neighbor, and she looks exactly as I remember her, with dark and slightly wrinkled skin accompanied by a head of brown curls. She wears a large-brimmed hat with flowers on it, the same one she would use to garden. There was rarely a time in the spring or summer when she wasn't outside gardening. She looks so out of place in here. She didn't have a husband or any grandchildren, so on many days I would help her with her gardening, usually doing the more strenuous work for her, like lifting soil bags and carrying pots. I never minded, though, because she was always so nice and pleasant to be around.

I carefully approach her table and smile. "Hello, Ms. Evalia. It's me, Haylyn," I say as I watch her whole face brighten up.

"Oh, Haylyn! It's so good to see you looking well!" I suddenly feel guilty when I see how happy she is to see me.

"Ms. Evalia, it's my fault that you were brought here," I blurt out, unable to hold it in anymore. "I made the Laves mad, and as a warning to me about acting out again, the Laves brought you here." I'm hoping that whoever her mentor is has explained to her all about the Laves.

Ms. Evalia gives me a funny look. "Now, why are you so upset? I don't see what the big deal is. I planted flowers in Denver, and I'll plant flowers here. I don't see the problem."

Guilt blooms inside me like one of Ms. Evalia's flowers. "But you were *kidnapped* because of me. And," I add, "I haven't seen anyone have a successful flower bed here."

"Then it will be a challenge!" she responds. "Now, hush child. I don't want to hear another word about it."

Feeling resigned, I take a seat in the chair across from her and motion for Sam to do the same.

"Why, this is just so odd!" Ms. Evalia says, chuckling. "Everyone back home is in a fit trying to find you, and you've just been here all along. Who would have thought that I would be the one to find you?"

"How is everyone?" I ask, even though I dread the answer.

"Well, they haven't been the best," she starts. Sam flicks his eyes over to me worriedly, waiting for my reaction. I keep my expression placid and nod. It's not like I expected anything different.

"But they're okay, physically and all?" I ask. "Avery doesn't have a cold or anything?" I think over my question and stifle a laugh. Before I was brought here, I didn't give a rat's ass about Avery's possible cold symptoms. But now I can't even bear the thought that he has the hiccups and I'm not there to make them better for him. I just want his and my parents' lives to go on perfectly without me.

"No, Avery is fine—practically in depression over the fact that you're missing, but physically, he's fit as can be." My heart is heavy over Ms. Evalia's words. Avery shouldn't have to deal with this; middle school is hard enough.

"Who's Avery?" Sam suddenly asks, a sharp edge to his voice. I glance at him with shock. *Is he jealous?*

"He's my little brother," I explain.

Sam relaxes again. "Oh, okay," he says, settling back into his chair.

"And my parents?" I press her.

Ms. Evalia gives me a dismal look. "They lost their firstborn. Their only girl. I think they're doing the best they can, all things considered."

I take a deep breath and try to tell myself that this is good news—the best I could have hoped for.

"Well, I hate to leave so soon," Ms. Evalia says as she stands up, "but I have an initiation something-or-other to take care of this morning. Wish me luck to stay awake; I'm going to need it!" We wish her luck, and she walks out of the food court, humming happily. I stare after her and start laughing. I turn back around to face Sam, who is smiling so wide his white teeth glitter in the light.

"I like her," he declares.

"Well, that's good because I like her, too," I say, standing up. I start to head toward the door when Sam catches my wrist.

"Shouldn't we get something to eat?" he asks a little too innocently.

"I'm not that hungry," I reply.

Sam frowns. "Haylyn."

"Sam."

"You need to eat something. I can't just sit back and watch you waste away," he says.

"I get that, but you have to trust that when I say I'm not hungry, I really am not hungry."

Sam purses his lips in an expression that is a little too close to a pout for my serious expression. "Fine."

I laugh and head out the door, but not before I see Sam sneak what looks to be an English muffin into his pocket. I roll my eyes.

"Where to now?" he asks nonchalantly.

I give him a look. "Just give it to me."

"I don't know what you're referring to."

"Sam. Just give it to me, and I'll eat it later when I'm actually hungry."

At this, Sam finally reveals the hidden food item. I take it and, in turn, put it into my pocket. "Happy?" I ask.

Sam shrugs but does seem slightly comforted by the fact that I have taken the food. "So really, where to now?" he asks as we start to walk away from the food court.

"My cabin, I guess."

Sam nods and we start to walk in the direction of my cabin. The slight breeze ruffles our hair, and I think back to my conversation with Ms. Evalia. "You know, I can't believe I'm saying this, but I think Ms. Evalia actually seems fine being here."

"Well, I don't know what she was like before, but she did look pretty happy. Happier than you, at least," Sam points out, giving me a concerned look.

"What, are you kidding me? I'm happier than Natalie in a shoe store," I say sarcastically. "The scowl is just my natural expression."

"You don't scowl; you just don't seem to be adjusting to this place."

"So? That doesn't mean I'm not happy. It just means I'm slow at adapting," I respond, provoking a sour look from Sam. "I'm fine," I add more sternly.

Sam continues to glare down at me with disbelief, but, luckily, I am spared from having to add any further comment by the ringing of my phone. At first I don't know what's happening; I haven't heard it in so long. I look around frantically for the culprit making the noise when finally I realize that it's coming from my pocket. I slide my phone out and hold it up to my ear. "Hello?"

"Hey! It's Natalie!" calls the other end of the line.

"Oh, hey, what's up?"

"Well, me and the girls are going to go shopping and were wondering if you wanted to come!"

I ponder this a second. I treasure every moment I have with Sam, but he is asking too many questions right now, and I don't know how much longer I can lie to him. Every time I do lie, it feels like my insides are twisting into knots. Which is weird because usually I am great at lying. Besides, I need to prove to Sam that I am adjusting, and this is the perfect opportunity.

"Yeah, sure, I'll be at your place in fifteen," I reply.

"Great! See you then!" she calls and then hangs up. I return my phone to my pocket and look back up to Sam, who looks disappointed.

"What was that all about?" he asks, already knowing how I plan on ditching him.

"Natalie, Tana, and Emily are going shopping," I reply, shrugging. "And I thought, what the heck, it could be fun, so I said yes."

Sam smiles slightly; this is what he wants me to be doing and I know it. He wants me to make friends and adjust. Even though I am doing what he wants, he still seems slightly upset that I am ditching him.

"That does sound fun," he agrees. "So I guess I won't see you until tomorrow night when I get back from the Hunt?"

"No, I want to see you off!" I protest. It could be the last time I ever see him if things go badly with the bird.

"We're leaving pretty early," Sam argues.

"I don't care; just come inside my cabin and wake me up!"

Sam smiles broadly; I love when he does that. Two dimples curve into his cheeks like perfect apostrophes quoting his smile.

"Well, I will see you in the morning then," he agrees. Sam leans in and, very sweetly, he kisses my cheek. My heart soars at the touch of his lips and butterflies dance in my chest. There is no better feeling in the world than when Sam kisses me. I only wish he would kiss me full on like he did at the dance.

I close my eyes, trying to savor the moment. When I open them again, Sam is no longer in front of me and his silhouette is shrinking in the distance. I sigh loudly. I miss him already.

Shopping is exhausting. I had forgotten just how exhausting it is, but today cleared that right up. It was strange to be doing such a mundane thing as shopping, especially when tomorrow I have plans to kill a giant bird. But now, lying on my bed, staring up at the ceiling, I realize just how fun it was. I almost felt normal, just like regular old me shopping in Denver, when it was a weekend and I needed a new shirt or a dress. It was nice to feel normal, because it was familiar.

Even though Natalie, Tana, and Emily aren't my real friends, shopping with them still felt comfortable. It was like sliding into a worn pair of jeans. I may miss my real friends and family like crazy, but I also miss just waking up and knowing I had school in the morning. Or even better, waking up to that golden sunlight of the late morning on a weekend. It may have been a dull sort of happiness, one that I hated at the time, but now I crave that. I crave feeling safe.

That won't happen for a while, I think bitterly. But one day I will feel safe again; I'll make sure of it. And I will make sure that Sam does, too.

Chapter 22

"Haylyn," a sweet voice calls. I moan and roll over in my bed to seek out the voice.

"Mmm," I grumble.

"I'm leaving for the Hunt," the voice says.

Suddenly I snap into consciousness. "Oh yeah!" I leap up from my bed and try to stand, nearly falling over after standing up too fast. "Good luck, and be careful," I say, my tired eyes trying to focus on Sam as he gives me a bemused look and steadies me.

"I will. So what are you going to do today?" Sam asks, turning strangely tense. "I don't want you to get into trouble." This explains his tension.

"I won't, I'm just going over to Natalie's to hang out and stuff," I say, forcing the lie out of my mouth. Sam gives a small smile of relief, and I feel sick to my stomach.

"Well, that's good. Have fun."

"Thanks! You too! And do try to be careful," I add. Sam smiles a warm smile down at me.

"I'll see you tonight," he says as he pulls me into a tight hug. I wrap my arms around his chest and breathe him in. I love that spicy smell that always clings to him. I try to memorize every curve of his body against mine. I shudder at the idea that this could be the last time I ever touch him. Sam mumbles something into my hair, but his words are incoherent. I should be upset that I don't hear them, but it's almost better this way. If this is the last time I ever get to see him, I can imagine a better replacement for whatever he really said.

It feels too soon when Sam lets go. I sadly return my arms to my own side, even though I can feel them trying to reach for Sam again. I know

I can't act all sentimental; he would know that something is up if I were to get all clingy.

"See you then," I reply, hoping desperately that it will be true.

Sam gives me one last look and makes his way out of my cabin, my door clicking shut quietly behind him. I run over to my window and shove the curtains out of the way to watch Sam until I can't see him anymore. I don't want to miss what could be the last sight I ever get of Sam.

I close the curtains again and try not to cry, but taste the salt on my lips anyway. Why do I feel like I'm going on a suicide mission? Probably because I am. I don't want to become another tragedy in Sam's life, and I don't want to hurt my family, but someone has to do this. If I don't, then all these people will be stuck here forever, continuously tormented by the Laves. If that's not a cause to die for, then what is?

I wait until my tears stop falling and then stand up abruptly. This is war. I quickly take a shower and pull my hair into a high ponytail to keep it out of my face. I shove my legs into a pair of exercise pants and throw on a long-sleeved shirt. I lace up my hiking boots nice and tight and take the time to double knot them. I really can't be bending down to retie a shoelace in the middle of a fight to the death.

I reach my hands under my mattress and pull out the dagger contained in its sheath. I give it one hesitant look before tucking it into the straps of my boot. At home I would be sticking my phone in there; this is a little different.

I glance at myself for a second in the mirror, and the person who looks out at me can't possibly be capable of killing something so great. The eyes staring at me are still my eyes, despite everything I've been through. When Callock told me that I would be fighting this bird, the first thought I had was that I couldn't do it, but now that I actually am, I don't know what to think. He said that I could beat the bird with intelligence, but what if he overestimated how smart I am? Whether I live or die all depends on me.

I drink a big cup of water to keep hydrated and have to resist the urge to put on Sam's necklace; I don't want to lose it. I turn away from it with haste and feel myself turning away from everything I care about in my life. I eye my door and try to shove down a rush of emotion. *It's now or never*, I think and then stride purposefully through the door.

I weave my way through the cabins, and I feel as if I'm the last person alive in a decimated city, about to join the others in their violent deaths. The sound of my shoes is the only noise for miles; everything else is as still as a held breath. This feels like it's my death march.

Crunch, crunch, crunch. My footsteps, like my first night here. *Pound, pound, pound.* My heartbeat is like the ticking of a clock, counting down. My breath billows in clouds as the forest rises up before me. Every step I take toward the menacing trees makes me want to take a thousand steps backward to safety, but safety is not an option.

I reach the forest's edge twenty minutes after I have left town. The dark trees loom high above me, jabbing into the hollow air. The smoky sky that signals daytime has yet to break. This forest feels nothing like my forest at home. These trees seem to carry dark secrets, as if they've seen a thousand crimes and have remained silent to justice. The branches are like hands, waiting to grab me and pull me in, drowning me in their demonic calls.

Calm down, Haylyn! I snap at myself. *You haven't even seen the thing you should really be afraid of yet. You can't get scared by a bunch of trees!*

With a hesitant step, I move my foot into the line of trees; the dead needles crunch under my feet, a deafening cry in the silent morning. I take another small step in and become encased by skeletal branches. This forest is unlike any I've ever seen. It ends in one sharp, clean line. One second I'm in the open; the next I'm in the maze. I feel like the door has slammed shut behind me.

The thick foliage overhead makes it impossible to see more than three feet in front of me. I feel vulnerable without my vision. I clasp my sweating palms together into tight fists, my nails biting into my flesh. My mouth goes dry and my eyes open wide, searching for any sign of life lurking in the darkness in front of me.

I feel like I'm walking through a haunted house. It's that feeling where your legs shuffle along the ground as you sense the actor about to jump out at you. But the scary monster hasn't popped out yet, and it's the anticipation and uncertainty that's killing you—not knowing where it's going to come from, looking ahead while waiting for the hands to come down on your shoulders.

This feeling lasts for hours as I walk aimlessly around. I feel like a mental patient let loose in the wild after years in a windowless room. The hairs on my neck are probably exhausted from standing on edge all day. The white sky is up and illuminating the forest in a gray haze, but now the air looks more like fog than anything else, which does little to ease my fear. Callock said that the bird should attack me within an hour—what bull.

My feet drag through the dead leaves on the ground, creating the only noise in this eerily quiet nightmare. I continue walking straight, praying that I won't be lost in this forest. I'd rather be killed by the bird than be stuck in here.

This place screams that every shadow is waiting for its chance to choke me, and that every misshapen shrub has a horrible surprise inside that ends with me being a mangled, dead heap. I feel like I'm going insane. The forest looks the same in every direction I look, as if it goes on forever in never-ending horror. If I do get stuck in here, I will most likely die of fright rather than anything actually killing me. That is just how disturbing this place is. I am actually looking forward to killing this bird now. The faster I kill it, the faster I get out of this place.

I take another small step, and as my foot comes down, it is met by a sickening snap. I look at my shoe and see that I have broken a bone—someone else's. My heart rate peaks as I quickly pull my foot off it. I study it, feeling sick to my stomach, but I cannot tell what kind of bone it is or whether or not it's human.

I edge around it and force myself to calm down; it could just be an animal bone. I walk forward, using all of my self-control to keep from turning around and running as fast as I can out of here. Taking another step, I nearly cry out when the ground begins to quake. My whole body is shaking as my bones vibrate like they do when Cassie blasts dubstep on her fancy stereo. I freeze. I hear several branches snap; they sound like the cracking of bones, like the one I just stepped on. It's the first noise I've heard in hours that wasn't created by me. I whirl around, yanking my dagger from its sheath in a sting of metal.

When my eyes find my opponent, I struggle to suppress the scream that is trying to climb out of my throat. Before me stands a monster, one even more horrible than the Laves. The creature stands at about thirty feet tall, with a body similar to a T-Rex. Its long black beak curves out so that it nearly touches the ground. Sharp grooves line the edges of its beak, similar to the ridges on a knife. Its wings look relatively useless, but its legs make up for that. They are as thick as tree trunks, covered in thunderous muscle and a dry, thick pelt. Its feet are coated in rotten scales with sharp talons. The eyes are the size of basketballs and solid black like the Laves'.

I stand still and watch as the creature studies me intently, looking like it's about to pounce. I start to move away when it opens its beak and lets out a howling cry before leaping at me. I jump out of the way and hit the ground, rolling directly into a tree with a painful crunch. I force myself to get up and move just as the bird slams into the tree I lay next to only moments ago.

The tree shakes with the force of the hit, and the bird squawks in response. I crawl away at a frenzied rate. The pine needles stab into my hands, but I barely even feel it. I haul myself behind a different tree as my chest heaves.

I don't even have time to catch my breath before the bird is sticking its long beak around the tree, snapping for my leg. I yank it back, but I'm not quick enough; it catches my shoe, and I fall to the ground as it starts to drag me back around. I jerk and kick my foot, my heart running wild, and I claw my hands into the ground, my nails ripping in little paper cuts of pain in my struggle to grab hold of anything I can.

As I am dragged along the forest floor, I pick up a pinecone and get an idea. I pray to the god of good aim and chuck it at the creature's eye, and by some miracle it hits its target. It screeches and drops me. I don't waste a moment before flinging myself off the ground and booking it out of there. Luckily, my shoe protects my foot from any damage, but I am done playing hero. I can't do this.

I run for a few seconds before the ground starts to shake behind me: It's coming. I push my legs harder and swing my arms. My throat feels like its collapsing and my eyes water. I won't be able to outrun it much longer, but I have to keep going.

I continue to sprint through the forest, my legs starting to wobble from the ground shaking so much. Suddenly, the creature's foot is crashing down right next to me, and I am thrown off my feet by the force of it.

I hit the ground and roll like a log away as the bird pecks viciously into the ground a few inches from me, leaving a gaping hole. My lungs are now gasping for air from fear and exhaustion. I can't keep this up much longer.

Tired of feeling so scared and alone, but being too stubborn to give up, I army crawl behind another tree. I reach for a fistful of pine needles, trying to do what little I can to ready myself for when the bird comes, but instead my fingers find a stringy, dry material. I look down and feel bile rising up my throat. My hand has just reached into the hair of one of the bird's victims. A human victim. Its body is pecked clean, but its head is still intact, its hair not yet disintegrated.

I dry heave and drag myself over to another tree, staring at the empty eyes of the corpse a few feet away from me. I edge around the tree so that I won't have to look at him and try to shove the image of my own dead body decaying on the forest floor like his out of my mind, but fail. I can see what would be left of my body: a heap of bones with the flesh barely hanging on where the bird's beak ripped it off. The flies crowd me as I become their new lord.

The bark of the tree digs into my back, and my hands tighten around the clumps of needles I have grabbed as I await my fate. I'll die just like he did. I expect to feel the thunderous footsteps getting closer to me, but instead they seem to be going off in the same spot over and over again. Curiosity getting the best of me, I slowly poke my head out from behind the tree.

I now understand what Callock said about it going into a frenzy. The monstrous thing is spinning in maddening circles looking for me. It looks like a small child trying to become dizzy and fall. Despite the situation, I let out a small laugh. This is a big mistake. As soon as the noise comes out, the bird stops spinning and locks its massive eyes on me. But after seeing in person how dumb it is, I'm ready. Time to play dirty.

The bird begins to charge at me again, but this time, instead of diving far out of the way, I move barely a foot and hold out my blade. The dagger slices the bird's ankle, and a black, sludgy fluid covers my blade. My heart leaps with excitement over my victory before I realize that this is its blood and start to gag. My heart is pounding at a panic-filled rate, I feel as if someone is pouring adrenaline into my body.

This isn't going to work, I think with frustration. I won't be able to kill it like this. Its body is too high up from the ground for me to do any real damage from down here. I look at the trees surrounding me and get the nerve to smile. *Perfect*. I run over to a tree, clasp the clean part of the dagger with my teeth, and start to climb.

My plan is pretty simple: Jump on the bird from above. Then I will stab it and use the friction from the blade as it cuts downward to slow my fall—a lot like what pirates do with sails in movies, a sort of "blade brake." I may be crazy, but desperate times call for desperate measures.

I keep climbing until I reach the proper height I need to reach in order to have leverage on the bird. Sap covers my hands, and needles are stuck in my hair. Below me, the bird is frantically looking for me but doesn't bother to look up. I guess when you're so tall, having to look up isn't typically a problem.

I ready myself against the tree, trying hard not to look down. I'm not particularly afraid of heights, but I don't need another thing to have to worry about right now. I take the dagger from my teeth and grip it in my hand. The bird is slowly getting closer, and I am itching in anticipation.

"Come on, just a little bit closer," I murmur to the bird, willing it telepathically to walk up next to my tree.

Luckily, the bird seems to hear me, for it begins to walk closer to me. The bird is only three feet away from the tree now, and I am about five feet above it. Now is my chance. I let go of my hold on the tree and take a giant leap forward, hitting the bird's back with a heavy thud.

The bird screeches in protest at my presence on its back, and I make no hesitation before digging the knife into its flesh. The bird lets out another cry and snaps its powerful beak at my leg. I clasp my teeth in pain as the bird wrenches away skin from my calf.

I shake my head, trying to clear away the pain. I dig my blade deeper into the bird and start to slide over the edge, slowly slitting the bird's throat. It is a gruesome task, I think, as blood spatters onto my face. I am inching closer to the end of the bird when I realize the flaw to my plan. Its body ends, and I am still twenty feet in the air. When I reach the end of its ribcage, my blade will come out, and I will be free falling.

I am only a foot away from the end now, and I am trying desperately to hold on to something, anything. But it is too late. My blade has run out of bird to cut, and I am left to fall. My stomach shoots into my head and my limbs are flailing frantically. I watch in horror as the ground comes up fast.

I hit the ground in a sickening crunch. Every inch of me hurts. The fall knocks the wind out of me, and for a few scary seconds, I can't see. When my vision comes back, I almost cry with relief. I greedily try to suck air back in, but when I do, a sharp pain stabs my side. I sit up slightly to see if I am cut or something, but instead, the very end of my ribcage looks as though it has collapsed. I gasp, which only causes my ribs to flare up in another wave of pain.

I slowly lower myself to the ground again, trying to ease the pounding in my skull. My ribs are definitely broken, and who knows what else I've hurt? Every inch of me roars with pain.

I try to stand up, and the pain is almost unbearable. It is worse than anything I have ever felt. The leg that the bird bit can't take any weight, and the blood from it is starting to flood my shoe. I stare, nauseated, at my leg before remembering that I am in the middle of something.

I look around wildly for the bird, only to see its body a few feet away, disintegrating. It is starting to vanish right before my eyes. I try to run forward, to grab the heart before the body is completely gone, but this turns out to not be a good idea. I fall to the ground in a heap of hurt. Pain is a fire that is burning me alive, and I can barely get enough air in with my broken rib arguing against every breath.

When I finally manage to push myself back up, the bird is completely gone. In its place sits a shiny black rock that resembles obsidian. I hobble forward, forcing myself to ignore the pain and pick it up with the arm that hurts less. I grasp it tightly and find it, surprisingly, to be lightweight. I know that this rock must be the bird's heart. I dig out a cloth bag from the waistband on my pants and put the basketball-sized rock inside.

I did it, I think. I probably would be happier if it weren't taking all of my energy not to fall over. I turn around slowly and start to walk in the direction I think I came from. It's nearly impossible to tell, though. Every direction looks exactly the same—eerily terrifying.

I don't know how long I have been walking; it can't be more than a couple of minutes, but it feels like days. Pain is clouding all other thoughts, and the ground is starting to move beneath me. My shoe makes a squishy noise every time I walk because it is filled with blood.

My eyes survey the ground as it bucks around me, and they notice something in the distance; a cluster of pine needles and branches making a raised circle on the forest floor. It almost looks like a nest. *That's interesting,* I think as the ground sways even more violently, as a palm tree does in the wind, making me stumble around like a drunk.

I drop to my knees with a sudden thud. Pain sparks up my legs and I crumple completely. I know that I have to get back, but I can't remember why. And these pine needles feel like a cloud. My vision leaves, and before I know it, I am unconscious.

CHAPTER 23

MY EYES FLUTTER OPEN AND try to focus on the blurry figure in front of me. After a moment, I recognize the face as Sam's; he is staring down at me with a peculiar expression on his face. I look around to see where we are, but I can't tell. It's a strange room that smells like rubbing alcohol.

"Where am I?" I croak. Sudden alarm rings through me when I remember what happened before I lost consciousness. "Where's my bag?"

Sam points to a bedside table, where the bird's heart sits. I let out a sigh of relief, only to wince as I notice that my whole body still hurts.

"You're in Callock's guest room," Sam answers. I look around and see Callock sitting in a corner. He gives me a quick smile and I feel better. I let my eyes graze over the room once more and notice a window with dark sky showing through it.

"What day is it?"

"The first," Callock replies. My head spins at his answer. *I've been out a whole day? Oh my God!* I give Sam a nervous look. Why is he here? What happened? Did he know about our plans to escape?

I study Sam's face, looking for answers. He glares down at me, concern thick in his features. His hair is sticking out every which way as if he's been nervously running his fingers through it for hours.

"Haylyn, what is going on?" he demands, his voice filled with distress. I look over at Callock, asking him for permission to tell Sam. Callock's face remains placid, and Sam's eyes are hooked on mine, trying to pull the answer from them. I glare at Callock again, urging him to speak first since I don't know how much Sam knows.

"Well, Sam, Haylyn and I are trying to make a portal to get back to earth," Callock says nonchalantly.

I nearly smack myself. *Well, let's just come out and say it then!*

Sam's eyes fly open with surprise. "What?" he cries angrily. I try to sit up, despite the pain, so I can look Sam in the eyes.

"I am half Lave," Callock explains further, "so I have the ability to open portals."

"Then why is Haylyn hurt?" he asks. His hands fly over and point at me as if I can't hear a word they're saying.

"I got hurt because Callock is half Lave, so he needed the heart of the bird that the Laves worship. He couldn't do it, so I killed it for him," I tell Sam. His eyes widen with anger, and then suddenly he launches himself at Callock. I shout in surprise as Sam pins Callock against the wall, holding him by a fistful of his shirt.

"You did this to her?" Sam growls angrily at Callock, preparing to punch him.

"Sam, no, stop! I did it on my own accord. He didn't force me to do it!" I call out, stopping Sam's fist from crashing into a bewildered-looking Callock.

"You said you were going to go to Natalie's," he says, hurt filling his voice as he lowers Callock back to the ground. He turns to face me again, his bright green eyes raining with betrayal.

"I'm sorry that I lied, but I had to," I say.

Sam just shakes his head. "It isn't just that you lie; it's that I believe you," he cries. My heart stops in confusion. "I care about you too much," he says with remorse. "I tried so hard to push you away when I knew that I had fallen for you. The Laves have a personal interest in me, and I knew that if I ever acted out, and they found out how I felt about you, they would hurt you to keep me in line. I did everything I could to protect you, and this is how you repay me? You go on a suicide mission behind my back?"

"Sam, I'm sorry, I would have told you if I could, but Callock wouldn't let me," I plead. Sam gives Callock another hateful glance. "He didn't do it to spite you; he did it because he had to. You would have tried to stop me if you had known."

Sam looks at me with hard eyes. "Well, gee, I wonder why? I mean, look at you! Of course I would have tried to stop this from happening! You almost died!" he yells.

Once again, guilt blooms up inside me, and I look at my hands shamefully. "I had to," I mumble.

"Why couldn't you just have a happy life here, with me?" he asks.

"Sam, a life without my family just wouldn't be a happy one," I say. "It's not like I was trying to leave you, though! I wanted you to come with me!"

"Oh yeah? How was not telling me anything about it supposed to help with me coming?" he spits out bitterly. "Have you been lying to me this whole time?"

"Sam, it wasn't like that," I start, but he cuts me off.

"You lied and I ate it all up! I believed everything that you told me!" he cries angrily.

"I only lied because I had to!"

"You ignored everything that I told you!"

"And why should I have listened? You don't get to tell me what to do! You can't expect me to be happy here with you when there is a chance of me getting home again!"

"Is getting home really worth you dying?"

"Yes! Maybe you don't get it because all your family is dead, but mine needs me!" I scream back. As soon as the words are out, I regret them. Sam's face isn't sad; it's broken. I feel my heart is cracking just looking at it. I didn't mean for it to come out like that.

"I gave my heart to you, and you just threw it away," he says and turns to walk out the door.

"Sam," I call as I fling myself from the bed. I cry out in pain as soon as my feet touch the floor, and I start to collapse. Sam is there in a second, catching me before I hit the ground. I am crying now as I look at the hurt on his face, but this time Sam doesn't wipe away the tears.

"I thought you were good, but clearly I was right before: No good can live here," he says. "Goodbye, Haylyn."

I try to call out to him again, but he is already gone. "Sam no," I whisper as I choke back a sob. My heart feels like it's just been ripped apart, and Sam has just left with the other half. I feel broken. Not hollow—now I am all too aware of my emotions. Broken is much worse than hollow. Why did I have to say that? Sam cared for his family more than anything, and I just went and slapped him in the face with their deaths.

I stand on a cold, hard floor, wearing a strange blue and white night-gown. I let myself fall to the floor, cover my face with my hands, and just cry. I am so absorbed by my tears that I completely forget that Callock is still in the room until he clears his throat awkwardly. I turn toward him, embarrassed, and wipe the tears from my cheeks.

"So you were successful, obviously," he says, gesturing to the heart on the small bedside table.

"There was a body," I say coldly, sitting back on the bed and wincing in pain, an image of the body flashing behind my eyes.

Callock looks down momentarily, a sign of guilt. "I figured that might happen; sometimes the Laves make human sacrifices."

"If that full-grown man couldn't survive the bird, how did you expect me to?"

"Well, you did, didn't you? I knew you could and I was right," Callock replies.

I sigh; this is a losing argument. "How did you find me? And why was Sam here?" I ask, moving on from the fact that I almost died doing a task that others have died from.

"Well, after the Hunt, I went back to your cabin to see if you had com-pleted the task. When I got there, you were nowhere in sight. I checked the food court and the park, but you weren't there either, so I figured that something had happened. I went into the woods a short way and found you curled up on the ground, unconscious and bleeding. I scooped you up and took you back to my cabin to treat your wounds. Once you were stable, I went over to your cabin to pick you up some extra clothes, but when I got there, Mr. Pretty Boy was there freaking out.

"He was looking for you, and as soon as I walked inside, he knew something was up. I tried to shake him, claiming that I was just looking for you, too, but he saw the blood on my shirt from carrying you. So he followed me back here and threw a complete fit when he saw you. I tried to shoo him away, but he stayed with you all last night and today," Callock explains.

My heart feels the pang of hurt when he talks about Sam staying with me. "Why take me to your place instead of the infirmary?" I ask. "Wouldn't that have been easier?"

Callock shakes his head. "No. If I had taken you there, they would have reported your injuries, and the fact that I took you there, to the Laves, and we can't have them knowing about this."

I nod; that makes sense.

"So what are my injuries?" I ask, hoping that they aren't too serious. I still have lots of things to do; I don't have time to be slowed down by a few broken bones.

"You have a concussion, two broken ribs, a fractured wrist, and a huge gash in your calf that needed stitches. I wrapped your ribs, but there wasn't much more I could do, so you'll need to be careful with those. You sure are lucky that I used to be a doctor," Callock says.

"Not too bad for a twenty-foot free fall," I comment. Callock's eyes widen with surprise.

"That's what happened? That's not bad at all. You could have died," he remarks.

"I am already well aware of that fact," I say, rolling my eyes. *Does he think I don't realize that? I saw the body, after all.*

"So what exactly happened that caused you to fall twenty feet?" Callock is curious.

"I fell off the bird," I reply. Callock gives me one look and then starts to laugh. I cross my arms over my chest, only to have the brace on my wrist get caught on my nightgown, and the movement sends another flare of pain down my side. "What's so funny?" I demand.

"Haylyn, you were just supposed to kill the bird, not ride it like it's a rodeo!" Callock blurts out while continuing his cackle.

"I didn't ride it for fun! I couldn't reach its vitals from the ground, so I had to jump on it from above and stab it from up there!" I say in protest.

Callock stops laughing and nods his head, looking impressed. "Smart thinking, and either way I thank you for doing this. I am forever in your debt."

I let out a small smile, despite how torn up I am about Sam. "So what do I do now?"

"Well, now you need to pick some people to go through the portal with us," Callock answers, looking hesitant about something.

"Well, that shouldn't be too hard; there's going to be a stampede!" I declare.

Callock shakes his head solemnly. "You would be surprised; many people won't believe you."

"Well, yeah, maybe at first, but I'll be very persistent. Soon we'll have at least nine hundred people escaping!" I say happily.

"Well, you see, Haylyn, that's the thing. We can't take a lot of people with us. The portal will only be open for about ten minutes," he says.

I feel my smile fall back down again. "I thought you said the heart would allow you to hold open the portal for a long time?"

Callock hangs his head, and I feel devastated.

"Ten minutes is a lot longer than what I could do before," he explains. "And I am not using the whole heart. I will be using most of it for necklaces to protect everyone who does escape and their families from being brought back here. The heart's properties make it so that anyone who is wearing it can't be transported back here."

"Oh, I guess that makes sense," I mumble. And it does; it was a smart idea, but I just wish that we could free more people.

"Haylyn, it isn't over. Once we get back to earth, we will come up with a new plan to free everyone."

I nod. That will have to do.

"And remember, you can't get too upset if someone doesn't want to go. They could be afraid."

I let this sink in. What if nobody wants to come? What if Sam doesn't want to come? The thought makes a new group of tears collect in my eyes. When the time comes, will I be able to leave without Sam? I don't know if I can.

"Then we will try to fit as many as we can in that time frame," I say determinedly.

"And don't pick anyone that might rat us out to the Laves for a reward. You need to pick people that you can trust."

I nod my understanding to Callock.

"I will have the portal set up to go to Denver; that's where you're from, right?"

I give a quick smile at the thought of going home.

"Yeah, that's where I'm from," I say, smiling tentatively, as though just the thought of being able to go home can make every worry slip away again.

"I say that this calls for a celebration!" Callock declares.

"Okay, how should we celebrate?" I say, raising an eyebrow and being in no mood to celebrate.

"Well, we can eat meat all the way from today until the sixth. But the sixth also happens to be when we are leaving!"

"That's so soon!" I say excitedly.

"Yes, six a.m., in front of the park. Now, I am going to the food court. Would you like anything?" Callock asks politely as he starts to put on his coat to leave.

I shake my head sadly. When I first got here, I would have done anything for some meat. Now all that I want seems to be the one thing I can't have: Sam.

CHAPTER 24

WAKING UP TODAY IS A whole other story from waking up yesterday, and the day before that. Then, I had Sam as motivation, but now I have nothing. I lay dead as a rock on my bed, filled with both mental and physical pain.

Last night I fell asleep crying. I woke up several times from nightmares where I saw the dead body again, where it talked to me, where I was the dead body. The dreams made me scream and gasp, which then made my ribs start up in fiery pain. I had to roll over very carefully and calm myself down by taking deep breaths, despite the pain. Then my stitches would be grazed during my unconscious flailing from the nightmares, which would bring on a different kind of pain. Callock gave me some pain medicine, but I hate to take it. It makes me all loopy and nauseous. I can't stand it, so I try to stand the pain instead. Both options are turning out to be no fun.

As if the nightmares weren't enough, a war is raging within my head. Most of me wants to run to Sam, to apologize for everything that I ever did and will do. But the smaller part of my head, the stubborn part, keeps me still. It tells me that I did what I had to and Sam should understand that. So I stay, sitting all alone in my cabin, hating myself for not going, but still not making any plans to move.

Callock dropped me off at my cabin last night, leaving me to my own thoughts. I sort of wish he would have kept me there at his place. Then at least I would have someone to talk to occasionally and bring me out of the battle ravaging my mind.

I think about going to breakfast, but I've felt sick to my stomach ever since my fight with Sam. Besides, I don't think I have the strength to walk all the way there yet. So I continue to lie here, staring up at my unchanging ceiling as if it's a television show. Every breath hurts and every thought of Sam hurts ten times worse. I am a hot mess.

This continues for the rest of the day and the next, with Callock checking in on me every so often. I use the majority of that time to feel miserable over Sam. I know that I am just throwing myself a pity party, but I can't seem to stop. It's like I am punishing myself for making Sam hate me.

The worst part is the hate I feel for myself. I never wanted to be one of those girls who is obsessed with a guy. Personally, I've always thought that I would die alone, laughing as I watched all those girls who were once so desperately in love getting divorces. But look at me now, crying over a guy I haven't even known for a month.

I am just about to start the second phase of my pity party, which includes angry pillow throwing, when a knock sounds on my door. I sit up abruptly, shoving aside the pain. All I can think is that maybe it is Sam. When Natalie walks through the door, to say I feel disappointment is the understatement of the year.

"Oh my God, Haylyn, what happened?" Natalie cries as soon as she sees me.

"I took a nasty spill in the park yesterday," I lie. Something tells me that Natalie wouldn't take my bird-killing story too well.

"Oh, you poor baby," she coos, giving me a sympathetic look. I roll my eyes. I have enough pity for myself; I don't need it from her, too. "Well, I was going to ask if you wanted to come to dinner, but I'll just bring the dinner back to you!" she says, smiling like she has just solved all of my problems.

"Thanks," I grumble

"So what would you like?"

I think about my upset stomach again, but I decide that I do need to eat something. "Steak," I reply. If all the food here is going to be free, I might as well get what would have been the most expensive thing.

Natalie's face falls a little. "Um, little problem: The meat of the night is corned beef, so…"

I sigh. I should have known the Laves wouldn't give us good meat. "It's fine, just get me some of that," I say reluctantly.

"Okay, I'll be back in ten!" Natalie exclaims as she flounces her way back out of my cabin.

The next two hours are spent gnawing on corned beef and listening to Natalie chatter. I know that she is just trying to be nice, so I tolerate her. But make no mistake, I was ready for her to leave one hour and fifty-nine minutes ago. What with hating myself, worrying about something going wrong with the plan, and thinking about possible people to ask to come with us, I just want to be left alone to my thoughts.

Natalie gives me a big hug before leaving—one that my ribs do not enjoy at all. I close my eyes and try to get some sleep, but all I end up doing is tossing and turning until my ribs feel like they are on fire. I finally give in to the call of the pain medication and fall asleep swiftly afterward.

I am jarred awake by the sound of my door being swung violently open. I scream as three Laves file inside. My heart pounds louder with every step closer to me that they take. My mind reels with fear. *Do they know I killed the Retter? How did they find out? Are they going to kill me now?*

"Haylyn Jones, our leader has requested an audience with you. It will be easier if you come quietly, but your cooperation isn't necessary," the Lave in the front informs me in a scratchy voice.

"I don't have to go anywhere with you. Leave my room at once!" I say with confidence I don't feel. Who is this leader they're talking about? What does he want with me?

The Lave who just spoke makes a clicking noise, and the two other Laves behind him rush toward me and clamp their rotting hands on my arms. I scream again and struggle in their steely grip.

"Like I said, your cooperation isn't necessary. Though, it would have made this more pleasant for you," the Laves snarls. I glare at him with hatred in my eyes and decide that if I am going to die at the hands of these people, I am not going to die screaming and looking weak. I will die my way: going out with a bang.

I break one hand from their hold and get one good hit in before the Laves pull me from my bed, causing my ribs to flare up in fiery pain. I hit the ground with another slap of pain, and they start to drag me out like a ragdoll. They slide me along the carpet in my room and straight out the door into the chilly morning air.

I think about the woman with the red hair. *Will I suffer the same fate she did? Should I scream for help? Would anyone come? Nobody here would stand up to three Laves head-on like this. I am a goner.* I think about my family, how they will never know how I died. They won't even really know that I am dead for sure. I let myself have a minute of remorse for how difficult their lives will be from now on. That is why I must die honorably, so I can know that if my parents do ever find out how I died, they will be proud of me.

The Laves drag me by my arms along the gravel, and I have a vague thought that they are probably getting my blue pajama pants all dirty. If I do make it out of this alive, I am so making them buy me new ones. After that thought, I chuckle at myself; here I am, possibly being dragged to my doom, and all I can think about is my pajamas. At least I've got my priorities straight.

The Laves look down at me with hatred in their eyes as I laugh, so I clamp my mouth shut once again. I look up at their long, curving beaks and suppress a shudder. I try to look at the ground again because when I look at them, this seems all too real. I really am facing the possibility of death at the hands of these monsters. I am living a real nightmare here.

A sense of dread starts to pool into me like a hose filling up a watering can. My heart is pumping painfully in my chest, and I think about how, just minutes from now, it could be silent—that I will have no more thoughts; there will be no more rising and falling of my chest, no more pain. How will they kill me? Will it be quick and painless? I sure hope it is. I realize that all this dread is coming from the unknown. I need some answers. I take a deep breath, ignoring the pain it causes, and muster my courage.

"Where are you taking me?" I ask. "Who is this leader person? What do you want from me?"

The three Laves turn their heads and look at me with their beady black eyes. "Gag her," the leader snaps.

"No, no," I argue nervously, "let's not gag me."

The Laves give me no thought, and I let out a cry as they get even closer. I clamp my mouth shut and shake my head, but the two Laves who were gripping my arms shove a dirty cloth into my mouth and tie it around my head. Unwanted tears start to stream down my cheeks. I want to wipe them away, to look brave as I meet my end, but my hands are being clamped by the Laves' bony fingers.

The cloth tastes stale and aged in my mouth, like those old rags you keep around the house that you cleaned something with a long time ago and still keep around to clean something else, but whenever the time comes, you never pick them up because they are just too gross. I wish they would take it out already. It is just one more factor that makes this horrible. I try to spit it out, but they have tied it too tightly. Tears are starting to soak into the cloth, adding a salty taste. I wonder if this will be the last thing I will taste while I am still alive—my tears. There is something sad about that prospect.

The pain in my leg, wrist, and ribs is starting to become unbearable. My mind clouds with the agony, and I know that if they keep dragging me, I will be unconscious soon. I can't decide if this is a good or bad thing. Do I want to meet my death head on? Or is it better if I am already unconscious so I don't have to feel the pain?

The Laves start to grumble amongst themselves, and I twist my head to see where we are going. I feel my eyes widen in surprise as I see the Watching building loom into sight. I suppose that I would prefer coming here than the main city, where the Laves live.

They haul me through the doors and down a hallway that I have never been in before. Time seems to slow as they pull me down a hall where an open door sits at the end. I somehow know that the door is where we are going. I wonder if this will be the room where I will die. I try to hold in tears at the thought, but they continue to spill over. What does it matter anyway? My cheeks are already stained with tear trails by this point.

The Laves haul me into the room and drop me in the corner, removing the gag from my mouth but tying my hands together in front of me. I take in the room and see four plain white walls with a huge desk and chair in the middle. Over the desk hangs a large portrait of a particularly horrid-looking Lave. The Lave has an evil gleam that starts in his eyes and creeps down into his smile. At the top of the portrait it says, "Our Leader." The big chair remains facing away from me, but I just know that this leader of the Laves sits in it. And I know that I also hate him the most out of all Laves.

"We have brought her, Leader," the main Lave stammers as he gives a stout bow to the chair.

"Good," a deep, rattling voice replies from the chair. "Wait in the hall until I call for you." I watch as the three Laves quickly fall in line and make their way out the door, closing it behind them. I feel a tremor as the door clicks shut. Now I am all alone with the leader of the worst species known to man. I wonder how exactly this Lave became leader. I highly doubt that the Laves run a democracy, so my money's on a dictatorship.

"Why am I here? I haven't done anything wrong," I say sternly, hoping for the off chance that he doesn't know I killed their Retter and that maybe this is for some other thing.

"That's what we need to figure out—whether or not you have done something wrong," the voice growls.

"What do you mean?" I question. The chair slowly turns around so that I am face to face with a real-life demon. His eyes threaten to swallow me whole as he looks at me. His skin looks like baggy old rubber, and a few stray hairs stick out of his head. "Well, aren't you a looker," I say sarcastically under my breath, making him scowl.

"We want to know where you were during the Hunt, and why you are so banged up. Have you been up to something that you shouldn't have?" he purrs, taking out a long file and beginning to sharpen his curling black nails into points.

Oh crap. What do I tell him? These aren't exactly easy injuries to acquire, and I doubt he would be as easily fooled as Natalie. How does he even know I'm hurt?

I sit there with my mouth opening and closing. Usually I am very good at getting out of situations like this, but his black eyes bare down on me, pinning me down as all my logical thoughts scamper away and hide.

"Well, you see," I start before I dwindle off, having no idea where I am going with this. The Lave leans forward, looking malicious, when suddenly a loud, clear voice is ringing around the room.

"It's my fault!"

I look behind me at the door and feel my heart drop when I see Sam standing there and the three Laves that were waiting in the hall starting to close around him. What is he doing here? If I go down, I don't want Sam to go down with me!

"What exactly is your fault, dear Sam?" the leader hisses out.

"Haylyn's injuries," Sam answers flatly.

No! They aren't his fault! What the hell does he think he's doing? I try with my eyes to beg him to leave, but he is deliberately looking away from me. Why is he doing this? I thought he was mad at me.

"Oh, and how exactly did you manage to cause them? Not to mention, why did you attack the one person whose wellbeing we put you in charge of?" the leader spits out, making every innocent word sound like a curse.

Sam looks at his hands, still avoiding my gaze. "I had finally had enough of her whiney behavior; she was getting on my nerves. A couple of days ago, she wouldn't quit asking me to show her around the park, so I did. I thought that would shut her up, but she only got more annoying and kept getting way too close to me. Eventually, I needed some space, so I tried to push her away from me, but I used more strength than I'd thought, and she hit the ground hard, cutting her leg on a jagged rock.

"I took her to my friend Natalie's place because she knows some medical stuff, and she got Haylyn all fixed up. I left her with Natalie and thought everything would be fine until I saw her getting dragged here. I may hate the bitch, but I don't want the guilt of having her killed when it was my fault," Sam explains, giving a very believable speech.

I want to scream that this is a lie. I want shield him from the Laves' wrath, but when Sam finally looks at me, it is a look filled with force, begging me to keep my mouth shut, and for once I listen to him. Maybe this is all part of his plan, and he will be okay.

"Sam Eveland, I must say that I am disappointed in you," the Lave drawls, sounding closer to pleased, if you ask me. "You know that hurting another human can't go unpunished. We must punish you now."

What? No! You can't hurt Sam! "I really don't think that punishment is necessary," I protest. "I mean, he only pushed me because I was bothering him. It's my fault."

Sam gives me a hard look, but I can't just sit back and let him take the blame for something he had nothing to do with.

"Either way, the main rule here is no hurting other humans, and he broke that rule. He must be punished," the Lave leader says, making my heart drop.

Sam stands there like a statue, not showing an ounce of fear.

"I think we should go with a barring," the leader says, making Sam's eyes widen slightly, but otherwise he does not move. This makes me worry about what a barring is.

"It's my fault! I should be the one getting punished!" I argue, making everyone's attention snap back to me, including Sam's, who now looks furious with me.

"Doesn't matter. We have a zero-tolerance policy for violence," the leader of the Laves replies, making me snort. *Oh yeah, the Laves are real peace loving.*

"Please don't!" I beg as the Laves start to grab Sam's arms, and he just stands there letting them.

The leader turns his attention back toward me. "How cute. The girl has a crush on you, Sam," he sneers before walking right up to me and glaring into my eyes as I struggle not to flinch. "Don't you realize that he doesn't care for you at all?"

I swallow hard, thinking that things would be better if Sam didn't ever care for me. He wouldn't be here right now if it weren't for me, but he is. Even after everything I said, he is still here, and that alone makes me know that the Lave leader is wrong.

"Gag the girl. I want her to see exactly what happens when she causes problems," the leader snaps. Within seconds, the third Lave gags me and starts to follow the other two Laves, who have Sam in their grip out the door and down the hall. I struggle, twisting my body as the Lave drags me by my tied hands. I have to try to do something. I swing my legs out and manage to trip one of the Laves holding onto Sam. I stifle a laugh as he releases Sam and catches himself.

The Lave barely stumbles, and I manage to see Sam's worried look before a hand cracks against my face. Stars flash before my eyes, and I look up to see the Lave that I tripped towering over me. I try to tell him that he didn't even fall and that he's being a big baby, but it only comes out as garbled noises.

The leader clicks something at the Lave, who continues to steam above me, and the Lave's eyes instantly calm down. He blinks once before moving back over to Sam and roughly grabbing his arm again. I wince for Sam and start to struggle again, but this time the Laves make sure to stay far away from my flailing legs as we continue to be forced down the hall.

After a few feet, we reach another unlabeled door. The leader scans something in front of it and it swings open for him to walk in first, followed by Sam and me. The room is dimly lit and is in the shape of a circle. A post stands out in the middle, and a few chairs line the room.

The leader sits down in a plush chair directly in front of the post. I am thrown at his feet, making my wrist and ribs flare up in pain. I watch helplessly as Sam's hands are tied to the post and his shirt is ripped from his back. The two Laves tighten the ropes, and the third is opening some kind of oven on the other side of the room. At this point, I am begging the leader to punish me instead, but in my despair it all just sounds like nonsense.

I start screaming when I see them heating up something in the fire. What are they going to do to him? I writhe around, trying to stand up from my awkward position, when the leader of the Laves catches me and shoves me back to the ground, making my shoulder take most of the hit. I cry out in pain as it hits the ground, but then I try to stand up again, only to be shoved back down again. This time my face catches my fall.

"Haylyn!" Sam whispers sharply, while the other Laves are distracted watching what is going on near the red-hot oven thing. "It's okay," he mouths.

I shake my head. *It's not! It's not okay!* I start to struggle even more when one of the minion Laves shoves a strip of leather in Sam's mouth and explains that it is for him to bite down on. I start to clamber up again, but this time the leader has had enough with me and whistles at one of the Laves. Within minutes, I am tied to a chair, completely immobile while Sam's eyes plead with mine to quit being so difficult.

I watch with horror as the Laves pull out a red-hot bar of metal from the oven and start to approach Sam with it. They walk behind him so he can't see what's coming. I start to thrash around like a madman, but the ropes don't give me any leeway. Sam watches me and knows by my reaction that it must be coming. I expect him to look scared, but he just keeps staring at me with a pleading look. His look doesn't plead with me to help him; it pleads for me to stay calm. Suddenly, Sam's eyes snap shut, and this is when the screaming begins.

It is muffled by the leather, but it still pierces my heart like nothing else can. The Laves have the red-hot piece of metal horizontal across his back, and they continue to hold there as he writhes under the pain. I can hear his skin sizzling from here as it crisps to a strip of black. I thrash and scream so much that eventually my chair crashes to the ground with me still tied to it.

Slowly, the Laves remove the bar, and the smell of burnt skin permeates the room. There, all the way across his back, just below his shoulder blades, is a long strip of charred skin. It is at least ten inches long and one inch wide. Before Sam has any time to recover, they are bringing over another newly heated rod and pressing it into his back again. This time he doesn't scream; he just writhes around like an ant burning under a magnifying glass.

I scream for him, tears falling down my face and onto the cold hard concrete that my face is pressed up against. Why did he ever take the blame for my injuries? My throat burns as I continue to yell and attempt to thrash within the confines of my chair.

The Laves remove the rod, and parallel to his first mark is another identical line of charred skin just below it. Sam's back is gleaming with sweat, and it looks like he is just clinging to consciousness. I scream again as the Laves bring over another red hot bar and press it into his skin. I scream as every muscle in his back is flexing and shaking under the unfathomable amounts of pain. *Oh God, when will this end?*

After ten more minutes of watching him writhe, the Laves remove the bar. He now has three parallel burn marks down his back. They start to grab another one when the leader's voice cuts through the air.

"That is enough. I believe he has learned his lesson," the Lave announces. I nearly cry in relief at those words. Sam's eyes are nearly shut all the way as they untie him, causing him to groan out in pain again as his back protests the movement. Two of the Laves carry him out and the third unties me. The leader has already left to move on to better things. As soon as am free, I leap up, despite my own injuries, and follow the two Laves that carry Sam down the hall.

I creep behind them until they stop at a door that says "Nurse" and push inside. I walk into the room with them, not caring if they know I'm following them now. Inside there is a petite, elderly human woman sitting at a desk in a room that looks a lot like a regular nurse's office at school. The woman gives a squeak when she sees Sam being carried in.

"Oh, place him down over here, on his stomach please," she clucks at the Laves, pointing to one of the beds in the corner. They lower him down as she requested, and Sam groans yet again at the new position. "You're lucky I'm here doing paperwork, or else I would be off like everyone else for the holiday."

The two Laves grumble at this, not seeming too particularly interested. I am, however. If she weren't here, Sam would have to be carried all the way to the hospital, and anything that saves him from more pain I am thankful for.

The Laves shuffle out without any comment, leaving the nurse to get to work. I sit down next to the low cot and help her lay out cold washcloths on Sam's back. The smell of disinfectant floats around the room, but it is better than the smell of Sam's burning flesh, so I welcome the scent. I am pretty sure that Sam is unconscious by now, but I am glad for it. At least he can escape from the pain for a little while this way.

"Poor boy," the nurse coos, "nobody deserves this." She gets out some ice and starts to rub it on his back.

"He really didn't. It was my fault; he took the blame," I say shamefully, having to tell someone of Sam's heroics.

The nurse gives a small smile and hands me a washcloth. "What are your names?"

"That's Sam, and I'm Haylyn," I reply as I push Sam's hair away from his forehead and press the cold washcloth to it instead. He looks so vulnerable in sleep. So young.

"I'm Marybeth," she says with a smile. "Well, Haylyn, this is one of the Laves' favorite punishment methods, so I have developed a really good solvent for it. He'll have scars, but if he puts it on twice a day as instructed and only takes cold showers for the next two weeks, there should be little pain left in a week."

"That is great news!" I exclaim. "Thank you so much!" My heart leaps at this news; at least he won't have to be in pain for too long. I hate that this happened to him, and it is all my fault. I should have stopped this from happening while I was still ungagged.

"No problem, sweetie," the nurse says, standing up. "I have to go run to the supply closet a few stories up to grab the solvent and some pain meds. Keep putting fresh ice on his back while I'm gone, and I'll be back in a couple of minutes." She is already walking out the door, leaving me alone with Sam.

"I'm so sorry, Sam," I say when she's gone, my words filled with regret. "You didn't deserve this. I did. This is all my fault; you weren't even involved." I stare at my hands, unable to face his unconscious form, knowing that I did this to him. "I wish that I could have prevented this. I wish that you would have never come in and saved me," I whisper.

"I don't," Sam says in a weak voice, suddenly making my head snap up to meet his glowing green eyes. "I would have taken that five times over again to know that you would be safe."

"Sam, don't say that! You shouldn't have done it. You didn't owe me anything!" I say hoarsely.

"It wasn't a selfless act; it was a selfish one," Sam mumbles, his long lashes shadowing his cheeks.

I remain silent for a few minutes as I try to understand the entirety of that statement. Sam's eyes start to drop again when I finally find my voice. "I know you think that being here has crushed all the good in you, Sam, but you have the most good out of anyone here."

Sam's eyes flick up to mine, and he gives me a weak smile.

I am about to add something when suddenly Sam lets out a groan. I look at him with concern as he suddenly seems to grow drowsier. I start to panic when I look up and see Marybeth standing over us with an empty shot in her hand.

"I figured it was better to give it to him while he was distracted," she says, looking slightly guilty.

"What did you give me?" Sam asks.

"Some really strong pain meds; you'll be out in a half-hour, once your adrenaline dies down, and you won't wake up for a few hours. It will give your body some time to rest and recover and give us some time to move you back to your cabin," Marybeth answers sweetly.

I look down, hating that I can't stay with him all day. As much as I don't want to leave his side, I know that recruiting people to leave with Callock and me is more important.

"Do you have any friends in mind that could pick you up and take you back to your place?" I ask Sam.

"Miles and Percy probably could; their numbers are in my phone," Sam replies, moving his heady gaze to his phone, which sticks up out of his pocket.

Trying not to think about how close I am to some seriously R-rated stuff, I slowly pry Sam's phone from his pocket and scroll through his contacts until I see Miles's name.

"Hello?" Miles picks up.

"Hey, Miles, it's Haylyn."

"Oh, hey, Haylyn." I hear a loud, garbled noise in the background. "Dude, will you shut up? I can't hear!" Miles yells, his voice sounding distant as he probably holds the phone away from his face. "Sorry, that was Percy," he says, finally returning to me. "What's up?"

"Actually, that's perfect; I needed to talk to both of you," I start. "Sam and I need your help."

Fifteen minutes later, Miles and Percy are crowding the nurses' small room with their arms crossed over their chests.

"How did this happen?" Percy demands.

Thinking that I probably won't be meeting any people anytime soon who would be better to ask, I look over to Marybeth, who is now watching me. "Can I trust you?" I ask.

"With your life," she says solidly.

"Okay, what I am about to tell you cannot ever fall on the wrong ears, understand?" The three of them nod soberly, and Sam looks at me with wariness. "On the sixth, at six o'clock a.m., in front of the park, there will be a portal opening into the real world. A half-Lave and I have figured out how to do it, and we're having a few people come with us. Would you like to come?"

The three of them gasp in shock as Sam simultaneously cries, "The sixth?"

I give Sam a look. "Yes, the sixth."

"But that's in two days!" he exclaims wildly, the medicine finally starting to take its toll.

"Yeah! Are those meds affecting your brain?" I ask playfully. Sam purses his lips, suddenly looking upset. "What's wrong with that?"

"I just thought I would have more time to convince you how bad this idea is," he spits out, his words slightly slurred as he tries to fight off the pain medication.

I just shake my head I don't have time to have this fight with him. I turn to the others and ask, "So you'll all be there?"

"Definitely!" Percy shouts.

"Of course!" Miles agrees.

"Yes, I can't believe it!" Marybeth cries.

"I'm so glad to hear that," I say, standing up. "I'll see you all at six in front of the park. You can bring one or two people, as long as you can trust them."

I start to walk out of the room when I turn back around and look at Sam, who is watching me through lidded eyes, barely staying conscious. "I really hope you come with me, Sam. I don't know what I would do if you didn't," I say.

Sam just stares at me. I hope he heard what I said.

"Thank you," I add to him in a hushed voice, and this time Sam's eyes fall for good, and he is out like a light.

CHAPTER 25

I SLOWLY LEAVE THE WATCHING building with my thoughts in a whirlwind. I can't even process everything that's happened. I can't believe that Sam chose to be tortured rather than see me get hurt. I can't believe that even after all that, we still didn't leave each other on a happy note. At least I got three people for the portal. Now, if only Sam would quit being so difficult. God, I hope he comes.

I wish that I could go back to the start, when I first met Sam. I would trust him right away, and tell him everything. I wish I could, but if there's one thing that this world has taught me, it's that wishing gets you nowhere. You have to live with the mistakes you make in life, whether you like it or not. He put so much faith in me, and I keep letting him down. *I'm sorry, Sam.*

I start walking, looking for people to recruit and only stopping once at my cabin to change out of my very ruined pajamas. After an hour of looking, I am about to give up and go get some breakfast when I see her: a young lady of around twenty-eight, pushing a stroller with a small child in it. I've seen her a few times before but never really took notice. It's not until right now that I realize what strikes me as odd about her. Of all those times I've seen her out and about, I have never seen the father of the child. I feel my heart sink grimly as I realize the answer. The Laves have separated them. She is the perfect person to ask.

I jog over to her nonchalantly, trying to act as if I've just seen the baby and have the sudden urge to coo over it. The woman smiles widely at me but also somewhat timidly. I don't blame her, really. It's awful enough for me being here; I can't imagine how much worse it must be to have a child and be separated from the father.

"Aww, isn't she just the prettiest little girl in the world!" I exclaim, slipping into my baby-talk voice.

"Well, thank you, that's nice of you to say!" the woman says, beaming. I quickly look up and down the street for any unwanted listeners.

"I assume that you were separated from the father?" I ask, taking a more serious tone. The woman's eyes round with emotion and shock at my question.

"Yes," she answers, eyes flashing back and forth.

"Would you like to get back to him?" I ask, lowering my voice.

"Of course!" she declares in a hushed voice, finally bringing her eyes back to me. "But it's not possible," she adds, her voice full of remorse.

"What if I told you that I have a way to get back? Would you be interested?"

"Very much so," she says, nodding her head vigorously.

"Well, I have teamed up with a half-Lave, and we have figured out a way to open a portal. The portal will be open on the sixth at six a.m. in front of the park. It will take us to Denver, and from there you can go back to your husband. The half-Lave has even invented a way to keep the Laves from kidnapping you, or your family, again," I inform her quickly, enjoying the spark of hope as it flames up in her eyes.

"Is this really true?" she cries.

"Yes. Are you in?" I ask, while motioning for her to keep her voice down.

"Yes," she says fiercely

"Great. I will see you in front of the park at six a.m. sharp," I confirm. "And remember, tell no one."

"Thank you so much! How can I ever repay you?" the woman asks, pulling out her wallet.

I shake my head. "You don't need to give me anything. I'm just happy that she will be able to see her father."

The woman gives me a warm look, and I smile at the baby one last time before turning and jogging away.

I'm heading down a new street when suddenly I think of the perfect person to ask. Of course! I quickly jog to the Living director's office to find out where Ms. Evalia's cabin is. Once I get the address, I run down the street as fast as my injured body can take me with a big smile on my face. I make a right at her cabin and already see that she has churned the soil so that it is ready to take plants. I can't see much of anything growing here, but you have to respect her for trying.

I skip up to the door and scrunch my eyebrows when I see that a piece of paper has been taped to the door. My heart pounding, I slowly peel the note off and read it: "Giovanna Evalia is dead. Sorry for your loss."

My hands shake as I read it over and over again. This can't be right! I slowly sink to the ground, too stunned to cry, my mind racing at a million times a minute. *No, this isn't true! It's a prank or something the Laves are using to mess with me!*

I crumple the note in my hand and sit on Ms. Evalia's walkway in shock. She can't be dead.

I don't know how long I have been sitting there when a voice calls out to me, "Oh, I see you've found the note. Did you know that woman?" A lady of about fifty years old asks me this from her own walkway, directly across from me.

I slowly nod.

"I'm sorry. It's quite sad. Yesterday morning they came for her. Today that was pasted to her door. The Laves' customary death notice."

I nearly choke on this information. I don't understand why they killed her. I hope it wasn't because they knew what I had done. I wrap my arms around myself and place my chin on my knee, ignoring the pain that accompanies every movement. Sadness crushes me like a vice. I feel as though I have just climbed to the top of a mountain and been told that I can't go back down again.

"Do you know why they took her?" the ignorant lady continues to engage me in conversation.

"I don't know," I manage to croak out. "She was just a nice old lady with dementia who didn't do anything."

"Ah, that explains it," the lady clucks.

"Explains what?"

"Why they killed her. She had dementia. The Laves always kill the ones with dementia. They claim that they're no good for studying or something."

My mind reels. They took her when they knew they would kill her here! I stand up and start to walk away, ignoring the lady's cries as she calls questioningly after me. Maybe I should have told her about the portal, but she annoyed me and she seemed like a snitch, so not today.

It's all my fault that Ms. Evalia was killed. They brought her here because of me, and by extension she was killed because of me. I'm not going to make myself feel better when I know the truth. I want to get revenge for her, or cry for her, but I can't. That may make me heartless, but I can't do anything to risk all of our plans when we are this close. The only thing I can do is get more people to come through the portal in Ms. Evalia's place. I will give her a proper funeral once we are back in Denver.

Over the next two hours, due to my new fervor to do this for Ms. Evalia, I get three more people to join. Two of them are a married couple, separated from their twin ten-year-old boys. They were so happy and thankful that I nearly cried tears of joy for them. The last one was Mr. McKulhan. I can honestly say that I didn't expect him to come with me. He was always just so nice and happy that I assumed he liked it here. However, after asking him, I learned that Mr. McKulhan has spent the last thirty years away from the love of his life. He desperately wants to get back to his wife, and I am excited to able to return some of the kindness that he showed to me when I first got here.

This is truly what makes the Laves such monsters. It's not because of their nightmarish appearances or how they treat us like lab rats. They could torture us and test us all they want, but the worst thing they have done is separate us from our loved ones.

It has been a long day full of accomplishment, but I don't feel a content exhaustion like I normally would when I get a lot done. Sam was tortured because of me, and Ms. Evalia died because of me. How can I feel content after that? I have a total of six people, and I know that none of them will rat me out. I want to call today a success, and I try to focus on recruiting people, but every time I let my guard down, I am bombarded with flashes of the note on Ms. Evalia's door and Sam's contorted face.

Finally, caving to my worries for Sam, I walk to his cabin. I try knocking on the door, but he never opens it. I bite my lip. He'd better be okay. I then walk to the food court, but he isn't there either. Is he still unconscious?

I want to worry some more over where Sam is, but I have to keep going. I force myself to choke down some of Die Andere Welt's best while I'm still at the food court before continuing on my way to Natalie's to talk to her about leaving.

Luckily, Tana and Emily are at Natalie's cabin, too, so I don't have to go to their houses as well. I explain to them the plan, and as I talk, Natalie starts to clench her hands in uncharacteristic anger.

"Of course we don't want to go! We're not falling for your little trap, Haylyn!" Natalie shouts as soon as I finish explaining.

I reel back in shock. "No, it isn't a trap! This is real! We can leave!" I plead. Emily tries to step forward, but Natalie wields an arm out to the side, stopping her.

"I can't believe that you are trying to trick us into getting in trouble with the Laves for your own benefit!" she hisses.

"No, I'm not. I wouldn't do that to you!" I argue. Natalie scowls viciously and I back up, trying to escape her wrath.

"Sure you wouldn't," she snaps. I try to open my mouth again, but Natalie grabs my arm sturdily and shoves me out the door hard. I fall to the ground and lie gasping in pain, my ribs on fire as I try to breathe. I look up at Natalie with shock, but she is giving me a hard death stare.

"I thought you were my friend," she spits in a deadly tone before slamming the door. I lie on the ground for several seconds trying to gather my breath. I stand up slowly, wincing with every inch I ascend.

When I am up on my feet again, I just stand there staring at Natalie's door. *Where did that come from?* Natalie is bubbly, if a little ignorant, not aggressive and doubtful. I hope she calms down and decides to come after all. She may not be my favorite person, but she has always been nice to me and definitely doesn't deserve to be stuck here.

After the shock of Natalie, I walk at a measured pace to my cabin, forcing myself to avoid knocking on Sam's door again. The brisk air feels smooth and crisp against my cheeks, a contrast to the combination of my heated emotions and fiery pain. I am so done with this injury. What's the point of getting injured if you can't milk it and have people sign your cast? Because right now I don't have a cast or anyone that cares.

I heave open the door to my cabin and collapse onto my bed, crying out as my ribs erupt in pain. Yep, *so* done with this injury.

I try not to think about the long day I've had, but memories fill me anyway. I hear Sam's muffled cries. I see his charred skin. I hear my own cries harmonizing with his. I see the note. I see Ms. Evalia confused and scared as the Laves drag her away. Every self-preserving part of me is trying to force the positives of today down my own throat, but the empathetic part sobs at the fact that two people went through a lot of pain because of me.

I close my eyes and worry that maybe Sam is right and this is all a bad idea. What if Callock is lying to me? What if this really is a trap? What if he is just a Lave going undercover, trying to get me in trouble? Or what if it just flat-out doesn't work? What if everyone's pain has been for nothing?

Well, Callock had better hope that all goes well because if it doesn't, I can't see it going well for him. I am not known for my calm attitude when being severely let down. But it *will* work. It has to.

CHAPTER 26

My eyes snap open when a raspy voice hisses into my ear. Without thinking, I immediately thrash my arms to hit the unknown entity, thinking that the Laves have come for me again.

"Ow," the voice snaps, then growls accusingly, "Haylyn." As my eyes adjust, I see Callock glowering down at me. Relief and confusion fill my head as I rub my waking eyes.

"Callock, what are you doing here?" I mumble, not entirely awake yet.

"I heard that you were dragged off to see the leader of the Laves," he replies shortly.

"Yeah, well," I say, unsure of what more he wants me to say.

"Well, did he find out anything?" Callock urges. So this is what he is so worried about.

"No, Sam took the blame, saying that he's the one who hurt me. He got severely punished for it, but we're safe because of him," I answer as I am reminded of yesterday's hellish morning.

"Did the leader give any hints that he's worried about me working with you?" he presses urgently.

"No. Why are you so worried? I thought you were all about giving the Lave society the middle finger and all?" I question with interest.

Callock sighs. "Because Laves have mind-persuasion abilities. The leader of the Laves becomes the leader by being the most powerful mind controller. If he found out what I was planning, he would simply force me to stop, and we would be stuck here forever; they would never trust me again. We can't have him knowing about me."

"If Laves can control each other, can they control humans?" I ask worriedly.

"Luckily no, the Laves don't know enough about the human mind to control it," he replies. I nod. That is one good thing, at least.

I thank my lucky stars that the Laves can't control me until something comes into my mind. The Laves don't know enough about the human mind to control us, but what are they doing all day during Watching?

They are studying our minds! Oh my God!

"Callock, you say that the Laves can't control us because they don't know our minds, but that's what they're doing all throughout Watching! That's why they study us! They want to control humans!" I exclaim.

Callock's eyes fly wide in shock. "By golly, you're right! This is terrible!"

"Not only that," I say, thinking back to the time Timothy got punished and everyone went blank for a few minutes, "but I think they're already starting to succeed a little."

"Really? What have you seen that makes you think that?" he asks with dread.

"Well, a little while ago, the Laves were punishing this kid by stabbing him, and then all of a sudden I felt this wave wash over me, but I just shoved it aside. Next thing I knew, everyone had blank faces and they didn't react at all. At the time, I just thought they were stronger than me, but now I realize there was more going on. I mean, they didn't even seem to notice what had happened!"

"My God, you're right. You're lucky that the Laves haven't mastered controlling humans yet. It sounds to me like they're still just practicing."

"Why was I able to resist it?" I ask, wondering if it has something to do with the amount of time a person has been here.

"Strong will?" Callock suggests.

I smile for a moment. My mom always thought my strong will was going to be my undoing. Now it's working in my favor. *Take that, Mom!*

"I can't believe it! Why would they want to control us?" I ask with disbelief.

"Who knows? Whatever it is, it can't be very good," Callock responds.

My imagination suddenly runs wild, making me feel sick to my stomach.

"We have to get people out of here," I declare.

"How many people have you gotten to come so far?" he inquires.

"Six."

"That's not enough. Every single person here could help the Laves further understand humans. If the Laves master the human mind and take over earth, then we are all done for. We have to get as many as we can fit in the ten-minute time frame and continue to try to free people when we get back to earth," he says.

"Well, it was always our plan to do that," I say, referring to freeing everybody from back on earth.

"Well, now it's a whole lot more urgent."

"I will try to get more people today," I say.

"Good. We'll have to get as many people as possible," Callock repeats.

I press my hands to my head as my brain starts to pound. I groan and fall back onto my bed. "Well, this just sucks."

"Agreed, but we have to do everything we can," Callock states as he heads for the door. "I will see you tomorrow at six a.m. You know where," he says. I think about asking him if he has seen Sam recently, but before I can, he is already striding out my door with a hurried gait.

I think back to how Ms. Evalia was killed for her dementia. It makes so much more sense now! I bet dementia doesn't work well with their studies on how to control our brains. I give a little prayer to Ms. Evalia, telling her how sorry I am and that I hope she is okay, wherever she is.

I sit up and push my hair from my face. I drop my feet to the floor, trying to ignore the dull pain in my leg. I take the fastest shower in history and throw on a random outfit of mismatched clothes. I stride out my door and waltz right into Emily. She blushes like she is embarrassed to be caught standing right outside my door.

"Sorry," she mumbles under her breath.

"Oh, hey, what's up?" I greet her, breaking the ice.

"I want to leave here and go home," she whispers, speaking so rapidly that I almost don't catch it.

"That's great!" I exclaim. "Why the change of heart?"

"Well, it wasn't really a change. I always wanted to leave and was going to say yes last night, but then Natalie went into psycho mode," Emily explains. "I'm sorry you had to see that; she can get a little touchy about the subject of leaving. She's had her hopes lifted so many times that this time she just snapped and tried to save herself from the hurt and having her dreams crushed again. And Tana won't do anything without Natalie."

"Her dreams crushed *again*?" I ask.

"Yeah, some of the kids in our class had a lot of fun convincing Natalie over and over again that they had figured out a way to get home. She used to be so trusting that she would believe them every time and then get punished by the Laves for it. I guess this time, in her mind, she wasn't going to fall for it again."

I take a minute to let this soak in, sympathy for Natalie flashing through me. "That's terrible; I would never do that!" I exclaim. "You believe me, don't you?"

Emily looks at me the way a puppy does—with complete trust. "That's why I'm here."

I smile at her and know that I will do whatever it takes to keep her trust and not let her become distrustful like Natalie.

"I'm so glad you're here, and I hope that Natalie will change her mind, too, because there is something a lot more sinister going on than the Laves are telling us."

"What are they up to?" Emily asks, her innocent face scrunching up.

"Well, the Laves are using us to try to control the minds of the entire human race," I admit.

"What!" she cries. I feel bad for being so blunt about it, but every second I waste on someone who has already agreed to go means that I could have less time convincing someone else to go.

"Yeah, so we have to get as many humans out as we can, because every human who stays helps the Laves get closer to unlocking our minds. I can't explain everything right now, but if there is someone you trust, bring them, too. I'll see you tomorrow at six a.m. in front of the park."

"Okay," she agrees, looking dazed and slightly confused from all the information I just piled onto her. I smile to myself. Emily may be the quietest of the three popular girls, but she is definitely my favorite.

After she is gone, I force myself to go to the food court for energy and eat silently. Sitting here by myself, it is impossible to ignore my thoughts of Sam. Every minute I don't see him, I become more and more worried about him. I know the nurse said that he should be fine in a couple of weeks, but what if something has happened?

I sigh dramatically, feeling helpless, and throw my food away. I walk outside and into the cold, stiff air, everything about Sam still haunting my mind—his laugh, the way he draws, how he has more reasons than anyone else I know to become what he tries to act like—cold, distant, and uncaring—but he hasn't. He is still so good inside, and I've done nothing but hurt him.

I pace up and down the gravel streets looking for more people to convince to leave. Pathetically, I also spend the time looking for any sign of Sam. I can't help myself. It is driving me crazy not knowing where he is or whether or not he is going to leave for earth, or if he's okay. It's not like I left him in the best shape. I wish I could talk to him, but I have to keep my head in the game.

I start to walk past the infirmary when I suddenly remember someone else that I can ask to come. I'm so stupid, why didn't I think of him before? I rush into the infirmary and quickly spot Timothy lying in one of the beds. He looks at me questioningly as I approach.

"Hey, how are you feeling?" I ask casually, wondering how long I'll have with him before the obnoxious nurses kick me out again. However, none of them seem to mind me at all, and the one who kicked me out before is nowhere to be seen.

"Okay," he replies shortly.

"Really?" I question. "Stabbing isn't exactly a flesh wound."

Timothy snorts and then winces. "I know, but nothing vital was punctured. The Laves made sure of that. All the pain with none of the permanent repercussions that randomly getting stabbed would cause."

"You're saying that the Laves know where to stab humans without killing them?"

"Yup."

I feel my stomach drop at this. The Laves stab kids where they know it won't kill them but will still hurt them. All for not turning in their homework. I think of how many trials and errors the Laves must have had to figure out exactly where to thrust the knife. The people who died merely as part of an experiment. The people who were maybe even dissected to see where our vitals are.

I shudder.

"Yeah, I know the feeling," Timothy remarks.

"Well, at least I come bearing good news," I comment, trying to regain my happiness after picturing the Laves digging around dead humans' bodies.

"Which is?"

"I'm going to get you back to earth. I have paired up with a half-Lave, and tomorrow at six a.m. we will be opening a portal and getting a bunch of people out of here. Do you want to come?"

"Can I bring someone?" he asks slowly, surprising me.

"Yeah, as long as they won't turn us in to the Laves," I reply.

"Great! Maddie is stopping by later, and then I can tell her everything, and she can help me get there tomorrow," he says, now growing excited. It doesn't take me long to realize that Maddie is the girl who called out his name when he was getting stabbed before the Laves started doing their mind-control thingy.

"I'll see you there, then! Don't be late," I say as I stand up.

"I won't! Thank you so much… wait, what is your name?" he asks.

"Haylyn," I reply with a smile.

"Thank you so much, Haylyn; you'll never know how much this means to me!" he calls after me, looking like he wants to cry.

I give him one look before responding, "I do." He smiles even wider at that, and I feel as if I just donated a million dollars to the animal shelter.

By dinner time I have picked out seven more people, all of whom say yes. I think about trying to find Kat and seeing if she wants to come, but something tells me not to. So I stick to my gut. Besides, I can't find her anyway. However, more importantly, I still haven't seen any proof that Sam is even alive. I try knocking on his door again, now becoming increasingly worried about his wellbeing, but he never answers it, leaving me standing there feeling like a loser before walking away again.

I am about to take another loop around the cabins when I fall to the ground in pain. My leg is twitching with uncontrollable spasms. I wince and try to soothe the overworked and injured muscle. The fall also reminds my wrist how it is injured and should also be crying out in pain, which it does.

I gather myself off the ground and limp my way back to my cabin. I hate to admit this to myself, but I need to rest. Besides, it has already been dark for at least three hours, and I haven't seen a soul in two. I slide out my phone and text Callock to let him know I have convinced everyone I can to come with us.

I haul myself inside my door and drop onto my bed. I stretch myself out on the covers and start thinking about Sam again, despite myself. Where is he? Is he okay? Does he not want to go back? Does he think avoiding me will be easier than telling me straight? I only wish I could know what is going on in that head of his. Does he plan on coming tomorrow or not?

I will drag him through if I have to, I think determinedly. Sam doesn't know what's best for him. He is too afraid of what the Laves will do to me, but he doesn't know what they will do to the whole human race if we stay! I can't leave him in a world where he could be stabbed methodically for some tiny infraction. You'd think that after being tortured, he would finally realize how life here is just as dangerous as, if not more than, trying to leave, but apparently he refuses to acknowledge that fact.

I roll over and set my alarm for five a.m. Normally, I would groan at the thought of waking up that early. Now, I can't wait for tomorrow to come. I can't wait to see my friends and family. I can't wait to be home.

CHAPTER 27

WHEN FIVE O'CLOCK ARRIVES, MY alarm starts to blare into life, ending the silent morning. I throw my arm onto the alarm, stopping the raging call. I sit up slowly, vaguely thinking about how this could be my last time ever waking up in this bed.

I take an indulgently long shower, trying to break myself out of this haze that I'm walking in. I just can't believe that this is really happening, that this day has finally come. I slide into the clothes that I was wearing when I was first brought here. The denim is slightly wrinkled from the water, but otherwise they fit just like the first day I put them on. It feels weird to be wearing them again. It is almost sad how all the fashionable clothes that Natalie picked out for me are going to waste, but I know I can't bring them back. Every time I would wear them, it would just bring painful memories back.

I look over at the clock and give a small sigh when I see that it reads five-thirty. I walk around my cabin one last time to see if I am forgetting anything, double checking that I have Sam's necklace resting on my chest. It is one happy memory that I can take with me.

I make my way over to the door and survey my room. If all goes well today, this will be the last time I ever see this place. The thought fills me with mixed emotions. I quickly stride out the door and try to not look back. This is the first place that has ever really been my own. I thought that it would happen in college, but life has its surprises, I guess.

I walk hesitantly down the street, eyeing everything in a new way now that I know this could be the last time I will see it all. I barely notice the chill in the air today; I know that it will be much colder when I get to Denver.

When I reach the park, almost everyone is there, milling around in a restless huddle. As I get closer, I can feel the bubbly emotions of everyone in the group. I can't believe that this is really happening! I can almost hear my parents calling my name and see Foxy tilting her head at my words like she is really listening and understands. Despite all that's happened, it feels like everything will be okay. I can't help but smile as I stride over to Callock.

"Hello," I greet him excitedly.

He eyes me over and gives a small smile in return. "Hello yourself," he replies, watching over the anxious people.

"What time is it?"

"Ten 'til six," he answers. I nod and look around nervously. Where is Sam? I gnaw with panic at my fingernails as Callock explains to the group how the bird necklaces work. All of them are nodding along with his words and excitedly murmuring to each other. Callock hands five necklaces out to each person; they greedily take them, staring at them with awe.

I try to smile as I watch new hope dawn on their faces. I raise an eyebrow when Callock walks over to me and hands me ten necklaces.

"The Laves are going to be after you most of all. You're going to need all the protection you can get," he informs me. I chuckle at Callock's lighthearted tone and gratefully take the clump of necklaces. They aren't that pretty, really; each is just a leather string with a small rock hanging from it. But that doesn't matter. They symbolize protection against the one nightmare all these people thought they would never escape from.

"Thank you so much!" says a small voice from behind me. I turn around and face Emily, who looks like she is about to cry from happiness.

"Oh, you're welcome!" I say, feeling bashful.

"But really, you're changing my life," she insists. I give a small, embarrassed smile.

"That's good," I say encouragingly, glancing around for Sam.

"Oh, look, it's starting!" Emily cries. I turn around to see what she's looking at. Callock stands a few feet away holding the glowing orb that is the bird's heart. He chants rapidly under his breath, and I feel like I am watching some kind of voodoo sacrifice. Callock clasps his mouth shut again, and as soon as his words stop, a glowing sphere starts to form in front of him. It shimmers and moves like water floating in air. When it stops growing, it is about seven feet tall and three feet wide. I hope that it will show me an image of Denver, but it just looks like a swirling patch of air, colors reflecting and contorting within it.

My heart leaps with joy as people start to walk into it without hesitation, disappearing inside like it's a doorway. But two people are still missing: Mr. McKulhan and Sam.

"Your turn, my dear." Callock says, turning to me.

"No, we have to wait for Sam!" I cry.

"Haylyn, you have to realize that he may not come," Callock says gently.

"He will," I state and search the scenery around me again. I pray that he isn't too injured to get here.

"Haylyn, we only have a few minutes now," Callock says, sounding strained. I ignore him and keep looking around until I see a thin, dark figure walking this way with his hands in his pockets.

"Sam!" I call out to him. Sam strolls up, his face looking worried. I smile to see that he is standing perfectly normally and doesn't seem to be in too much pain. "Are you coming?"

"I just came by to see if it works," he states coldly.

"Well, obviously, it works! Now come on!" I say, reaching for his arm. Sam pulls his arm away from my hand and looks at me with an odd expression.

"Four minutes," Callock says.

"I don't know, Haylyn. What if it kills you?" Sam asks.

"Sam, we have to go. The Laves are trying to control our minds!" I plead. A quick flash of surprise splashes over Sam's features, but he doesn't say anything. "Come on, Sam! Don't you miss the real world? Don't you just miss everything about it?" Sam's mouth opens and he looks like he is about to say something negative, so I continue. "Don't you miss music, Sam? Don't you miss listening to a song over and over so many times that you memorize the lyrics?" I ask desperately. Sam mulls this over like he is tasting a fine wine.

"Three minutes," Callock informs us.

"Well—" he starts, but I cut him off again.

"Don't you miss the sun and the stars?" I ask.

Sam still looks unconvinced. I open my mouth again to suggest more things that he should miss when I am spared by a voice suddenly calling my name.

"Haylyn, get through the portal!" the voice yells. I turn around in confusion and see Mr. McKulhan running toward us at top speed, looking disheveled. His clothes are torn and his graying hair is a wild mess. *What happened to him?*

"Mr. McKulhan, are you all right?" I ask him worriedly.

He shakes his bright red face as he heaves for breath from his running. "I'm fine," he finally manages to say. "But you need to go through the portal right now."

"Why?" Sam asks, surprising me.

"The Laves. They found Haylyn's fingerprints on the dagger. They're on their way right now to kill her!" he cries. I look at him wildly in complete shock. How did they get the dagger? Sam reels back and looks at me protectively.

I open my mouth to beg Sam to come with me when, suddenly, a Lave launches itself out of the trees and tries to throw itself at me. I scream, but Sam is there in an instant, taking the blow for me. I scream again as Sam hits the ground with a groan of pain from his injured back, with the Lave on top of him. The two start throwing punches and before I can even do anything, Callock is there, punching the Lave in the temple so that he crumbles into an unconscious heap.

"Are you okay?" I ask, rushing to Sam's aid as I help him off the ground. He nods once, brushing off dirt, his face slightly pinched in pain.

"There will be more Laves coming; you have to go now!" Mr. McKulhan declares.

I try to look up at Sam to plead with him to leave, but something is grabbing my wrist. I look around and see that it is Sam who is holding my hand and pulling me toward the portal.

I always thought that I would be the one pulling Sam through the portal. But now he is pulling me, and together we fall.

ACKNOWLEDGMENTS

FIRST AND FOREMOST, I WOULD like to thank you—yes, you!—all the readers of my book. It's through you that my book gets to come to life, and I hope that you've had as much fun reading it as I did writing it!

Next, I would like to thank my family for listening to my crazed ramblings for the last four years about a book I was "going to get published." None of this would have been possible without you. Dad, it's because of you reading to me every night when I was little that I have the love for books that I do. Mom, thank you for reading the first cringe-worthy drafts of my novel and seeing the potential in it. To my sister, Michon, thank you for providing the inspiration for some of Haylyn's sassiest comments, and her love for Avery. Thank you Aunt Cathy, for editing my book when it had more mistakes than not.

To the fabulous Tracie Douglas, thank you so much for believing in me when I found it difficult to believe in myself. Your love and insight for *The Other World* helped make it what it is today.

To Ellen Hopkins and the fantastic writers at the Ventana Sierra Writing Workshop, it is because of you guys that I found my home with Lucky Bat Books and had faith that my age would not hold me back from publishing my book.

To Julia, thank you for being the first shipper of Sam and Haylyn, and for listening to all of my crazy ideas for this book and others. You were my first official fan, and I will always be thankful for that. And to Katrina, for reading one of the first drafts and still having the audacity to say it was good—same. To the rest of my friends, thank you for inspiring me every day with your hilarious shenanigans.

To Nuno Moreira, thank you so much for the amazing cover design. It brings the book to life in a way that words never could.

Last, but certainly not least, thank you Jessica Santina, my editing wizard. You and the rest of the wonderful people at Lucky Bat Books have supported my novel since the first three chapters. You have turned my dream into a reality, and for that I cannot thank you enough.

ABOUT THE AUTHOR

Photo by Reaney Photography

CALLISTA O'BRIEN STARTED WRITING THIS book in the eighth grade after a dream inspired her. Now, four years later, her dream is becoming a reality. This is her debut novel and, hopefully, the first of many. When she isn't writing, she is usually in school or reading one of the books that made her want to become a writer in the first place. She lives in Reno, Nevada, with her family and a sassy cat named Percy.

You can read more about this author at:
CallistaObrienAuthor.com